ONLY YOU

MELANIE HARLOW

Cover Design: Letitia Hasser, Romantic Book Affairs

http://designs.romanticbookaffairs.com/

Cover Photography: Lauren Watson Perry

https://www.instagram.com/perrywinklephoto/

Editing: Nancy Smay, Evident Ink

http://www.evidentink.com/

Publicity: Social Butterfly PR

http://www.socialbutterflypr.net/

Proofreading: Michele Ficht, Janice Owen, Karen Lawson

For my small but mighty tribe,
and you know who you are,

thank you for always believing in me.

"You don't find love, it finds you.
It's got a little bit to do with destiny, fate, and what's written in the stars."

ANAÏS NIN

ONE

EMME

It is true that I am *slightly* more prone to disaster than the average person, but even I was surprised by the fire.

I mean, it's not like I had a habit of igniting household goods—either on purpose or by accident. And certainly I had other options for destroying that invitation. Flushing it down the toilet, for example. Shredding it in the garbage disposal. Stabbing it repeatedly with an ice pick. All good ideas, and each would have been gratifying in its own way.

But in the end, I went with fire—and got slightly more than I bargained for in the process, which is often the case with me.

It happened on a Friday.

I'd come home from the Devine Events office a little early since I'd worked late at a corporate event the night before. Normally, I only handled weddings and my partner Coco managed corporate events and fundraisers, but she was way pregnant with her fourth child, had three rowdy boys under age six, and was beyond exhausted all the time. I didn't mind taking on a few extra projects here and there to help her out. Weddings were slow during March in Michigan anyway.

The funny thing is, it's actually my last name—Devine —on the business, because my cousin Mia Devine started it like ten years back, then partnered up with Coco, her college roommate, a year or so later. It was Mia who suggested I take her place when she and her husband moved up north to open a winery a few years ago. The timing had been perfect since I was fresh out of grad school with a business degree but didn't want a job where I'd be stuck at a desk.

Incidentally, you might think a person *slightly* prone to disaster would be ill-suited for handling the biggest (and most expensive) day of someone's life, but somehow misfortune never follows me to work. It's perfectly content to wait for me at home, however, and that particular afternoon, it practically greeted me at the door.

I'd picked up my mail in the lobby of my building and was idly sorting through it on the elevator ride up to my 23rd floor loft. There was the usual assortment of bills, coupons, special offers, appeals for donations, and crap addressed to the guy who'd lived in my apartment before me, but there, at the bottom of the pile, was something unexpected—a wedding invitation.

For a moment, I frowned. Did I know anyone getting married who wasn't a client? I attended all those weddings automatically and wouldn't normally have received an official invitation, since I wasn't technically a guest.

One glance at the return address and my jaw dropped.

They wouldn't.

They couldn't have.

A sweat broke out on my back and my pulse thundered in my head. When the doors opened, I dashed through them and hurried down the hall, my heels catching on the carpet. Once inside my apartment, I slammed the door behind me, dropped my bag and the other pieces of mail to the floor, and tore open the fancy engraved envelope.

Then I gasped.

They *had*. They actually *had*.

My blood boiled as I stared in disbelief at the thick ivory card stock in my hand, its elaborate black script requesting the *honour of my presence* (what a joke) at the marriage of my ex-boyfriend, Richard the Turd, and my former assistant, Lucy the Traitor.

I'd known they were getting married, of course. Before she'd quit working for me "to focus on the wedding," Lucy was constantly flashing her big diamond and pitiful-yet-smug expression my way. I'd spent months pretending it didn't bother me that I'd been dumped for my younger, skinnier, prettier assistant.

Of course I understand.

You can't help who you love.

I'm not angry. I'm happy for you. Really.

It was all an act, though. Of course I was angry—who wouldn't be? I'd dated that asshole for almost a year and he'd never *once* mentioned marriage, yet he'd proposed to Lucy after only a few weeks! And she'd worked for me for *two years* and had known how I felt about him. I'd wanted to scream, bite their heads off, throw things when they'd told me. But I didn't want them to know I was hurt, so I summoned my dignity, smiled, and played the role of the Bigger Person as I congratulated them.

Then I *literally* became a bigger person, since the whole situation drove me to eat my way through the holidays. I'd probably put on ten pounds between Halloween and New Year's, and let me tell you, there is nowhere—*nowhere*—on my five-foot-two frame to hide an extra ten pounds. I'd spent hours in the gym this year trying to take it off, and I *loathe* the gym.

It was all their fault.

I shoved the invite back into the envelope and whipped it across the room like a Frisbee. Then I shrugged off my coat, dug my phone from my bag, and wondered which of my sisters I should call first to rant about this. I decided on my younger sister, Maren, only because our older sister, Stella, was a therapist and might try to analyze my anger rather than indulge it. Maren, a free-spirit who believed that everything happened for a reason and gluten-free pancakes tasted as good as regular pancakes, might not share my outrage either, but she seemed a better bet to start with.

"Hello?"

"They invited me," I said.

"What?"

"Lucy and Richard! They sent me a fucking wedding invitation!" I gestured wildly with my free hand.

She gasped. "They didn't."

"They did."

"Why would they do such a thing?" Maren kept her voice low, which meant she was likely still at the yoga studio where she worked.

"To show off, obviously," I huffed. "To rub my face in the fact that I am a loser and they are the winners."

"Emme, come on. You're not a loser."

I began to pace back and forth in front of the big picture window overlooking downtown Detroit. Normally the view of the city lights coming on at twilight cheered me up, but not today. "Then why can't I find someone nice? Why do I keep dating assholes who disappoint me? Why don't my pants fit?"

She lowered her voice to a whisper. "Listen, can we talk about this later? I would be happy to help you find answers to some of these questions you have about yourself, but I'm at the desk and the studio is getting busy with the after-work crowd. Hey, why don't you come down and take a class? I think it would be great for you, really help you find some peace and balance."

I wrinkled my nose. I didn't want peace and balance. I wanted wine and cheese. Maybe a cupcake. "I can't," I lied. "I have to work tonight."

"Okay. Maybe tomorrow?"

"Maybe. I'll call you."

We hung up, and I stood there fuming for a moment, eyeballing the invitation, which lay on the floor in front of the television. Tossing my phone onto the couch, I picked up the envelope and took it into the kitchen, holding it away from me between my thumb and forefinger like it was a rotting vegetable. Then I set it on the counter while I yanked the cork from a bottle of Merlot I'd opened last night. Since no one was looking, I took a few swills straight from the bottle.

"Lousy motherfuckers," I seethed, my nostrils flaring. "No class whatsoever." After a few more mouthfuls, I set the bottle on the counter and pulled the RSVP card from the envelope. It gave me two choices—I could *regretfully decline* or *accept with pleasure.*

If I were really the bigger person, I thought, I would put an X on the *regretfully decline* line and simply send the RSVP card back. That's what Stella would have done, but Stella has *way* better control of her emotions than I do. It's easier for her to be a bigger person because she hogged all the sensible, rational genes. I got all the wild, unbalanced ones, which was great for enthusiasm and creativity, but meant my feelings occasionally got the better of me.

Okay, *often* got the better of me.

Better make that usually.

Maren says this is because I am not centered and lack inner homeostasis (which I think sounds like some sort of infection, so I'm pretty glad I don't have it). If this had happened to Maren, she might have gotten angry, but then she would have gathered herself with a few deep breaths, repeated some sort of soulful affirmation about letting it go, and tossed the invite into the recycling bin. But while I agreed that the tree deserved a better purpose in its next life, there was no way in hell I could let this go—not without a retaliatory move.

Lifting the bottle to my lips again, I considered my options. I could show up at their stupid wedding and cause some kind of disturbance, but that would be a little bit public, and I prefer to keep my crazy hidden whenever possible. So that was no good. But maybe I could send the RSVP card back with a little message from me. Like I could cross out *regretfully* and pencil in a more accurate word, like *disgustedly*. Or *revoltingly*. That might be satisfying.

I set the bottle aside, pulled a thick black Sharpie marker from a drawer, and stuck the cap between my teeth. But instead of merely adding a word, I decided to add my own response.

Kindly Respond

M s. Emme Devine

___ ACCEPTS WITH PLEASURE
___ REGRETFULLY DECLINES
X *SAYS GO FUCK YOURSELF*

____ Steak ____ Chicken ____ Pasta

There. That was better.

But it still wasn't enough.

Maybe it would have been enough if I hadn't told him I loved him. If I hadn't thought he might be the one. If I hadn't confided all this in Lucy, who'd probably been sleeping with him at the time.

No, I couldn't send this back. I didn't want them to think they had broken me in some way, or shaken my faith in love. They'd shaken my faith in *humanity*, perhaps, but I still believed in love. I still believed in soul mates. I still wished on stars and blew the fluff off dandelions and read my horoscope every morning, hoping for romance on the horizon.

I just wasn't sure I believed in *myself*.

I mean, I must be doing *something* wrong to be single at thirty when I didn't want to be. And this wedding invitation felt like a kick in the gut, a reminder that I was the butt of the joke, a giant signpost from the universe that said YOU CAN'T HAVE NICE THINGS.

It had to be destroyed.

It was while I was opening a second bottle of wine, a Firesteed pinot noir, that it came to me—fire.

Fire was the answer.

It was symbolic!

I would *burn* that invitation, ignite one little corner and watch the flames eat away at their fancy paper and their pretentious words and their choice of chicken or steak. I'd turn their love to ashes, exactly like they'd done to my pride. Then I would *truly* be over the betrayal, and I'd let it go. I'd move on. I'd rise from the embers like a phoenix, triumphant and strong!

I put the RSVP card back into the envelope and opened the kitchen drawer again. My hands shook as I pulled out a utility lighter. It ignited with a gratifying click. I picked up the invitation in the other hand, my lower lip caught between my teeth. Then I carefully set it ablaze, my heart racing as the flames crept toward my fingers, much quicker than I'd expected. In fact, the thing was burning so fast that it startled me, and I dropped it.

This probably would have been okay except for the fact that I had this Easter bunny decoration sitting on my counter that turned out to be *highly* flammable. It was cute —at least, it had been before I barbecued it—a white rabbit standing on its hind legs with big floppy ears, faux fur, and a straw pack on its back with colored eggs in it that said HOPPY EASTER.

Before I knew it, there was a raging rabbit inferno right in front of me. I totally panicked, screaming at the top of my lungs and frantically looking around for something to put out the fire with. The only thing at hand was the bottle of wine, but thankfully I at least had the good sense not to pour that on the flames.

In hindsight, of course, there were any number of things I could have done. Aimed the faucet nozzle at the blaze and drowned the bunny. Smothered the bunny with the kitchen rug. Recalled that there was a fire extinguisher right below the sink.

I did none of those things.

Instead, I stood there freaking out, flailing my arms and continuing to shriek, imagining the headlines: BITTER OLD MAID BURNS DOWN HISTORIC BUILDING IN JEALOUS RAGE. I wondered if I should dial 911 or run into the hall and pull the fire alarm. It seemed like I might save more lives if I got everyone out of the building, so I bolted for the door. I was halfway there when I remembered the lesson from visiting the firehouse in kindergarten—you were supposed to crawl if your house was on fire so you wouldn't breathe in the smoke! Immediately I dropped to my hands and knees and kept moving.

Right at that moment, the door to my apartment swung open and my neighbor from across the hall burst in. He wore a suit and tie and a worried expression.

I looked up at him from my hands and knees. "Nate! Help!"

"Emme, what the hell? Why are you screaming?"

"Fire! In the kitchen!"

He moved past me with long, quick strides. Scrambling to my feet, I followed behind. The rabbit was still engulfed in flames on the counter. Without a word, Nate went straight for the extinguisher under the sink and sprayed the poor creature with huge clouds of white. When the fire was out, the two of us stood next to each other, staring at the mess on the counter.

"Jesus, Em. What did the bunny ever do to you?"

I flattened a palm over my chest. My heart was beating way too fast. "I think I'm having a heart attack."

"You're not having a heart attack. Do I even want to know how this happened?" Nate gave me a sidelong look.

Closing my eyes, I took a deep, slow breath and exhaled. "Probably not."

"And yet I'm oddly curious." Nate, maddeningly calm as usual, returned the fire extinguisher to the cabinet and closed the door. "Fire is one calamity from which I *haven't* had to rescue you. And there aren't many of those left." He straightened and leaned back against the sink, crossing his arms over his chest. Not a speck of dust on his black suit. Not a hair out of place.

Smoothing back the wayward strands that had escaped my bun, I opened my mouth to defend myself, but wasn't sure how to do it. *Rescue* seemed too strong a word for the way Nate occasionally helped me out, but I will admit to calling him whenever I saw a big spider in my apartment or heard a strange noise in the night or locked myself out. And he always answered the call, even if he had to come home from work to resc—

Ahem. To help me out. I wasn't the kind of girl who needed or wanted to be *rescued*.

"It was an accident," I said, brushing dust off my skirt.

"I assumed that much. You're a little crazy, but not that kind of crazy." His smile widened and he cocked his head. "And why, exactly, were you crawling on the floor?"

My face got hot, but I lifted my chin and defended my knowledge of kindergarten fire safety. "You're supposed to crawl when your house is on fire. Everybody knows that."

He burst out laughing. "I see. And where were you planning to crawl?"

"Into the hallway to pull the fire alarm," I said, like it

was obvious. "So I could save everyone, including you, I might add."

That made him laugh even harder, which made me feel even smaller next to his six-foot frame. "Thank you for that. Can I ask why you didn't simply use the fire extinguisher?"

"I don't know. I couldn't think, okay? I forgot it was there."

"Ah. Well, next time you play with matches, try to remember it."

"I wasn't playing with matches," I said irritably. "I was trying to burn something, and set the rabbit on fire by mistake."

"What were you trying to burn?"

I ignored the question and went to the upper cabinet where I kept my wine glasses. Taking two out, I set them on the island and reached for the bottle of wine on the counter behind Nate. He didn't move out of my way, and I came close enough to smell him.

Nate always smelled good, even when he'd just come from the gym. It was totally unfair—if the universe was going to give a man the kind of good looks it had bestowed upon Nate Pearson, the chiseled jaw, blue-eyed movie star kind that melted hearts, willpower, and panties with a single glance, then it could have at *least* given him overactive sweat glands or something. But no. As far as the male species went, he was about as perfect a specimen as you could imagine, at least physically. Yet another example of how the universe favors some people more than others.

Not that I had anything against Nate, other than the fact that he was a divorce attorney and thought it was insane that people spent a fortune on their weddings—including my fee—when half of those marriages were going to fail. Needless to say, we disagreed on things like marriage, love, soul mates, and wishing on stars. Actually, we disagreed on almost everything. But I'd never been one to shy away from conflict, and both of us liked a good argument.

That said, I didn't particularly feel like arguing about this. Nate was not going to understand my feelings.

"Well?" he prompted.

"Let's just say I had a bad day," I told him as I poured us some wine.

"Don't tell me—the mother of the groom refuses to wear beige."

"Very funny." I handed him his glass. "Are we ever going to have a conversation where you don't make fun of what I do?"

"I doubt it." He took a sip. "Thanks. Now what were you trying to burn? And don't bother lying because you're horrible at it, and you know I'll get the truth out of you anyway."

It was true. I swear, the man could talk the bark off a tree. I steeled myself and gave in. "A wedding invitation."

A grin tugged at his mouth. "Only you." This is his favorite thing to say when I get myself into troublesome situations.

"It wasn't just any wedding invitation," I said defensively.

"Do go on."

"It was for Lucy and Richard's wedding."

He gasped dramatically. "Lucy the Traitor and Richard the Turd are getting married?"

"Yes! And they had the audacity to invite me!" Thinking about it made me angry all over again. "Talk about rude. They don't really want me there. They did it to spite me. To shove it in my face."

"I see. And burning their wedding invitation was going to make you feel better?"

"I don't know. I just got so mad, I needed to express it somehow. Don't you ever get that mad?" I asked him, although I knew the answer. Nate could always keep his cool. He probably didn't even sweat in the sauna.

"Nope. I don't give anyone that sort of power over me."

I rolled my eyes. "I know, I know. Feelings are bad."

"I never said feelings are bad."

"You just don't have them," I prodded.

"I have them. But I'm careful with them—not like some people I know who hand them over at every opportunity." He gave me a pointed look over the rim of his wine glass.

"I don't hand them over," I said in a huff.

"You're at least buy one, get one free." He took a drink, enjoying this a little too much.

"Well, how am I supposed to turn it off? When I feel something, I feel it deeply." I paused and took another drink, then studied the toes of my shoes. "My sister says I'm not balanced, that I lack inner peace." I peeked up at him. "Do you think that?"

"Normally, I think all that stuff is a bunch of BS." A smile tugged at his lips as he glanced behind him at the charred rabbit. "But in your case, I think it might be true."

I bristled. "Sorry I'm not as perfect as you."

"No one is." He countered my dirty look with a wink. "Look. Did it ever occur to you that maybe the invitation was sincere? Maybe they thought you'd want to come."

"Are you being serious right now?"

He shrugged. "You told them you didn't care about their relationship. You told them you were happy for them."

"I was lying, Nate! I didn't want them to see how hurt I felt. How stupid I was."

"You weren't stupid, Emme." Nate shook his head. "You trusted people you shouldn't have. It happens all the time. Have you seen my car? My flat screen? My wristwatch collection? All paid for with disappointment and broken trust."

I frowned. "That doesn't help. I feel like a fool."

"So you've learned a lesson. Don't be so trusting next time. Don't get so carried away."

"I guess." But somehow his advice didn't make me feel any better. Why wouldn't I trust someone who claimed to care about me? Who said he loved me? Who gave me every indication, at least outwardly, that he was happy? How was I supposed to know who to trust and who would disappoint me? My eyes filled with tears. Embarrassed, I tried to blink them away.

Nate tapped me on the nose. "Hey. Cheer up, Calamity. It's Friday night. Let's do something fun." He finished the wine in his glass and set it on the counter.

"No date tonight?" I asked, surprised. Rare was the weekend night Nate wasn't out on the town with a beautiful woman—or several—on his arm. I'd seen them leaving his apartment the next morning on multiple occasions. He definitely had a type: tall, bombshell brunettes with long legs and big chests. Needless to say, I did not fit the bill, which was just as well. I didn't want a man who was "careful" with his feelings. I wanted a man who was generous with them. And I liked being different from all those one-nighters. Our friendship felt special.

He shook his head. "Originally, I was going to have dinner with my mother, but she wasn't feeling well enough to make the drive down."

"Oh. Nothing serious, I hope."

"Nothing serious. Anyway, lucky for you, that means

my evening is free. Do you want to go out? Or come over and watch a movie? I'll even watch Skyfall."

We both loved Bond flicks, but Nate considered every Bond actor other than Sean Connery a personal affront. I happened to prefer Daniel Craig. "That's big of you."

"What can I say? I'm that kind of guy. And I don't like to see you so upset." He grabbed my head and wobbled it side to side. "So let's do something to put a smile on that face. Preferably something that does not involve fire."

I tried to push his hands away, but I was laughing. "That could have happened to anybody."

"Nope. Only you." He started for the door, and I trailed at his heels. "Come over whenever."

"You're telling me you've never started a fire in the kitchen by mistake? Not even a small one?"

Reaching the door, he pulled it open and tossed a rakish grin over his shoulder. "I set my fires in the bedroom, Calamity. And they're *never* small."

My stomach flipped as the door shut behind him, his words setting off a stirring deep inside me. *Relax, you silly fool. He's not flirting with you—he's bragging.*

Back in the kitchen, I got some paper towels and started to clean up the mess on the counter, shoving the thought of Nate in his bedroom from my mind.

But the fluttery feeling in my belly lingered.

TWO

NATE

I made sure the door to Emme's apartment locked behind me. As of yet she had not called me to save her from a masked intruder, but no sense inviting disaster. Emme did that well enough on her own.

Still smiling at the thought of her crawling frantically toward the door to "save" me, I let myself into my apartment across the hall. Like Emme's, it was open and spacious, lots of dark wood and exposed brick, and nearly an entire wall of old-fashioned, multi-paned windows, arched at the top. Her apartment and mine were actually mirror images of each other, with the kitchen at one end, above which was a loft bedroom, and the rest of the living space open all the way up to the exposed ducts and pipes and beams reminiscent of the building's industrial history. But other than the bones and layout, our lofts were completely different.

Mine was masculine but sophisticated—leather uphol-stery, chrome finishes, sturdy-legged tables and chairs with hard edges and straight lines. This was not a frat-boy man cave with fucking futons and bean bags and plastic cup rings on the coffee table. At thirty-five, I was over that shit.

This was a classy-as-fuck bachelor pad. I had framed art on the walls, expensive rugs on the floor, and guests drank good booze out of real fucking glasses they could set on stone coasters while they relaxed on deep, comfortable couches.

Emme's apartment was nice, too, but her style was much more girly and dramatic. A pink velvet sofa. Curvy tables and chairs. Fluffy cream-colored blankets and pillows and rugs. Gold accents. A crystal chandelier over her table. I'd never seen her bedroom, but I imagined it was much the same—a big bed covered by a puffy, ruffled down comforter and heaped with pink and ivory pillows she had to tunnel through to get in. She probably had a crystal chandelier up there, too. I once teased her that her apartment looked like it had been decorated by Marie Antoinette. She punched my shoulder, but secretly I think she took it as a compliment.

Inside my loft, I saw the leather bag containing my laptop and a few files sitting right where I'd dropped it on the floor. I'd just gotten in the door from work when I'd heard Emme's screams and took off running. Given the girl's propensity to overreact, I thought maybe she'd found a gray hair or broken a nail. One time I heard her shrieking and shouting obscenities at the top of her lungs, and went over there only to find her rolling around on the living room rug in agony trying to zip up her skinny jeans.

But I'll admit to a fearful adrenaline rush tonight as I'd fumbled for my key to her apartment and raced across the hall. Those screams had sounded real, and I'd had this anxious feeling all day I hadn't been able to shake, like something was going to go wrong. I'm not a superstitious person by any means, but I don't believe in ignoring gut instincts. I might not talk about them, but I have them, and they're usually spot on.

Emme had given me a key to her place because she

locked herself out so frequently. She had one to mine as well, but the only time she'd used it was to water my plants when I traveled. I'd never locked myself out. How hard was it to check that you had your keys before you shut the door?

Loosening my tie with one hand, I headed up the stairs to my bedroom. While I changed out of my suit and into jeans and a light gray sweater, I wondered what would have happened if I hadn't come home when I did. Would she really have pulled the fire alarm?

Probably.

I shook my head, laughing a little as I hung up my suit pants and jacket—trousers from the hem on a felt clamp hanger so the wrinkles would fall out (I fucking hate wrinkles).

After sniffing the white shirt I'd worn to work, I decided it could use a cleaning, so I tucked it into the bag destined for the dry cleaners. In the bathroom on the other side of my closet, I checked to see that my neatly-tended scruff wasn't veering too close to mangy hipster territory and ran a hand through my dark hair, pleased to see I hadn't grown any additional grays since this morning. Lately, it felt like they'd been cropping up overnight. Going gray didn't worry me because I was getting older—I had no problem with aging. I had the job, the apartment, the car, the social life, the bank account. But I was vain as fuck and liked to look good. The minute I thought the gray was cramping my style, it'd be gone.

Downstairs in the kitchen, I filled a martini glass with crushed ice for Emme and let it chill on the counter, then poured myself a few fingers of bourbon. I was about to text Emme to ask what kind of takeout she felt like having when she messaged me.

Emme: Do you have enough vodka?

Me: Enough for what?

Emme: For my bitterness, my jealousy, my fat ass, my broken heart, and my vengeful soul.

Me: Maybe not for your vengeful soul. But for all the rest, yes.

Emme: Good. There in 20.

A minute later I got on Grubhub and decided to order Chinese from The Peterboro without asking her. She loved the crab rangoon at one of our favorite local places, but if I asked her, she'd probably squawk about having to watch her weight, which was ridiculous. I thought she looked better with a few more curves on her, anyway, but I couldn't tell her that.

Occasionally I wondered what the fuck the guys she dated were saying or not saying to her to make her anything less than one hundred percent confident in her skin when she was so confident about other parts of her life—her job, style, her family relationships, her opinions. But then I'd remember the kinds of guys she chose—nothing but douchebags and assholes, none of whom were worse than fucking Richard the Turd, and that's saying a lot. The entire time she was with him, I wanted to tell her what a weasel he would turn out to be.

I've known a million guys like him, guys who lie and cheat and don't give a shit about anyone but themselves. (I swear to God, half of them are lawyers in this city. And their pants are *always* wrinkled.) But I never said a word because it wasn't my place, and she wouldn't have believed me, anyway. The last time I tried to give her dating advice, our conversation went something like this:

Me: What do you see in that guy?

Her: Potential.

Me: Potential is not sexy.

Her: Relationships take time and effort. It's not only about sex. You wouldn't understand because you are not a relationship person; therefore, you are not qualified to give advice on them—not that I asked for it.

But I didn't need to be a relationship person to smell Richard's bullshit. It stunk to high heaven. It was amazing to me that someone as smart and sexy as Emme would fall for a guy like that.

But what could you expect from a woman who thought Daniel Craig made a good James Bond?

After ordering the food, I wandered over to the windows with my drink and looked out at the city while I waited for her knock. It was kind of surprising to me how much I liked spending an evening with her, given that our relationship was not now and had never been sexual, and sex was usually the way I preferred to connect with women. Our friendship was pretty unlikely on all levels, really. I didn't generally gravitate toward needy women, preferring those who were independent, maybe even a little aloof or reserved, those looking for short-term pleasure rather than long-term connection—the total opposite of Emme. That woman was a no-holding-back, no-poker-face-whatsoever, here-have-some-feelings Seeker of The One. I always teased her that she wore her heart on her sleeve and a sign on her heart that said HOMELESS—PLEASE HELP.

Not that she was needy in a clingy sort of way, because she wasn't. There was something kind of nice about the way she needed me, actually—I think it was that she didn't *want* to need me, and she would have argued until her dying breath that she didn't need me, not *really*. It made it kind of fun in an antagonistic way to be the one she turned to all the time. Mostly I liked to make fun of her for it, sort of like the way you'd poke at your best friend's younger sister.

But no matter how cute that sister was in her own hot-tempered-girl-next-door way (and probably a firecracker in bed), you couldn't sleep with her.

Even if you sometimes thought about it.

Even if you sometimes sneaked a peek at her legs in that short black skirt. Or her ass in her tight jeans. Or that little, accidental glimpse of a bra strap when a sleeve slipped from her shoulder.

Even if you sometimes had to work really, really hard not to fantasize about her while you were in the shower. Or alone in bed on a Saturday morning. Or not alone in bed on a Saturday night with a woman who turned out to be a little *too* reserved and aloof and you needed a little fiery inspiration to get the job done.

Fiery inspiration. Fuck, that was funny.

And hot.

Grimacing, I adjusted the crotch of my pants as they threatened to grow too tight for comfort. I didn't want to have to hide an erection from Emme when she arrived. I'd never live it down.

I closed my eyes and tried to think of something else, something not sexy. This morning's contentious arbitration. This afternoon's tense phone call with my mother. That ridiculous blackened rabbit. Those things distracted me for maybe five seconds, but then my mind took an unauthorized detour to Emme crawling toward me on her hands and knees, slowly this time, her eyes hooded and hungry instead of wide and panicked.

Oh, fuck.

Heat rushed my chest, making my sweater feel tight and itchy. I couldn't breathe for a second. My stomach muscles were clenched tight as blood rushed between my legs. I imagined her looking up at me. Her hands sliding up my thighs. Her fingers unbuckling my belt. Her tongue wetting her lips. The sound of a zipper being lowered.

My cock jumped.

"Not gonna happen, pal," I muttered to my dick, focusing on a church spire in the big arched window. "Not in a million years. That girl is off limits. She falls in love *way* too easily. And it's not like you don't get enough attention." Although lately, all the attention had been from me. I was in one of my rare dry spells. Maybe that was my problem. Tomorrow night, I'd do something about that.

Tonight, it was out of the question.

Because Emme was one of those girls who could not separate love from sex—I saw that the first night we hung out together (she was locked out of her apartment, and I'd invited her to hang out in mine until the building manager could bring her another key). For her, the emotional and the physical were inextricably linked. For me, that was like a neon sign screaming "RUN! RUN AWAY!" I'd made the mistake of sleeping with one or two of those girls in college... never again. Sex was a great way to feel good and make someone else feel good. But it wasn't emotional. Not for me. I made sure of it.

I went into the kitchen, opened the freezer, and stuck my head in as far as it would go. A couple minutes later, I pulled out the bottle of vodka I kept in there and began to make Emme's martini—three olives, extra dry, and extra dirty. I concentrated on mixing the cocktail exactly right, and by the time she knocked, her drink was ready, my breathing had slowed, my body temperature had returned to normal, and my pants fit just fine.

See? All it took to control your feelings was a little discipline.

―――――――

"SO WAS it any better the second time?" From her end of the couch, Emme looked at me hopefully before eating the last olive from her martini off the stainless steel cocktail pick. Her shoes were off, her denim-clad legs were tucked underneath her, and she'd taken her hair down. It spilled down over her shoulders, long and blond and wavy.

"You mean the third time?" As the credits rolled, I tossed back a little more bourbon, hoping it would take the edge off that uneasy feeling I'd had all day. I'd hoped putting out the fire in Emme's kitchen would make it go away, but it had lingered. "I've watched this for you before. And no, it wasn't."

She stretched out one leg and nudged me with her bare foot. Her toes were painted pink, of course. Not a soft pink like her velvet sofa, but a deep vibrant hue, more like a raspberry. "You just don't like Craig because he shows more vulnerability than Connery. He's more human. And you know he's a better actor."

"I don't know any such thing. And I don't need to see vulnerability in Bond because he's not a real person. Not that I think exhibiting vulnerability is an asset to real people, anyway, at least not usually. And definitely not men."

She made a disgusted noise at the back of her throat and poked me with her toes again. "Real men can be vulnerable, Nate."

"But they shouldn't show it."

"Why not?"

"Because it's a weakness, and weakness undermines power and authority and control." But I couldn't stop looking at her toes. What the fuck?

A sigh escaped her as she swirled the last few sips of her martini. "Well, I prefer men who *aren't* afraid to show weakness sometimes. That's what makes them real to me."

"But Bond is a fantasy, Emme. A fantasy." I got up off the couch, taking my empty glass with me. Partly it was to get a short refill, and partly it was to put a little distance between my thigh and her foot. It was disturbing how close to my dick it was. And why was I thinking about putting her toes in my mouth? I wasn't even a foot man. *Must be the dry spell.*

I went into the kitchen and reached for the bourbon bottle, pouring myself only a couple more swallows since I wanted to be at the gym first thing in the morning, and working out with a hangover was never a good time.

Emme followed me into the kitchen and kept arguing. "He's not a fantasy. A fantasy is a *thing*, a dream. Bond is a character—a *human* character."

"Fine, he's a character—the ultimate alpha male. No wife and kids, no honey-I'm-home. He eats and drinks what he wants when he wants, drives a cool car, sleeps with beautiful women, and kills bad people. No feelings involved."

Emme rolled her eyes before she finished her drink and placed her empty glass in the sink. Our dinner dishes were already in the dishwasher, the leftovers put away in the fridge. "And this is what you aspire to?"

"Why not?"

She gestured dramatically. "Because it's a cold and lonely life! You're going to die alone!"

I laughed. We had some variation of this argument all the time. I have no idea why she was so hell-bent on my having feelings, but she was. "I'm never cold, and I enjoy my alone time. As for dying, why not die alone? I'm going to spare a bunch of people a lot of grief and regret."

"That's sad. I'm sad for you."

"Of course you are."

"You know, even an alpha male can have feelings occasionally."

"Oh?"

She crossed her arms and leaned back against the counter, giving me the evil eye. "Yes. He doesn't have to be hard as granite all the way through, *all* the time."

Don't think about being hard. Don't think about being hard. Don't think about being hard. I leaned back against the opposite counter and sort of held my glass in front of my crotch. "Why are you even concerned with alpha males? You're never attracted to them."

"What? Yes, I am."

"No, you're not." I knew her type well. "You're always saying how you don't want to be rescued, you want someone willing to show affection and talk about feelings, you don't like arrogant or competitive guys or guys who always have to win, you like guys who get along with everyone—"

"What's wrong with that?"

"Nothing. But that's not an alpha male."

She chewed her bottom lip. "But look at Bond. Who is he so worried about protecting? Why is he so driven to kill the bad guys? There must be people he cares about more than himself to put himself in harm's way so often."

"Maybe he just likes the thrill of the chase."

"Maybe he's more selfless than you think."

"In this case, I think we're going to have to disagree."

She sighed heavily, and I knew I had disappointed her by ending the argument in a draw instead of winning or losing it. Any other night, I might have kept it going, but there was something odd going on with me, something that had me wanting to close the distance between us, set her up on the counter, slip my hands beneath that fuzzy white sweater she had on, see what her legs felt like wrapped around my hips. But I knew better.

Get her out of here before you do something stupid.

"Hey, you got fortune cookies? I didn't see those." She reached for the little cellophane bag.

"I forgot about them."

"Can I have one?"

"You can have them both."

She took one out and cracked it open. "A ship in harbor is safe, but that's not why ships are built."

"Very deep."

She ignored me and went on to the next one. "You have to keep breaking your heart until it opens." Her lips pursed. "Hm. I don't want a dangerous ship *or* a broken heart."

I laughed at the anguish in her tone and expression.

"It's not funny," she said, shoving pieces of cookie in her mouth. "It means I'm doomed to be unhappy. And then I'm going to die in a shipwreck."

"It means you take things way too seriously." I tipped back the last of the bourbon in my glass, and set it in the sink. "Well, I've got an early morning at the gym tomorrow."

She popped the rest of one cookie in her mouth and brushed off her hands. "I'm going. What time is it anyway?"

I checked the digital clock on the microwave. "It's 11:11."

Her face lit up. "Ooh! Make a wish!"

"What?"

"It's 11:11, you have to make a wish." She closed her

eyes for a couple seconds, her lips moving as if saying a silent prayer. Then she opened them. "Did you do it?"

I laughed. "No."

"Nate! Hurry up! Make a wish." She glanced at the clock and flapped her hands agitatedly.

"I don't have a wish to make."

"So make one for me, then. And do it fast, before it's 11:12."

This time it was my turn to roll my eyes, but secretly I wished that the next guy she fell in love with would love her back the way she deserved, and she'd be happy. But I didn't close my eyes, and I didn't move my lips, so she had no idea whether I'd made a wish or not.

"Did you do it?" She looked concerned.

"Yes."

"For me?"

"Yes."

Her mouth fell open for a second. "What was it? What did you wish for me?"

I started to laugh as I left the kitchen. "Nice try, Calamity. Even I know you don't tell a wish if you want it to come true." The credits were still rolling on the television, and I picked up the remote to turn everything off.

"Oh, *now* you believe in wishes?" She sat down on the couch and tugged on her fluffy boots.

No, I wanted to tell her. *I don't, because I learned a long time ago that wishes and prayers and hopes don't mean anything. No one is listening.* But I didn't tell her that, not only because she was looking up at me with my favorite expression of hers, the one daring me to fight back, but because at that very moment, I heard a noise in the hall.

A strange and oddly terrifying noise.

I looked over my shoulder toward the door, thinking I must have imagined the sound.

Then I heard it again—the unmistakable, ball-shrinking, cringe-inducing sound of a baby's wail.

I looked at Emme, who had paused mid-task, one foot off the ground. "Did you hear that?" I asked her.

"Yeah," she said, pulling the boot on and dropping her foot. "Was that a *baby*?"

"It couldn't be. Who's baby would it be?" Emme and I had the only two apartments at the end of this hall.

"Maybe someone's watching a movie really loud," she suggested.

But then we heard it again, and this time it wasn't an isolated cry but a plaintive howling that didn't stop.

Emme stood up. "We better go look."

I knew she was right, but I had a horrible, sick feeling in my stomach. That unease from earlier had grown into a bowling ball-sized bucket of dread.

Emme went to the door and opened it. Then she gasped. "Oh my God."

Paralyzed with fear, I didn't move. "What is it?"

"Come here."

Reluctantly, I walked to the door and peered over her shoulder at the screaming baby that had apparently been abandoned at my doorstep. "Oh my God. What the fuck?"

"Shh. It can hear you." Emme moved into the hall and stared down at the baby, which was red-faced and furious, its tiny fists waving in the air, a pink fleece hat slipping down over its eyes. It was covered with blankets and lying in some sort of contraption with a plastic base, a reclining seat, and a handlebar across the top. Next to it was a bag overflowing with items I didn't recognize. White things and pink things and fluffy things and plastic things.

I thought I might vomit.

"My God." Emme knelt down next to it and made shushing noises, removing the hat and smoothing its crazy tufts of dark hair back from its face. "It's a baby."

"I can see that." I braced myself in the doorway with a hand on either side of the frame. "But what's it doing here?"

"I don't know." On her knees, Emme looked up and down the hallway, but there was no one around. Getting to her feet again, she picked up the contraption by the handle, groaning as if it were heavy, although the baby didn't look as if it could weigh more than a bottle of whiskey. She set it down again, frowning as she studied the handle. Then she clicked some sort of lever or button, and the seat detached from the base. "Aha. Okay, grab the bag and the base to the car seat and bring it in."

"Why?" I stayed exactly where I was, with my hands bracketed on either side of the doorjamb, as if I wanted to block her entrance. Which, of course, I did. This baby was a harbinger of evil. I could feel it.

Emme gaped at me, struggling to get a better grip on the car seat using two hands. The baby continued to yowl, a shrill, ear-piercing sound. "What do you mean *why?* Because there is a *baby* in the hallway outside your apartment that appears to have been left on purpose. We can't just leave it here."

"Maybe it was left outside of *your* apartment. Why can't we take it there?"

Emme rolled her eyes. "Give me a break, Nate. It's not going to bite you or give you cooties or whatever it is you're afraid of."

"How do we even know it's a real baby? It could be a bomb. Is it ticking?"

Emme stared at me. "Are you insane? It's not a bomb;

it's a *baby*. Now get out of my way so I can come in. This thing is heavy."

She came at me and I had no choice but to step aside. Once she was in, I stepped out into the hall and walked all the way to one end. Opening the stairwell door, I went into it and looked up and down. "Hello?" I called, my voice echoing into the dark. I saw no one and heard nothing. I came out of the stairwell and walked toward the elevators, again seeing no one and hearing nothing. Scratching my head, I went back to my door and stared down at the over-stuffed canvas bag and plastic car seat base. My heart was hammering in my chest, and not in a good way.

Stop being ridiculous, Pearson. It's just a baby. And it's probably a complete coincidence that it was left at your door. Maybe even a mistake. But I still felt nervous as I picked up the bag and the base and brought them inside.

Emme had taken the baby from the seat and was cradling it in her arms as she paced back and forth in front of the couch, bouncing it gently and shushing it with soft, soothing sounds.

"We should call the police," I said, trying to sound authoritative as I set the bag and base on the floor. "We need to find out who this baby belongs to."

Emme stopped moving and looked up at me. "Brace yourself, Nate. I think she might belong to you."

"Me? That's impossible!"

Emme started the pace-and-bounce routine again, focusing her attention on the baby's face. "There's a letter in the car seat with your name on it."

I didn't want to see it. God help me, I didn't want to. If it were any other day, maybe I wouldn't have been so scared. But all day long, my gut had been trying to warn me about something.

Swallowing hard, I went over to the car seat and saw the white envelope at the bottom of it. My name was written on the front in black ink. Cursive letters. A feminine slant. I reached down, picked it up, and pulled out the handwritten letter inside.

Dear Nate,

I'm sorry. I should have told you about her. Trust me when I say she was just as much of a surprise to me as I'm sure she is to you. I thought I would give her up, but found I couldn't. I thought I could do it on my own, but find I can't. I just need a break, okay? Some air. I'll come back for her, I promise. She is healthy, has had all her shots, and eats well, about four ounces every three hours. Her formula and a couple bottles are in the diaper bag, along with some diapers, wipes, some clothes, and a couple toys. She can sleep in her car seat, although she is not a good sleeper.

She is eight weeks old.

Her name is Paisley.

Sincerely,

Rachel

I read the letter once, twice, five times, ten times, twenty. I wanted it to be lies. I wanted to deny I'd ever known a Rachel. I wanted to pretend I didn't remember the boozy weekend we'd spent in her downtown hotel room after blowing off the boring tax law seminar we were supposed to attend.

But I couldn't.

My vision clouded.

I have a daughter.

She's eight weeks old.

Her name is Paisley.

I swayed forward.

Is Paisley even a name?

I thought it was a tie pattern.

I prefer stripes.

Something was wrong with my legs.

"Well?"

I looked up from the letter to find Emme staring at me intently. "Is it true? Is the baby yours?"

"Yes," I said, my voice cracking, my world cracking. "I think she is."

And then I fucking fainted.

THREE

EMME

"Oh my God! Nate!"

His eyes had rolled back in his head, his knees had buckled, and he'd dropped forward in a heap, his upper body slumped over the car seat. I hurried over to him and knelt by his side.

"Nate. Hey, wake up." Hitching the baby over to one arm, I slapped his face a few times, not too hard, but not too gently either.

He moaned and his eyes fluttered open.

"Nate, can you hear me?"

"Yeah." He blinked a few times and sat back on his heels. "What happened?"

"You fainted."

He looked distressed. "No, I didn't."

I bit my tongue—he had *so* fainted—and took his hand, helping him to his feet and then leading him over to the couch. "Here, sit down. Do you need some water?"

"No. Yes. I don't know." He scratched his head, which left a few pieces sticking up in the back. His eyes were still dazed, and he was sitting in a way I had never seen him sit before, sort of slouched over, defeated. He looked like he'd been hit by a bus.

"I'll get you some water," I said, heading for the kitchen. The baby was finally quiet in my arms, as if distracted by the show. I found a glass in a cupboard, threw a few ice cubes in it, and filled it from the water dispenser in the freezer door.

Part of me simply couldn't believe it. Nate didn't seem like the kind of guy this could happen to—he was too clever, too together, too *lucky*. Another part of me wondered if, when you had as much casual sex as Nate did, your luck was bound to run out at some point.

I looked down at the baby in my arms. Her expression seemed to mirror Nate's—a mix of befuddlement, anger, and fear. I searched for a resemblance and thought I found one in the shape of her big gray-blue eyes. Holy shit, maybe she really was his daughter.

Back in the living room, I handed him the water and watched as he downed the entire glass without taking a breath. Then he lowered it to his lap and stared at the baby, blinking repeatedly as if he thought maybe he'd imagined the whole thing and she simply wouldn't be there when he opened his eyes.

"Are you okay?" I perched at the other end of the couch, but as soon as I sat still the baby started to fuss, so I stood up again and started twisting at the waist from side to side— one of my old nanny tricks for calming a fussy baby.

"I'm fine," Nate said, but it came out as more of a whisper. He cleared his throat and tried again. "I'm fine."

"Okay. But you should stay seated. Sometimes after you faint, you—"

His brow furrowed. "I didn't faint. I tripped, that's all. On that thing." He gestured toward the car seat.

Again, I bit my tongue. "So what did the letter say?"

But Nate didn't answer. Instead he stared straight ahead, murmuring something that sounded like *this can't be happening to me*. When it was obvious he wasn't going to tell me anything, I went over to where the note had slipped from his hand when he'd "tripped" and scooped it up off the floor, which wasn't easy while holding a baby in my arms. Planting my feet wide, I had to do sort of a grande plié, keeping my back upright and blindly reaching for it with my free hand. I made a mental note to thank Maren for dragging me with her to ballet class all those years.

I read the letter a few times, and found my heart beating faster each time through. "Holy shit, Nate. You've got a daughter."

He finally looked at me. "I changed my mind. I'm not fine. I'm dying."

"You're not dying."

"I am. My life is flashing before my eyes."

"You're not *dying*." I glanced at the letter once more. "You're just...a dad."

He groaned and clutched his stomach. "Don't say that word."

"Fine, I won't. But I think it might be true." I put the letter on a table near the door, right next to Nate's keys. "Who's Rachel?"

Nate sighed, his eyes closing a moment. "She's a woman I met at a tax law seminar last year."

"Met?"

Nate pressed his lips together. "Slept with."

"At a *tax law seminar*?"

"The seminar was boring. She had a hotel room."

I nodded, ignoring the quick dart of jealousy, the same one I sometimes felt when I saw women leaving his apartment in the morning. It made even less sense right now. "And was that"—I did some quick math—"roughly eleven months ago?"

He nodded slowly without meeting my eyes.

"And you weren't careful?"

"Of course I was careful," he scoffed. "I'm always careful."

"Right. Well, you'll forgive my confusion as I seem to be holding evidence to the contrary in my arms."

At that Nate jumped off the couch and began to pace back and forth in front of the window, grabbing onto fistfuls of his hair with both hands. "No. This can't be. I protected myself."

"Everyone gets carried away sometimes, Nate."

"Maybe you do, but I don't. Never. Not once. I'm always in control. Always." He stopped pacing and looked at me, his eyes bloodshot and glassy, his hair a disaster. The muscles in his neck flexed as he swallowed hard. "I wore a condom every time. I know I did, because I always do. It's a rule."

"No form of birth control is one hundred percent effective."

He opened his mouth like he was going to argue, but then closed it.

"Unless you think she's lying..." I challenged.

"I didn't say that."

"Did she seem like the kind of person who'd make this up? I mean, she's a lawyer too, right? She'd know paternity could be legally proven or disproven with a test."

He exhaled, his shoulders slumping. "I know. You're right. It's... She's..." He braved a glance at the baby in my arms. "She's more than likely mine. I just...can't believe this is happening."

I couldn't help feeling sorry for him. A lot of guys like Nate—especially lawyers—would probably be screaming *get me a paternity test right the fuck now!* He didn't need someone to scold him or shame him or be judgmental—he needed a friend. He needed a voice of reason. He needed confidence.

And frankly, I needed to see a man step up and be a man. It couldn't all be a fantasy.

"What am I going to do?" he moaned, dropping onto the couch again, holding his head in his hands.

"You're going to take care of her until her mother comes back," I said firmly, taking a seat next to him.

"When's that going to be?"

"I'm not sure, she didn't say. But I can't imagine more than a day or so."

"I know I'm an asshole for this, but I don't want a baby, Emme. Not even for a day or so, even if she is mine."

I kept trying. "What you *want* doesn't really matter. She's here."

Nate looked at his daughter. "I am the *least* qualified person in the universe to parent a child."

"What makes you so unqualified? You've got money. A good job. A place to live."

"That's economics, not parenting. I've never wanted kids. I know nothing about taking care of them, especially a girl. And a baby? Forget it." He stood up suddenly, fisted his hands at his sides, and stared down at me. "You have to take her."

I shook my head and stood up too. "No way, Nate. I'm not taking her. She's *your* daughter."

"God, this is such a nightmare." Nate yanked on his hair and started pacing again. "What the fuck was Rachel thinking? Why didn't she tell me? I could've...could've..."

"Could've what?" I asked. "What would you have told her to do?"

"I don't know," he admitted.

"Maybe she was scared of your reaction. Maybe she didn't want to tell you because she thought you wouldn't handle it well."

"I'd have handled it fine!" he yelled. "Because I'd have been prepared for this insanity, and not fucking blindsided!"

"Okay, okay." Paisley had started to fuss again. "Lower your voice. Look, let's focus on moving forward. Do you have contact information for Rachel? A cell phone number, or an email address?"

He shook his head. "No."

"Do you know what firm she works for?"

"No."

"She was staying at a hotel, so is she from out of state?"

"I don't think so. She might be from Kalamazoo. Or Battle Creek? Somewhere in the middle."

"How about a last name?" I was sort of kidding, so I was stunned when he shook his head again. "Jesus, Nate." I switched Paisley to my other arm and forgot not to be judgy. "You might think I date assholes, and maybe I do, but I at least know their last names and how to find them."

"That's because you're a little girl living in a fantasy world," he shot back. "You think every guy you have sex with is going to be your future husband. You think an orgasm is the equivalent of an engagement ring. Some of us exercise a little more restraint, because we are mature adults and understand that sometimes a fuck is just a fuck."

My nostrils flared. I no longer felt sorry for him. In fact, I kind of felt like punching him. "Wow," I said, blinking. "*I'm* immature?"

"Yes," he snapped, although he looked a little less sure of himself.

"*I'm* immature, and yet it's *you* refusing to face the consequences of your *mature adult* actions." I mocked his deep voice. "Well, guess what? Sometimes a fuck isn't just a fuck, Nate. And if you were really the alpha male you pretend to be, you'd take responsibility for this like a grown-ass man and not fall apart like the ridiculous boy I see in front of me. But then again, maybe you're just like the rest of them—all talk. Shame on me for thinking differently about you." With that, I shoved the baby into his arms, made sure he was holding onto her, and headed for the door. "Good luck, pal," I called over my shoulder. "You're gonna need it."

I let myself into my apartment and allowed the door to slam noisily behind me. Then I stood there, arms crossed over my chest, wondering if leaving that baby alone with Nate was akin to child abuse, or at the very least, neglect. Was she all right with him? Would he know how to feed her tonight? Change her? Get her to sleep? Would he even try, or would he just take her to the fire station and hand her over because he saw that in a movie once? I bet he wouldn't even show them the letter. He'd say he found her somewhere. What an asshole.

Closing my eyes, I inhaled and exhaled slowly. I couldn't help being disappointed in Nate. It would almost be laughable, if there weren't a child involved. Nate was always scolding me for trusting too easily or believing a guy to be something more than he really was, leading me to believe he held himself to a higher standard, but here it was *Nate* letting me down. I didn't even really understand why. He had never made a secret of the fact that he wasn't husband/father material, but somehow he had seemed like he was made of better stuff. The kind of guy who would step the fuck up. The kind of guy you called in a crisis, because he would be there for you. A gentleman. A hero. A real man.

Maybe I should be glad he's just like the rest of them. It's not like he was anything more than a friend to me, anyway.

So why did this feel so shitty?

A knock on my door. I walked toward it slowly. "Yes?" I called out warily. I could hear the baby fussing on the other side.

"I'm sorry. Please open the door, Emme."

That was fast. "Sorry for what?"

"For what I said."

"You just want my help with the baby."

"No! I mean, yes, I do want your help, but I'm really, really sorry. I was angry with myself and I took it out on you."

Huh. That was actually acceptable, if he meant it. I opened the door a crack.

His expression was contrite. "I'm sorry. I was...in shock." He stood up taller, thrust his chest out. "But I'm man enough to handle this, dammit. I'm all fucking man."

"Oh really?"

"Yes." His posture drooped slightly. "I just...need a little help getting started. Will you come back over?"

I considered it. Part of me was still upset about what he'd said, and I've never been particularly quick to forgive (it's something Maren says I need to work on), but I liked his apology, and considering how often he helped me out, I definitely owed him. "Okay," I agreed.

He exhaled with relief, his eyes closing. "Thank God."

Back in his apartment, I picked up the diaper bag from

the floor and brought it over to the coffee table. "Look in there for a bottle and her formula."

"Her formula for what?"

"Infant formula. It's what you put in her bottle. What she eats. It will be a powder you mix with water."

He shook his head. "How do you know all this?"

"I used to be a nanny during summers home from college. It was great money, and it was under the table. But it was a lot of work, and you've got a lot to learn, so let's get started. Find the bottle." I took the baby from his arms. "And she probably needs to be changed."

All the color—what was left of it, anyway—drained from Nate's face. "You mean...her *diaper* needs to be changed?"

"Yes. See if there's a changing pad or blanket in the bag."

He gave me a deer-in-the-headlights look but sat on the couch and did as I asked, removing some diapers, a box of wipes, a pacifier new in the case (which he looked at as if he'd never seen such a thing before) and a large can of formula, before rooting around in the bottom of the bag. He pulled out a couple burp cloths, a few pairs of pajamas, and a stuffed bear before finally locating a pink and white striped flannel blanket. "This?"

"Spread it out on the couch," I said.

"The couch?" His expression was shocked. "This is a really nice couch, Emme."

"Jesus, Nate. The couch is the last thing you should be concerned about."

He swallowed hard, all the muscles in his neck flexing. "Right." He unfolded the blanket and laid it across the leather cushion, then stood up and moved out of the way, as if he expected me to sit down and do it.

"Uh uh. *You're* going to change her," I told him. I maneuvered Paisley from the crook of my arm into my hands and held her out, facing him.

"Me!" From his expression you'd have thought I asked him to breastfeed her. "I can't do that."

"Yes, you can, all-fucking-man. Take her. Put her on the blanket."

Nate pressed his lips together, inhaled through his nose, and reached for her. His hands covered mine beneath her arms. They were warm and solid and when I knew he had her, I took my hands away. For a moment he held her away from his body and studied her, and she looked back at him without making a sound or moving a muscle. Then she started to kick her feet, and he quickly sat down and gently laid her on her back. "I did it." He exhaled with relief.

"Good job," I told him, dropping down to my knees to make sure she didn't roll right off the couch. "But you have to keep a hand on her unless she's on the floor because she could squirm around and fall off."

He looked alarmed, and placed a palm over her belly, his fingers stretched wide. His hand looked gigantic on her little body. "Like this?"

"Yes. Now get her legs out of her pajamas."

"How am I supposed to do that with one hand on her stomach?"

"You can use two hands, Nate. You just sort of have to keep contact with her at all times." He looked nervous, so I touched him on the wrist. "Hey. You can do this."

We didn't usually touch each other in reassuring ways—mostly it was just to prod at each other when we were joking around or arguing. Maybe that's why Nate stared at my fingertips against his skin for a few heartbeats. "Okay."

With my coaching, he managed to get her legs out of

her pajamas, unsnap her onesie, and remove the wet diaper. I took pity on him and rolled it up, showing him how to tape it shut in a little ball. Next, I instructed him to hold her ankles in one hand, lift up gently, and slide the new diaper beneath her. He bit his lip and concentrated hard. "Jesus, her legs are so small. Her ankles are about as big around as my fingers. Are you sure I'm not hurting her?"

"I'm sure."

"Because she doesn't look like she likes this too much."

"No baby likes getting her diaper changed, but they like being wet even less, so keep going. You're doing fine, except you have to open up the diaper before you get it beneath her. Also, you placed it upside down. You have to make sure the opening is at the top and the tabs are on the bottom."

His eyes met mine. "I have no fucking idea what you're talking about."

I smiled. "You'll figure it out."

He exhaled in frustration but pulled the diaper out from beneath her, flipped it around, opened it up, checked the tabs, and pushed it underneath her little bottom all with one hand, still holding her by the ankles with the other. Then he looked at me. "Like this?"

"Yes, good job. The rest is easy. Let go of her legs, fold the top part up, peel back the tabs, and secure the sticky parts to the front."

He did as I instructed, but the diaper was way too loose when he was done. I reached over and tightened up the tabs. "You want to make sure it's snug enough, otherwise it will leak. Now get her legs back in her pajamas and snap them up."

It took him a while, mostly because he was so tentative with her and she was so squirmy, but he managed. By the time her jammies were done up again, he was sweating. "Damn. It's hot in here, isn't it?"

"Not really."

"I'm fucking roasting. Watch her for a second, okay? I have to take off my sweater."

"Okay." I made sure she stayed on the couch while Nate whipped off his sweater and tossed it aside. Beneath it he wore a white undershirt that hugged his muscular arms and chest. I let myself look for a moment, then refocused on Paisley, who was definitely working up to a big fuss. Getting to my feet, I scooped her up. "Let's feed you, huh? Does that sound good?"

To Nate, I said, "Grab one of those bottles and the can of formula from the bag. I'll show you how to feed her."

"Okay." He looked up at me from his seat on the couch. "Thank you. For being here. I don't know what I would've done if you hadn't come back."

"It's okay. You've gotten me out of a jam plenty of times."

"This is more than a jam, Emme. And I was a total dick to you earlier." He stood up. He stood *close*. "I'm sorry. I didn't mean what I said."

Oh, God. I could smell him, and the combination of man and baby smell does things to the body of a woman my age. Things that make the blood run faster, the heart beat quicker, and the ovaries send confusing signals to various other parts of the female anatomy. Parts that harden and tingle. Parts that flutter and whoosh. Parts that swell and pulse. For a moment, all I wanted in the universe was for him to touch me. Kiss me. Want me.

Was I going insane?

Paisley began to cry. I took a step back and headed for the kitchen. "Come on. She's hungry."

It took Nate much longer than it would've taken me to make a bottle for her, and she cried the whole time he carefully measured and poured and added water and mixed it up, but I wanted him to do it on his own.

"Not too tight," I warned him as he screwed on the cap, "or she won't be able to get anything out."

He immediately started loosening it.

"But not too loose, either, or it'll drip all over the place."

He grunted and tightened it a little before handing it to me.

I shook my head. "You have to warm it first," I told him. "No, no, no, not in there," I said as he popped the microwave door open. "Run the hot water on the tap and hold the bottle under it."

He looked at me blankly. "How will I know when it's warm?"

I shrugged. "You guess. Try 30 seconds, shake it up a little, and see if she takes it."

Nate did as I asked, but after shaking it, he held it out to me. "I don't know how," he said.

I took the bottle from him, and asked him to follow me into the living room, where I sat down on the couch. "Hey, see if there's a bib in the bag. You know what that is?"

"I think so." He dug around in the bag until he found one, and managed to get it snapped behind her neck while I held her. In doing so, the back of his hand accidentally brushed against my breast. "Sorry," he said, his cheeks going a little red.

"It's okay. Now sit." But my stupid nipple was tingling.

He hesitated, but eventually lowered himself to the couch,

and I transferred the baby to his muscular arms. It was the first time he'd held her that way, and she looked *so small* against his chest. I wondered if he felt any tug of paternal affection, or if he was still too stunned to feel anything at all.

"Hold her with her head in your left elbow so you can feed her with your right hand," I advised. When she was situated, I handed him the bottle. "Here you go. Tip it up gently at first in case the nipple is too fast."

He looked at me curiously. "There's such a thing as a fast nipple?"

"Only the rubber kind. Don't get excited."

For the first time since we'd discovered Paisley in the hall, he actually smiled. It didn't last long, though, because he was so nervous about feeding her. But she sucked eagerly at the bottle and made contented little noises as she drank.

"Is this right? Am I doing it right?" he asked.

"You're doing great. We'll let her drink a couple ounces and then you can burp her."

"Oh, Jesus."

I grinned. "You'll be fine."

And he was—sort of.

He managed to balance her on his knee, her stomach braced on one hand as he rubbed her back to encourage a burp, exactly like I showed him. He learned how to hold her against his chest, her head over one shoulder, as he walked around the room patting her back. He even talked to her a little bit as he moved around the room. "Sorry I'm not much good at this stuff, Paisley. Maybe I'll get better."

When she finally let out a pretty good-sized belch, he looked over at me, shocked. "Was that *her*?"

I nodded from where I sat on the couch. "Yep. Good job. Want to see if she'll take the last ounce?"

"Okay."

But she wouldn't, and Nate was frustrated. "She's not eating it. Why won't she eat it? What am I doing wrong?"

"Nothing," I said from beside him. "Babies don't always finish the entire bottle."

He set it aside and looked down at her for a moment. Her eyes were open and locked on his. "Do you think she's cute?"

"She's beautiful."

"Her hair is funny. Like an old man's."

I laughed. "It will grow."

"I don't think I've ever held a baby before. If I did...it was a long time ago." He spoke quietly, and Paisley seemed enthralled by the sound of his voice.

"I think she likes you."

"Who wouldn't?"

I poked his shoulder, and watched them taking each other in, both father and daughter wide-eyed and amazed. It was so sweet, my throat started to tighten. I could sense the bond taking hold and felt in my gut Nate would grow to love her.

Suddenly Paisley's face turned very red, and she gave a little grunt.

"What's she doing? Why is her face that color?" Nate sounded alarmed. "Is she choking?"

I smiled. "She's fine."

"But what's with—" He stopped talking and sniffed. "Jesus fucking Christ, what is that *smell*?"

"It's baby poop," I said, laughing.

"It can't be. There's no way." He inhaled, and his handsome features contorted. "Oh my God, that's *so bad*. How can something so tiny create such a disgusting stench? We should change her." He stood up and looked around. "Where's the bag?"

"You don't want to change her yet, Nate. Trust me. She's not done."

He looked down at me, aghast. "How long will it go on?"

I shrugged. "A few minutes, maybe."

"Oh my God." His eyes closed. "I don't think I can stand it."

"You can put her in the car seat if you want." I reached out. "Or I can hold her."

"No." He straightened his shoulders and sat down again. "No, I can take it."

"Very alpha male of you."

He nudged my leg with his. "Thanks."

But his confidence was shattered when he went to change her dirty diaper. He must have gone through fifty wipes and she still wasn't clean, he got poop all over her pajamas, and she screamed the whole time. Finally, I took over, but even when she was clean and dry and wearing a new onesie and sleeper, she refused to calm down.

I tried the pacing and bouncing while Nate threw her clothing in the washer, sealed the wet and dirty diapers in plastic grocery bags, and took them down to the trash bins in the basement. She still hadn't calmed down by the time he got back, so we turned off all the lights and tried the pacifier (she refused it), another bottle (*hell* no, she didn't want that), running the vacuum cleaner (did the trick on a couple of kids I used to sit, but Paisley wasn't having it), and even swinging her side to side in her car seat—but nothing worked. *Nothing.*

The hours crawled by.

"My God, what's wrong with her? Why won't she go to

sleep?" Nate asked, taking Paisley from me and placing her up over his shoulder. "It's going on three in the morning. Even an alpha male needs sleep."

"She's got colic, I guess."

"What the fuck is colic?"

"It's when a baby cries for hours on end with no reason, usually at night."

"What do you do for it?"

"Nothing."

"No, I refuse to accept that. There must be a solution."

God, he was such a *guy*, thinking every problem could be solved. "Sometimes motion helps. I wish we had a stroller," I said over the wailing. I was worn out too, and desperate for sleep, but I didn't want to leave him like this.

Our eyes met in the dark. "I've got a bar cart. Would that work?"

"Let's try it. But let's see if she'll eat first."

Nate held her while I prepared the bottle, then I fed and burped her while Nate cleared his Art Deco chrome bar cart of decanters, an ice bucket, glasses, coasters and some other random barware. We placed her car seat on top of the cart, strapped her in, and Nate held it in place as I pushed. It took some maneuvering to turn corners, but we managed to wheel her around the living room, circle the kitchen island, loop around the couch. Eventually, it worked.

"Oh my God," Nate whispered. "It's a miracle. She's asleep."

"For now, anyway." I knew from experience an eight-week-old wasn't going to sleep long. Stifling a yawn, I said, "Keep her in the seat, okay? You can take her up to your room or sleep on the couch."

"Wait, you're leaving?" His voice was panicked.

"I have to get some sleep, Nate. I'm exhausted."

"I know, but...don't leave," he whispered frantically. "I still need you. Please."

I was nearly asleep on my feet, but hearing him say those four words did something to me. Usually it was the other way around with us—me needing him. And as bad as I felt for Nate tonight, I sort of liked the role reversal. When had any man ever needed me, unless it was to plan his wedding?

"Okay," I agreed. "But we both need to sleep while she does." I figured I'd crash on the couch, so I was surprised at his next words.

"Come upstairs."

It was ridiculous, but my heart tripped a little quicker.

Don't make this into something it's not, Emme. He doesn't want to be alone with the baby. It has nothing to do with you and him. "Okay. You bring the car seat up —*carefully.*"

You'd have thought the seat was made of blown glass, he was so gentle with it on the trek up the stairs. I'd never been in Nate's bedroom before, but it was laid out like mine—sleeping area, walk-through closet, master bath on the other side. I was a little surprised the decor was so normal, no mirrors or restraints or sex swings hanging from the ceiling. Just plain white bedding, unadorned brick walls, a bed, and nightstand.

"You can use the bathroom first," he said softly, setting the car seat on the floor next to the king-sized bed and switching on his bedside lamp. "There are spare toothbrushes in the second drawer down."

"Thanks." I walked through his closet—it smelled like him—to the bathroom and shut the door softly behind me. I turned on the light, scorching my retinas since we'd been in the dark for hours, and frowning at my bloodshot eyes and smudged mascara. After using the bathroom and washing my hands and face, I located a spare toothbrush (refusing to think about why he had a stash of them), and brushed my teeth. Normally, I'd have been more curious about what else I'd find in his bathroom, but I was too tired to even snoop in his cabinets.

When I came out, Nate stood at the foot of the bed holding out something folded and white. "You can sleep in this if you want."

"Okay, thanks." I noticed he'd traded his jeans for a pair of loose black pajama pants, but he'd kept his T-shirt on.

While he was in the bathroom, I slipped out of my jeans and sweater and quickly pulled the cotton T-shirt he'd given me over my head, keeping my bra on. The shirt was big and comfortable, but a sniff of the collar disappointed me, because it smelled like fabric softener and not him.

Don't be fucking weird. Just get in bed.

It looked like Nate slept on the left side of the bed, so I quickly turned back the covers on the right, scrambled beneath them, and pulled them up to my chin.

A moment later, the bathroom door opened. Nate came into the room and went around to the other side of the bed, moving Paisley a little closer to it. He removed his wrist watch and turned off the lamp, but then he hesitated. "Would you rather I slept downstairs?"

"No," I said. Then I couldn't resist a joke. "Despite your reputation, I don't think you're going to try anything."

He climbed into bed. "In this particular case, you're right. Don't tell anyone."

"Your secret is safe with me."

When both of us were under the covers, Nate on his

back, me on my side, facing him, he whispered, "I still can't believe this."

"I can't either. It's so huge."

"That's what she said," he whispered a moment later.

Despite my exhaustion, I giggled. He might be a dad, but he was still a *guy*.

"Sorry. Couldn't resist." He was quiet for a minute, and I was nearly asleep before he spoke again. "Emme."

"Yeah?"

"I'm scared."

I opened my eyes. He was still on his back, arms at his sides above the covers. Automatically, I reached out, placing my hand on his bicep. "I know."

He looked at me. "Thanks for staying."

"You're welcome."

I fell asleep with my hand on him.

FOUR

NATE

My body was begging my brain to shut down, but even with my eyes closed, my muscles relaxed, and the room dark and silent, my mind refused to quiet.

I had a daughter.

My life would never be the same.

As the shock wore off and reality set in, I felt more and more panicked. What if Rachel didn't come back? What would I do? Alpha masculinity aside, how was I going to reconcile the person I had been, a person I liked and enjoyed being, with being a father to this child? Was it even possible? And what about work? The gym? My social life? Travel? I had plans, for fuck's sake. Goals. A bucket list. I wanted to run with the bulls and climb Kilimanjaro and skydive over Dubai. I couldn't do any of that with a baby strapped to my back.

And I had no idea how to be a dad.

I thought about my own father, who'd died three years ago of heart disease, but who had retreated from the family long before, so long ago that I'd barely registered the loss. But I had never blamed him for his distance, nor my mother for her nervous frailty. It was another loss, an earlier, unthinkable tragedy, that had done us all in. It was that loss that was responsible for who we became—an absent alcoholic, and agoraphobic hypochondriac, and a divorce lawyer with an iron cage around his heart. I had made up my mind long ago that love was something to be feared. Avoided. And if necessary, sabotaged.

Otherwise it would destroy you.

The problem wasn't love itself. The problem was allowing yourself to care for someone so deeply that the loss of them cut you deep to the bone, so deep you lost a piece of yourself. And that piece was your trust in God, your faith in the universe, your belief that if you wished hard enough and prayed long enough and loved fiercely enough, it would save a life. It would save your family. It would save you.

So you had to be vigilant if you wanted to protect yourself. And I was. I did. I had hardened my heart to the point where nothing and nobody could get to me. I'd never fallen in love. I'd never been tempted to get married. And I'd certainly never planned on being a father. I know some guys who think spreading their seed is the ultimate act of manhood, but *fuck that*. As far as I was concerned, my seed could stay in the vault where it belonged. Maybe I'd get a vasectomy after this; that is, if having a baby didn't ruin my sex life forever.

I looked over at Emme.

Her breathing was deep and slow. She'd rolled over and was facing the other direction, but her long hair was trailing over toward my pillow. It smelled so fucking good—like cake or something. Every now and again, she mumbled something that I couldn't make out, but it almost made me smile. *Ten bucks says she's arguing with me, even in her sleep.* Thank God she'd agreed to stay here tonight—I'd never wanted a woman to spend the night so badly, and there wasn't even sex involved.

And it was fucking surreal to think that Rachel and I had created a life during our marathon, whiskey-fueled sexcapade last year. Part of me still couldn't believe it. What were the odds? Weren't condoms like ninety-nine percent effective when used properly? How had I fucked that up? Was the condom defective? Or did I have some sort of bionic sperm that was able to penetrate latex? For a moment, I felt kind of proud of my herculean swimmers, but the feeling quickly vanished when I remembered the end result.

Speaking of which, she hadn't made any noise in a while.

My heart started to pound and I immediately checked to see that she was breathing. She was perfectly fine, but something in me couldn't believe I hadn't fucked up yet. How the hell did people do this? Were you supposed to just go to sleep and trust you'd wake up if your baby needed something? What if you were a sound sleeper? I wasn't, not particularly, but what if I was? And how could she be comfortable in that thing, all strapped in that way? I'd have unbuckled her, except then I would've been scared about her falling out somehow. So far, parenting seemed to me like nothing but worry, panic, doubt, and guilt. Why the fuck would anyone *choose* this? I certainly hadn't. And I didn't want it.

But like Emme said, what I wanted no longer mattered.

"Everything okay?" Emme whispered behind me.

I turned to see her propped up on one elbow. "Yeah. Just checking on her."

She put her head down again and lay facing me. "What a good dad."

I rolled to face her too, bunching my pillow beneath my head. "I have no fucking idea how to be a good dad."

"You don't have to have all the answers tonight, Nate. Give yourself some time."

"What if Rachel doesn't come back?"

"Then you'll find her. And in the meantime—" she reached out and took my hand—"you're not alone. Okay?"

"Okay." I squeezed her hand. "Thanks."

She closed her eyes and fell back asleep, and I thought about how lucky I was to have her as my friend. How peaceful she looked in her sleep. How pretty she was. How she'd left her hand nestled in mine, and it fit there so perfectly. I'd slept with my fair share of women, but I couldn't think of one time I'd held someone's hand during the night. In fact, if one of them had reached for my hand, I'd most likely have pulled away.

Tonight, it was oddly comforting.

At some point I must have fallen asleep, because I was awakened a few hours later by my phone vibrating on the nightstand. I rolled over and looked at the screen.

It's Rachel. How is she?

In a split second I was out of bed and halfway down the stairs, calling back the number she had texted from. It rang twice before she answered.

"Nate?"

"Yes," I said, trying to keep my voice down, squinting at the early morning sunlight pouring through the windows.

"Is she okay?"

"She's fine, which you would know if you hadn't abandoned her at my doorstep." I began pacing the living room floor. "What the hell were you thinking?"

"I was thinking that it's your turn," she said, starting to

cry. "So don't attack me. I've had to do it alone all this time. Do you think that was easy?"

"I don't know how it was, because you never told me. I would have helped you."

"Bullshit. You made it perfectly clear that all you wanted was no-strings sex. You would've thrown some money at me and then you would've been gone. Don't pretend otherwise."

"You don't know what I would've done! You don't know anything about me." Which had been on purpose, of course. I was surprised I'd even given her my number.

"I know your type. Big spender, big talker, big dick. But beyond money and sex and a good time, nothing matters to you."

"That's not true," I said, wondering if she was right and also if it was wrong to feel a little bit good that she'd said I have a big dick.

"Then prove it. Be a father to her for one week."

My heart pounded harder. "A week? I can't have her for a whole week."

"Why not?"

"Because I've got work and plans and life." I turned around to pace in the other direction and saw Emme coming down the stairs, her arms folded across her chest. She still wore my T-shirt, her legs and feet bare, her hair a long tangled mess. But the sunlight lit her beautifully, almost angelically. My body warmed, our eyes locked, and in my head I heard her words from last night. *Maybe you're just like the rest of them—all talk.*

Fuck that. I wasn't like those spineless douchebags she dated. I wasn't.

"Well, guess what?" Rachel went on. "Your life now includes a baby. One week, Nate. That's all I'm asking. If you want to walk away after that, fine. I'll take full responsibility, since I was the one who made the choice not to tell you at the start. But if you can't even handle that—"

"I can," I declared out of nowhere, my eyes still on Emme, her voice still in my head. "So you can go take your rest or whatever, and come back for her in a week. You know what? Make it two weeks."

At that, Emme's eyes bugged out.

"Two weeks?" Rachel laughed cruelly. "You can't handle two weeks. I bet you barely handled one night."

"Actually, make it a month."

Emme's mouth fell open. She covered it with one hand.

"What?" Rachel squawked.

"You heard me. Make it a month."

"You're crazy."

"No, I'm not. I'm a grown-ass man taking responsibility for my actions."

Emme's hand fell from her mouth, and she smiled.

"So you can call if you want to know how she's doing, but other than that, I can handle this all on my own. Good-bye, Rachel."

I ended the call, praying I wouldn't faint. Just in case, I went into the kitchen and braced myself against the island with both hands. Took a few deep breaths.

Emme came into the kitchen. "So," she said, arms still folded over her chest. "A month."

I tried to appear calm and collected, turning toward her and propping one hand on my hip like I was leaning against the counter in a casual way and not for support. My body was tilted at a strange and uncomfortable forty-five degree angle. "I've been thinking of taking some time off work anyway."

Her eyebrows went up. I was a total workaholic and she knew it. "Oh?"

"Yeah. And I think... I think it could be good for me. You know, not to be so selfish for a while." A sweat had broken out on my forehead.

She nodded. "Of course."

"And it's only for a month. A month isn't that long." I said it, but already I was wondering if a month meant four weeks or 31 days. And was yesterday day one or was today?

Paisley began to cry, and both of us looked in the direction of the stairs.

"She's probably hungry," Emme said.

"Already?" It was barely seven, and we'd just fed her at three.

"Babies her age eat often. Every few hours."

"Seriously?"

She grinned ruefully. "We need to get you a few baby books so you can learn all this stuff. And you probably need some baby items—a stroller, some kind of crib, maybe a swing, or at least a bouncy chair."

Inwardly I groaned, picturing my awesome, manly loft with baby furniture in it. "Really? Even if it's just for a month?"

Emme cocked her head. "It's not just for a month, Nate. Even if Rachel came back for her today, you are still her father. For *life*."

There was something fierce in her eyes, something that dared me to disagree with her. Or maybe something that suspected I would disagree with her, and prove that she had been right about me. That I was all talk, and not really man enough to handle being a father. I didn't want her to think that, even if I was scared it was the truth.

Gathering my courage, I pushed myself off the counter

and stood up straight. "I'll go get her. I'm sure you have things to do today." Feeling proud of myself, I left the kitchen and went upstairs.

"Good morning," I said to the angry baby in the car seat next to my bed. Not that I blamed her. Who'd want to sleep like that? I picked it up by the handle and went back downstairs. "Don't worry Paisley, I'm going to get you something better to sleep in today." Except I had no idea where they even sold baby shit. Maybe Emme would know.

She was still in the kitchen when I got down there. "Want some help?" she asked as I set the car seat on the island and began washing my hands.

"Nope. I've got this." I dried my hands on a towel and picked up one of the plastic bottles Emme had washed last night and left on a paper towel to dry. "You should feel very special, Paisley. Not only am I giving up my Saturday morning workout for you, but I am making your breakfast before I even make coffee." I hoped I sounded relaxed and confident, which was the complete opposite of how I felt. "Okay now, what was it again? Two level scoops of this stinky powder?" I took the cap off the can of formula.

"Well, seems like you're doing okay," Emme said hesitantly. "I'll go get dressed."

"Okay," I said breezily. She left the kitchen and I exhaled, my chest collapsing. Pretending to know what I was doing was tiring. I measured two level scoops of formula and dumped it into the bottle. "Next I add four ounces of water."

But when I went to the sink, I realized that I probably should have added the water first since the formula took up some space in the bottle. In the interest of doing things exactly right, I dumped the powder back in the can and started over. "I made a mistake, Paisley. Sorry to say, it's going to happen a lot." I glanced at her, and it was kind of amusing how interested her expression was. She wasn't even fussing while I spoke to her. "Don't tell anyone."

I got it right the second time, and I even used warm water, which seemed smart to me because it allowed me to skip a step (heating up the bottle). Congratulating myself on a job well done, I brought the bottle and the car seat into the living room, set them both on the coffee table, and unbuckled the car seat straps. As soon as I lifted her out, I could tell that she needed to be changed.

"You stink," I told her. "Maybe not as bad as last night, but that is not a pleasant odor about you. I thought babies were supposed to smell good." I was more confident in my bottle-making skills than my diaper-changing skills, but I figured I'd give it a shot. Keeping Paisley in place against my chest with one arm, I laid the blanket on the couch with the other. Before I set her down I grabbed a clean diaper from the bag. There were only two left, which meant shopping was first up on the agenda today. As I changed her, I started making a list of things I would need. Since she seemed to like my voice, I talked it out.

"We'll need diapers for sure, and more formula, and probably a few more bottles. We'll need a stroller and some-thing for you to sleep in," I said, swapping the old diaper for the new one, "and maybe some kind of lounge chair for you to sit in instead of that car seat. Speaking of which, I'm going to have to figure out how to buckle you into my car. Okay, let's see how I did."

I finished zipping up her sleeper and picked her up, holding her out in front of me and turning her this way and that. "Well, you're still in one piece and still breathing, so that's a good sign." I placed her in the crook of my arm, grabbed the bottle from the coffee table, and fed her a couple ounces. She probably would have eaten more, but I remembered that Emme said it was good to burp her about halfway through. Setting the bottle aside, I sat her on my knee and propped her up over one hand like Emme had shown me last night. With the other hand I rubbed her back, and I only had to wait about thirty seconds for her to give me a decent-sized belch.

"Look at you." Emme's voice came from the direction of the stairs. I turned around and saw her coming down, dressed again in her jeans and sweater.

I settled Paisley into my arms once more and began feeding her the rest of the bottle, crossing my legs so one ankle rested on one knee. I was determined to look like I could handle this. "Not bad, right?"

"Not bad at all." She came over and sat next to us, reaching over to brush Paisley's hair off her forehead. "Is your daddy taking good care of you?"

My stomach heaved. *Daddy*. Jesus fucking Christ. I cleared my throat. "I need to shop for her. Can you point me in the right direction?"

"Probably Target, or maybe Babies"R"Us."

"There's a place called Babies"R"Us?" I asked incredulously.

She giggled. "Yes. Do you want me to go with you?"

Of course I did. In fact, what I really wanted was to give her my credit card and have her do it all. "Only if you have time."

"I have a wedding tonight, so I do have to work eventually, but I could help you out later this morning." She sighed and fell back against my couch. "Although I definitely need a nap."

"A nap sounds fucking amazing." I set the empty bottle aside and sat Paisley up to burp her again.

"Do it while she takes hers. I'm telling you, that's the only time you will be able to sleep." She got to her feet. "I guess I'll go home for a bit. Anything you need before I go?"

I couldn't think of anything, although I was tempted to make something up so she would stay a little longer. What was I going to do with this baby all by myself? What if she started crying and I couldn't get her to stop? "Not that I can think of."

She must have sensed my fear, because she patted me on the shoulder. "You'll be fine, Nate. You're doing awesome, all things considered."

I took a deep breath and exhaled. "Thanks. I think I'm still running on adrenaline."

Emme nodded. "Are you going to tell anybody? Your family? Your work?"

The thought of telling my mother terrified me. This was a woman who was scared to leave the house and buy groceries because she worried about having a panic attack at Kroger. She wore gloves if she went absolutely anywhere, because the thought of touching germs terrified her. She had her doctor on speed dial because she was always convinced she had picked up some awful, incurable disease if she'd been out in public.

Thankfully, she had a longtime neighbor that often checked in on her, a good Samaritan who made sure there was food in the house, drove her anywhere she needed to go, and made the occasional phone call to me when things got bad. I would talk to my mom, assess the situation, and depending on her mental state, I sometimes had to make the nearly three-hour drive to Grand Rapids and get her out of the house. Usually, it was just that she had stopped taking her medication due to some irrational fear that someone at the pharmacy was trying to poison her. Once I could convince her that wasn't the case, she would take it again and improve within days. I tried to be patient with her, reminding myself that she hadn't always been this way, that once upon a time, she'd been a happy, well-adjusted woman with a beautiful home, a solid marriage, plenty of money in the bank, and two healthy sons. She must have thought it would all last forever. Hadn't we all?

Paisley still hadn't burped yet, so I stood and put her up on one shoulder. "I haven't really thought that far ahead yet. My brain is a bit overwhelmed. I guess I'll have to tell them all eventually, but for now, it's just you." I frowned. "Although if we see anyone while we're out shopping today, we better have a good explanation handy for why you and I suddenly have a baby."

She laughed. "We'll think of something. See you in a bit."

As soon she was gone, I realized I should've gone to the bathroom while she was here. Now what was I supposed to do? I couldn't just set Paisley down. My apartment was full of hard surfaces and sharp objects, a parental nightmare. But I couldn't bring her in the bathroom with me either. That didn't seem right. In the end, I ended up strapping her into the car seat and leaving it in my closet right outside the bathroom door. But I felt guilty about it because she cried the whole time, even though I was in there for less than a minute. I opened the door as soon as my hands were clean and picked her up again. "I'm still here," I told her. "See? I'm still here."

She stopped crying, and I marveled at how quickly a baby could become attached to someone. How easily they trusted. Yesterday at this time, she had never seen me, never heard my voice, never even knew I existed. Now I had the power to calm her just by holding her and talking to her. It was sort of sweet, but also scary as hell. I wasn't sure I deserved that kind of trust, and I certainly didn't feel like I had earned it. But maybe I could make that up to her. For the first time, an overwhelming urge to protect her struck me, and I found myself furious at Rachel, not just for lying to me or springing this on me, but for abandoning our child. I was more aware every passing minute of what she must've been going through trying to parent on her own, but she should have reached out. There was no excuse for leaving Paisley alone the way she had.

"Paisley," I mused as I brought her downstairs. "Kind of a cute name, I guess. I wonder what your middle name is. And did she give you my last name or hers? It's kind of fucked up that I don't know my own kid's full name, don't you think? And maybe I should stop saying fuck."

Downstairs, I spread a blanket out on a rug and put her on it with her stuffed bear, stretching out next to her on my side. She lay happily on her back and wiggled around, making little sounds and drooling up a storm while I yawned and tried to stay awake. My God, was every night going to be like last night? I wouldn't survive. No one could.

Eventually, she started to cry again, and I picked her up, trying the bouncing thing Emme had done last night. She still wouldn't quiet down, so I tried singing her a song. I wasn't the best singer in the world but by the time I'd fudged my way through a few Christmas tunes, which were the only ones I knew all the words to, she had drifted off to sleep.

I looked longingly at the couch.

Maybe I could lie down for a few minutes. Close my eyes. That was all I needed, a few minutes with my eyes closed. But could I manage to do it without waking her up? Suddenly I thought of the thousands of times I had simply flopped onto the couch for a Saturday nap with *zero* appreciation for how easy it had been. Flopping was definitely not an option today. Instead, I eased myself into a sitting position so slowly that my leg muscles were shaking. Then I carefully pivoted, wincing at the sound my pajama pants made as they squeaked on the leather. Finally, I leaned back at the rate of about one inch every ten seconds, so that my abs were practically screaming when I was done. But I did it —I succeeded in lying down on the couch without waking the baby.

I carefully maneuvered Paisley so that she lay with her belly on mine, her head on my chest. I kept one hand on her back, one hand on her butt, and one foot on the floor just in case (in case of what I had no idea, but it seemed like a good idea), and closed my eyes.

Sweet Jesus, it was amazing.

"Nate." A hand on my shoulder. "Nate."

I opened my eyes, and saw Emme standing next to the couch. But I was confused, because she'd gone home wearing her jeans and sweater, and here she was wearing only my T-shirt again. The light was strange too. Some sort of golden glow seemed to shine from behind her, like it had on the stairway this morning, but that was impossible because there were no windows behind her. I tried to speak but couldn't. She smiled and put a finger to her lips. "Shhh-hhh." Then with no warning whatsoever, she whipped the shirt over her head, and stood there naked from the waist up. My cock jumped. My mouth watered. My hands trembled with the need to touch her skin. But I couldn't move—I was paralyzed. All I could do was look at her and groan with longing, like a teenage boy with a centerfold.

"Nate. Nate. Wake up." The hand was on my shoulder again, this time shaking me insistently. I opened my eyes, for real this time, but it took a moment for the fog to clear. I propped myself up on my elbows and blinked at Emme, who stood there—alas, fully clothed—holding Paisley in her arms and looking at me curiously. "You okay?"

"Yeah." My voice was scratchy, so I cleared my throat.

She smiled. "You must have been dreaming."

"Really? What makes you say that?" I swung myself into a seated position so fast my head spun.

"You were moaning and groaning and squirming around." She looked at Paisley and rubbed noses with her—an Eskimo kiss. "Wasn't he, peanut?"

The whole shirtless scenario came back to me in a heartbeat, and my skin felt hot beneath my clothes. Well, my pajamas, since I hadn't gotten dressed yet.

"What were you dreaming about?" she asked me.

I feigned ignorance. "I can't remember. Did you just get here?"

"About ten minutes ago. Paisley was starting to fuss, but you were sound asleep, so I picked her up and changed her. I'll get a bottle going while you shower, if you want. It's been about four hours since she last ate."

"Has it really?"

She laughed. "Yeah. You guys had, like, a three-hour nap. I'm jealous. Mine was only about an hour."

Emme headed for the kitchen with Paisley in her arms, so I stood up and quickly headed for the stairs, hoping she wouldn't notice my erection. I went up to my bedroom, undressed, and got in the shower, feeling increasingly bad about the dream I'd just had—especially since she'd been watching me have it. It felt like getting caught doing something inappropriate.

But I couldn't stop thinking about it. I stood under the spray, letting it pummel my face and chest for a solid five minutes as I relived that magical moment in my dream when Emme had removed her shirt. Had I ever wanted to touch someone so badly, even in real life? Had I ever been so frustrated that I couldn't? Had I ever felt so guilty about wanting to know what someone's curves felt like beneath my palms? My lips? My tongue?

I turned around and braced myself on the opposite wall, letting the water hit my back and rain down my body. I wasn't used to feeling guilty about wanting anything. Not money, not status, not success, not women. Not even about fantasizing about Emme, which I had done plenty of times before without really thinking twice.

So why did I feel bad about it now? What was different? Was it because she was helping me? Was it because I was a father now and fathers weren't supposed to act that way? Was it because I suddenly didn't know who I was or how I was supposed to think or what to do with these strange feelings that were threatening to upset the careful balance of my life?

Stop it, I told myself. *This kind of self-pity is beneath you. Yes, your world is different, but you are still you. Maybe this fatherhood thing wasn't in the script you wrote for your life, but you still have control over your actions.*

Control. That was the key. I wanted a measure of control.

I straightened up and took my rock hard dick in my hand, determined to feel like my fucking self, even if it was for five stolen minutes in the shower. I pictured Emme on purpose, reclaiming the dream, the way she'd looked last night sipping a martini on my couch, leaning back on the counter in my kitchen, sleeping next to me in my bed. Behind closed eyes I watched her come down the stairs this morning in my T-shirt, her legs bare, her hair messy.

But she doesn't stop there. She comes over to where I am lying on the couch (I slept there because I'm such a gentleman, although there is no baby in this fantasy, so I'm not sure why she slept over at all but this is my fantasy dammit and I say what goes, and also I am naked) and this time, when she takes off her shirt, she stretches out above me straddling my hips with her thighs, taking me inside her, rocking her body over mine. She says my name softly, over and over again, her long hair grazing my chest, her eyes locked on mine, as she works us both into a frenzy, and gradually my name gets louder and louder and louder, her hips moving faster and faster and faster until —

"Fuck..." The orgasm hit me suddenly and ferociously, and I groaned all the way through it, my hand yanking furiously on my cock.

A few minutes later, I was toweling off and feeling much better about myself, even if I was still slightly out of breath. Clearly that was all I needed—to feel in command of my thoughts, my body, my life.

Everything was going to be fine.

FIVE

EMME

"Are you sure I need all this?" Nate looked suspiciously at the two full carts of baby gear we'd collected in our two hours at Babies"R"Us and shook his head. "She's only one baby. How can one baby need so much stuff?"

"It's not that much stuff. It's the basics." I pushed the cart that held Paisley and some of the smaller things, while Nate followed behind with a cart full of bigger items. He had decided on a Pack 'n Play with a detachable bedside sleeper instead of a crib, a swing, a stroller, a changing table, and a video monitor system. In my cart were bottles, formula, diapers, wipes, diaper cream, onesies and sleepers, baby shampoo, detergent and dish soap, baby wash, bottle scrubbers, burp cloths, towels, sheets for the sleeper, a few baby care books, and a sling.

"What is that?" Nate asked when I added the sling to the cart. "Some kind of backpack?"

"It's a sling," I explained, "so you can carry her around but still have your hands free."

He took it out of the cart and put it back on the shelf.

"No way. I am not *wearing* my baby. I've got to draw the line somewhere."

I took it down again and put it back in. "Just get it. If you don't want to use it, fine, but you are going to get very tired of carrying her around all the time, and there won't always be room to push a stroller."

He grumbled, but he let me keep it in the cart. What he did insist on was a little brush for her hair.

"It looks silly all sticking up like that," he said, frowning at his daughter. "I think I can do better."

Paisley did well while we shopped, fussing only once or twice, but she seemed to like the car ride and fell asleep on the way there. As for Nate, he was holding up pretty well, I thought. His color was good, he had lost that wide-eyed, I-can't-believe-this-is-happening look, and outwardly at least, seem to have accepted his new reality. There was a moment of panic at the checkout, however, as he watched all of the bath items being scanned.

"I don't even have a bathtub," he said, his voice shaking a little. "What am I going to do?"

"Kitchen sink," answered the elderly woman ringing him up. She shrugged. "That's how we always did it in my family."

"Kitchen sink. Right." At that point, Nate went a little pale. He looked at me, desperation in his eyes. "Are you... Can you help me the first time?"

I checked my phone. It was going on two, and I really needed to check in with my bride. The ceremony wasn't until five, but there were pictures at four, and I had to be there. "Maybe," I told him. "Let's finish up here, and see what time it is when we get back."

He nodded, handing over his credit card when every-thing had been rung up, and he didn't even blink at the total. Whether it was because his pockets were that deep or he was simply distracted by the terrifying thought of giving Paisley a bath in his kitchen sink on his own, I had no idea.

Back at his apartment, I changed, fed, and burped Paisley while he unpacked the bags and assembled the swing and the Pack 'n Play. They looked totally incongruous in his bachelor pad living room. "I have to say, I never saw this coming," I told him with a grin. "Nate Pearson putting together baby furniture."

He grimaced. "I didn't either."

"I think she's ready for a nap," I said, looking down at Paisley in my arms. "And I have to go. Want to try the swing?"

"Aren't we going to give her a bath?" His expression was a little panicked.

"We don't really have time, Nate. I'm sorry. I have to get to work." But at that moment, I wished I could blow off work and stay here with him all night.

"Oh. Okay."

"You'll be fine, I know it. You're so gentle with her, and babies are actually pretty resilient. Just fill the sink up a little ways with warm water, keep her sitting up with one hand, and use the other one to wash her."

"What about her hair?"

"Use a cup. Tip her back, let her lean into your inner arm, and pour the water over her hair to get it wet and rinse it afterward. If you get a little water in her eyes, it won't hurt. And Nate?"

He looked over at me as if he were afraid to hear what was coming next. "Yeah?"

"You really have to wash her well. All the...nooks and crannies. Know what I mean?" I looked at him pointedly. "It's really important for a baby girl so she doesn't get infections."

Nate went completely white, but he nodded.

"You okay? Maybe you should sit down." For a moment I was afraid he might faint again.

He took a deep breath. "I'm fine. I'm fine, and you can go."

He didn't look fine, but I couldn't stay any longer. I walked over and placed the drowsy Paisley in his arms. "I'll check in on you tonight, okay?"

"Okay."

I squeezed his shoulder. "I'm really proud of you. A lot of guys would not be doing this."

"Truth?" he asked quietly, his eyes on the baby in his arms. "Right now, I wish I was more like a lot of guys."

"Well, you're not." I slid my hand from his shoulder to his back and rubbed it, trying to ignore the way my heart quickened at the feel of his solid, warm muscles. "But you know what? It's okay to admit that."

He looked at me, and my hand stilled. "Thank you," he said.

Kiss me, I thought. And before I could do anything stupid, I took my hand off him, gave him an encouraging smile, and got the hell out of there.

Resisting Nate Pearson, handsome playboy, was one thing.

Resisting Nate Pearson, handsome single dad, was quite another.

I wasn't sure I was up to the task.

———

I went home and changed into work clothes, trading my

jeans, tank, and cardigan for one of the understated suits I wore to client weddings. I tucked my hair into a low chignon and refreshed my makeup, keeping it subtle and soft. My job was to blend into the background, not stand out. While I got ready, I thought of nothing but Nate and Paisley across the hall, and I had to stop myself from knocking on his door to check on him before I got in the elevator. I still couldn't believe he had offered to keep her for an entire month. A *month*. What had possessed him?

I kept thinking about it as I headed for the Ford Piquette Plant, where the wedding was being held. Was it Rachel's insinuating that he wouldn't be able to handle it? Was it her accusation that he would have tried to pay her off instead of support her? Nate had only given me the bare bones of their conversation on the way to Babies"R"Us, but even from his thirty-second explanation, I thought I had a decent feel for what had been said. Nate had felt insulted enough to go on the offensive, to make an outrageous offer that he'd probably thought she would never accept—I imagined him operating much the same way in divorce arbitrations.

Or was there more to it? I know it sounds crazy, but the way he'd looked at me the entire time he'd been on the phone with her made me feel like his posturing might have had something to do with me, or at least what I had said to him the night before. Was he showing off for me? Could he possibly care that much what I thought?

Maybe I was reading too much into this. Maybe he was just a hot dude with a big ego who couldn't stand for anyone, especially a woman, to get the better of him. And maybe all these fleeting romantic feelings on my part were a silly, biological response to seeing a man with a baby. After all, I hadn't had these urges around him before Paisley showed up. Not very many of them anyway. A handful—okay, a couple dozen maybe, and I blamed good genetics for that. Who wouldn't be attracted to him, with that face and that body? Of course, there was also his sense of humor, his brain, his reliability, his generosity, and his knack for mixing the perfect dirty martini, but those were all good qualities in a friend. And that's what we were. Friends.

That's why he cares what you think, silly. Because you're friends. He knows you were being honest with him last night, because there has never been any bullshit between you. No sex to cloud judgment. No jealousy. No reason for either of you to cut the other down.

And we had, hadn't we? As much as we liked to bicker, last night had been our first real fight, the first personal insults hurled, the first hurtful "punches" thrown. But we'd gotten through it.

That's true, you did. So when are you going to deal with what he said about you?

I frowned as I signaled and changed lanes on Woodward Avenue. Since last night, I had done a good job ignoring the voice in my head demanding I take a closer look at what he'd said about me. I really didn't want to, mostly because it was sort of true. I *did* tend to fall in love with anyone I slept with. I *did* want each lover to be the one. Why else would I be with him?

My sisters had all kinds of opinions about this. Analytical Stella thought I chose the wrong guys on purpose, some crap about my subconscious self being afraid the kind of love I wanted didn't really exist. She thought this probably stemmed from our parents' divorce, but I constantly reminded her that their split had been amicable, and no one blamed Dad for leaving, least of all Mom. For crying out loud, he was married to a man now, a wonderful guy named

Roberto, who we all adored—even our mother. Free-spirited Maren thought I was simply trying too hard, moving too fast. She was always telling me I needed to take time for myself, turn my focus inward, and concentrate on achieving harmony within my body and mind. Sometimes I tried to do what she said, but it never worked. For one thing, the inner workings of my mind were kind of frightening at times, and I never enjoyed examining them up close.

I pulled into the parking lot next to the old Model T factory, gathered my things, and checked my reflection in the rearview mirror one last time. Then I couldn't resist taking my phone out of my bag and texting Nate.

How's it going? Everything okay?

I gave it a minute but he didn't reply, and I really didn't have any extra time. My professional reputation was very important to me. Dropping my phone back in my bag, I got out of the car, locked it up, and hurried through the cold March wind into the building.

But when it was five o'clock and the ceremony was about to start and he *still* hadn't answered my message, I started to worry. Which was silly, right? He'd have called or texted if anything was wrong. Still, I was nervous enough to shoot off a quick question as the grandmothers were being seated.

You two okay?

Nothing.

The processional music started and I had no choice but to slip my phone into my pocket and concentrate on pulling off a smooth event, pleasing as many people as possible with as few delays or hitches as possible, answering everybody's questions, and ensuring that everything from the flowers to the music to the timing—the fucking *timing*—to the food to the drinks to the photography to the toast to the first dance to the cutting of the cake went off exactly as the bride had envisioned it. This was a fairly big, high-profile wedding, and pictures of the event were sure to make it into the glossy pages of local press. Since Coco wasn't here, I was working by myself, and felt the weight of our business's reputation on my shoulders. For that reason, I didn't get a chance to even look at my phone again until much later in the evening.

When I did, I gasped. I had 42 messages. All from Nate.

Many of them were questions.

Why won't she eat?

She's supposed to sleep on her back, right?

When do I give her a bath? Should I wait until she's messy?

How often am I supposed to change her?

Is it safe to leave her in that swing while I go to the bathroom?

Why won't she stop crying?

Why is her poop that color?

Fuck am I supposed to trim her nails?

Why doesn't like naps as much as I do?

Sometimes they were just frustrations.

She won't go to sleep.

She won't finish her bottle.

She won't burp.

She hates me.

She threw up on my sock.

I can't do this. Help me.

HELLLLPMEEEE.

Then he must have gotten her to go to sleep and started

reading his new books because his messages were full of things he was learning.

Did you know babies get acne?

Did you know you can predict how tall a baby will be?

Did you know she is supposed to be gaining half a pound a week?

Did you know most babies are born on a Tuesday? Did you know you could tell if your baby is the Dalai Lama or not by checking for large ears, long eyes, eyebrows curving up at the ends, streaks on the legs, and a mark in the shape of a conch shell on the palm of one hand? (Note: I do not believe Paisley is the Dalai Lama.)

Then there were actually some positive messages.

I take back what I said about the sling.

I think she just smiled at me.

She definitely likes my singing voice (she might be the only one).

She finished her bottle!

She is trying to roll over already, I think she might be a genius.

She's sleeping!

I was about to text him back when I heard the mother of the bride calling my name. Sighing, I dropped my phone into my jacket pocket and went back to work. Overall, it sounded like Nate and Paisley were doing okay. I'd check on them when I got home.

It ended up being close to midnight by the time I left the reception, and by then my phone was dead. I hadn't charged it last night at Nate's and I'd been so tired this morning that I'd neglected to plug it in. As I approached Nate's door, I could hear the sound of Paisley crying. Wincing, I knocked.

Nate opened the door, his hair a mess, his feet bare, his expression desperate, his daughter in the sling against his chest. His button-down from earlier was gone, and he wore only a navy T-shirt and jeans. "Oh thank God," he said. "I thought you were dead, and I need you."

"You didn't care that I was dead?" My heart was beating a little bit faster at the sight of him wearing that sling, but I ignored it as I went into his apartment and shrugged out of my suit jacket.

"I did, I swear. And I was going to mourn you properly as soon as possible."

I dropped my jacket onto a chrome and leather chair and reached for Paisley, pulling her from the sling. "Hey, you. What's the matter?"

Nate rubbed his face with both hands. "I have no idea why she won't stop crying. It's exactly like last night. She was relatively fine all evening, even took a pretty decent nap in the swing, but then it was like someone flipped a switch at ten o'clock and she turned into the devil. Her head has spun all the way around like five times."

Laughing, I stepped out of my heels and left them by the chair with my jacket. "When did she last eat?"

"I don't know. I kept trying to feed her, but I think that was a mistake because she ended up only taking like half an ounce to an ounce every so often. She never got hungry enough to drink a whole bottle." Nate ditched the sling, flopped onto the couch, and flung an arm over his eyes. "I keep reading about schedules, like you're supposed to get your baby on a schedule, but how the fuck is that even possible?"

"A schedule is a great idea, but she might be a little bit young for that." I bounced Paisley in my arms, holding her tight. "Did you try the pacifier?"

"I've tried everything."

"Did you ever give her a bath?"

He removed his arm from his head and gave me a guilty look. "No. I was too nervous."

"Why don't we try it together?" I suggested. "A warm bath can be nice and relaxing, and then we can try to feed her, and then maybe we can get her to sleep. This seems to be her worst time of night."

"I'll try anything." He stood up and cracked his knuckles. "What should I do to help?"

"Is your sink clean?" I asked.

"I think there are a couple half-finished bottles and it." He started for the kitchen. "I'll clean it out."

"Hey, before you do that, would you mind grabbing that shirt I slept in last night? I don't want to get my blouse wet." I glanced down at the lavender silk. "Either that, or I could run home and change."

Nate did an about-face. "No. Do not leave. I'll go get the shirt." He disappeared up the stairs while I walked and bounced Paisley a little, looking around the apartment, marveling at even more differences.

There was a changing table against one wall. The swing and Pack 'n Play. The sling lay discarded on the floor. A half-empty bottle and two burp cloths on the coffee table, next to a cup of coffee that had gone undrunk, and a little white rectangular box. Fudge? Curious, I lifted the lid, surprised to find something covered in chocolate. Nate wasn't really the type to eat sweets. "What's this, Paisley?

Was your daddy cheating on his diet?" I reached into the box, took one of the chocolate covered things, and nibbled on it. Potato chips? Oh my God, was that a thing? Chocolate-covered potato chips?

Nate came down the stairs, the shirt in his hands. "Here you go. Want me to hold her while you change?"

I finished the potato chip and looked longingly at the box. "I want you to take those things away from me and keep them away. I can't even believe you were eating those."

"Me either. They were a gift from a client and I stuck them in the pantry and forgot about them. But this afternoon I was dying for sugar for some reason."

"Welcome to being human." I handed him the baby, who was still howling. "Why don't you put her in the swing or something while you clean out the sink? I'll be right back."

I took the shirt into the first floor bathroom and changed into it, wishing I had some jeans—or even better, some sweatpants—to put on, but my work skirt would have to do. After tossing my blouse on the chair next to my jacket, I retrieved Paisley from the swing and went into the kitchen with her. When Nate was finished cleaning out the sink, I instructed him to grab a couple towels, a washcloth, a cup, and the baby wash while I filled the sink with some warm water. Together, we undressed her, got her in the water, and managed to soap, shampoo, and rinse her with a minimum of water in her eyes and on our clothing. Actually, she seemed to like the bath and splashed around a bit, making gurgling noises. I showed Nate how to carefully wash her, and how to rinse her hair. He paid close attention, took over for me when I asked if he wanted to, and when she was clean, he wrapped her up in a towel and took her into the other room to dry her off.

It was kind of crazy. Was this really the same guy who'd fainted at the thought of having a baby daughter?

I drained the sink, wiped up what water we'd spilled, and made a bottle. I happened to glance at the clock when it was 1:11 AM, so I quickly made a wish that Paisley would fall asleep fast instead of keeping us up until three in the morning again. When I came out into the living room, she was dry and dressed, and he was holding her against his chest, resting his lips on her head. My stomach flipped. Seeing him with her was definitely messing with me.

"She smells good," he said. "And she seems calmer."

"Good. Here's the bottle." I handed it to him, careful not to let our fingers touch.

He fed her as he walked slowly around the room, humming something that sounded like "White Christmas." I settled on the couch, my legs tucked beneath me, my cheek propped on my hand along the back of the couch. Watching him, I was disturbed by the way I couldn't seem to take my eyes off his butt in those jeans.

Stop it. This baby doesn't change things. This is still a man who doesn't believe in happy ever after.

"Oh my God," Nate whispered. "I think it worked. She's asleep."

"Great job, Bing Crosby. Where is she going to sleep tonight?"

"I put that bedside sleeper thing upstairs in my room. Should I try to put her in there?"

"Sure, why not?"

He nodded. "Come with me. She's better when you're there. *I'm* better when you're there."

"It's not me," I told him, getting off the couch, although secretly I was pleased he'd said it. "I made a wish at 1:11 that she would fall asleep fast tonight."

He glanced at me over his shoulder as we went up the stairs. "You mean it wasn't my awesome Christmas song?"

I stifled a giggle. "Maybe it was both."

At the top of the stairs, I scooted ahead of him to turn off the lamp in his bedroom. With the same slow, careful movement he had used carrying the car seat upstairs last night, he leaned over the sleeper and gently laid the sleeping baby inside it. For ten seconds, neither of us moved.

She stayed asleep.

Ten more seconds went by.

She stayed asleep.

Nate grabbed my hand in the dark, setting off a pounding inside my chest I thought might wake the baby. We exchanged a look of triumph in the silent dark, and Nate kept my hand in his as he led me down the stairs. He let it go at the bottom.

"Oh my God, the silence is like a fucking miracle," he said quietly, going over to the monitor on the coffee table and switching it on. "No wonder I never wanted kids. It's exhausting, my apartment is a mess, and I'm not any good at it."

"Stop it," I told him, starting to gather up all the bottles strewn around the living room. "You *are* good at it, and you're getting better. She's very lucky to have you as her dad."

"Well, we make a good team."

"We do." I bent down to pick up a burp cloth from the floor. "Although we had our first fight last night."

He rubbed the back of his neck. "Did we? Yeah, I guess we did."

"It's bound to happen when two people feel like they

can be really honest with each other. I think that's the sign of a solid friendship."

He didn't say anything else as he grabbed his coffee mug and the box of chips and followed me into the kitchen. It was dark in there, so I switched on the light above the sink and started scrubbing bottles. "You don't have to do that," he told me. "You worked all day, you were up half the night. You must be tired. Go home and sleep."

I *was* tired. And given my growing attraction to him, and the late hour, and the low light in the kitchen, I thought maybe it would be better if I left. "You sure?"

"I'm sure. You've done more than enough." He came over to put his mug in the sink, turned around and leaned back against it. "You think I'm crazy, don't you?"

"Why would I think that?" I turned off the water and dried my hands.

He shrugged. "Saying I'd keep her for a month was kind of a dumbass move."

"Are you having second thoughts?"

"Fuck yes, I am."

I looked up at him.

"But I'm not a guy who doesn't keep promises. When I say something, I mean it."

I spoke before I could think. "So did you mean what you said last night? About me?"

He grimaced, his eyes closing briefly. "I'm sorry about that. I shouldn't have said it."

"But you think it, right? That I'm a little girl living in a fantasy world?"

"No." He put a hand on my shoulder. "I think you're an optimist. I think you see good in people they don't even see themselves. You build people up—especially me."

"You?" I laughed a little. "You don't need me to build you up."

"Hell yes, I do. You think I'd have been able to handle this whole fatherhood bombshell if you hadn't been here? If you'd said, *'That's what you get for fucking around, asshole. Good luck.'*"

I shook my head, a strand of hair coming loose from my bun. "I'd never have done that."

"I know." He tucked the strand behind my ear and moved his hand to the back of my neck. His eyes dropped to my lips. "But I would have deserved it."

I held my breath. Things seemed to be happening in slow motion. His forehead came to rest on mine. And then our noses touched. Our eyes closed. An eternity passed, his lips a whisper from mine. Either one of us could have initiated a kiss. A slight lift of my chin. A little drop of his head. The question—will we or won't we?—hung there between us, even as his closed lips brushed mine, eyelash soft.

I wanted nothing more than to wrap my arms around his neck and fit my body flush against his, but my wrists lay inert on the edge of the sink. Suddenly he spoke, his breath warm against my mouth.

"You know that dream you have, the one where you really want to do something, you're desperate to do something, but you're paralyzed?"

"Yes," I whispered.

"I think I'm having that dream right now."

"Me too." And then I felt it, the gentle pressure at the back of my neck, pulling my head toward him.

It was all I needed. Our mouths came together firmly this time, our lips opening, and I angled my body toward his, throwing my arms around his neck. His hands explored my back while his tongue explored my mouth, and he backed me into the corner, his hips pinning mine against the hard stone counter. He kissed with a fervor and intensity that surprised me, his mouth traveling down my neck, his fingers threading through my hair, pulling the pins loose, his body giving off heat that mine hungrily absorbed. I wanted to get closer to him, wished I could feel his skin against mine. I rose up on tiptoe to press against him, my back arching to fit the question mark curve of his body.

He felt big and strong and reassuring, exactly how I wanted him to feel. I wasn't even sure what it was I wanted reassurance about... My desirability? Our chemistry? Something new and different happening between us? He swept his lips to the other side of my throat, a necklace of soft, insistent kisses that warmed my blood. When his mouth returned to mine, the kiss grew hot and frantic. He reached down and hiked the hem of my skirt to my waist, and I immediately jumped up, wrapping my legs around him. His hands moved under my ass and he carried me like that into the living room, never lifting his mouth off mine. When he reached the couch, he knelt on it and tipped me backward, stripping off his shirt and stretching out above me.

My hands moved lightning fast over hot skin, solid muscle. Chest and arms and back—I couldn't get enough. His hand stole beneath the T-shirt I wore and I arched my back so he could reach underneath me and unclasp my bra, then moaned softly at the feel of his palm over my breasts. Moving down, he shoved the shirt and bra up to my neck and put his mouth on me, his lips, his tongue, his teeth, my nipples hardening into tight little peaks that begged to be licked, sucked, teased, tortured.

What are we doing? What are we doing? What are we doing? screamed a voice in my head.

I ignored it, hooking my arms beneath his and pulling

him up so I could kiss him again. I didn't *care* what we were doing.

It felt way too good to stop.

SIX

NATE

My conscience had tried. It had talked to me as we stood there by the sink.

Don't touch her, it said.

Don't kiss her, it warned.

Don't let her get too close.

And I tried, I swear to God I tried to listen. I fought the urge. I told myself no for lots of good reasons.

She was my friend. She was my neighbor. She was someone whose well-being I genuinely cared about. She was a good, generous person helping me out. Beyond that, she trusted me. Trust was something I didn't take lightly, didn't offer easily, and didn't want to accept if I hadn't earned it.

But I couldn't resist her.

One kiss, I'd told myself as my lips hovered tantalizingly close to hers. One kiss to see what it was like. One kiss to satisfy the craving for her. One kiss to show her what it meant to me that she was here, that she cared, that she believed in me. I wasn't good with words, not those kinds of words anyway, but I could communicate my gratitude with a kiss, couldn't I? And she *wanted* me to kiss her. I knew she did. I could tell by the way she was holding her breath and standing so still. It would be okay this one time, right? We'd probably laugh about this later.

One kiss. And then we would stop.

Needless to say, that's not how it went down.

Five minutes after I put my lips on hers for the first time, we were horizontal on the couch and I was trying to reenact my dream from this morning and give it a better ending. Clearly I had way, *way* overestimated my willpower and underestimated her effect on me, from the scent of her hair to the taste of her skin to the feel of her chest against mine. Her breasts, small but perfectly plump, with sweet little raspberry nipples, drove me wild. Her perfume smelled like summer.

I bet she tastes like summer too. Like those strawberries right off the vine we used to pick when we were kids. The sweetest, juiciest, most luscious strawberries in the world.

I wanted that flavor on my tongue right the fuck now.

In three seconds flat, I'd slid down her body, hiked up her skirt and moved her underwear aside. At the first stroke she moaned aloud, then clapped both hands over her mouth. The more she struggled to stay silent, the more difficult I made the task. I clamped my hands on the outsides of her thighs, pinning her legs in place so she couldn't get away from my mouth. I got to my knees, hauling her lower body up with me so I could watch her while I worked her into a frenzy, her eyes wild and pleading above the hands that muffled her cries. I used every trick I had—long, lazy strokes up the middle with the flat of my tongue; quick, light flutters across her clit with the tip; swirling circles that made her eyes roll back in her head; fast, hard flicks as I sucked her into my mouth; long, low moans with my mouth sealed to her pussy. In no time at all, she was bucking beneath me, her legs locked around my neck, her head twisting from side to side.

And she was *not* silent.

She wasn't even quiet.

Her cries filled the room, bounced off the walls, shook the floor. I loved every fucking second of it. I felt like a million bucks. I might not know how to be a dad, but *goddamn*, I knew how to make a woman come.

And I was just getting started.

I let her wilted legs drop and reached for my belt.

"Oh my God." Emme's eyes opened halfway. She was breathing hard. "That was—"

A shrill, piercing wail cut her off.

No.

Emme looked at the monitor. I looked toward the stairs.

The keening seemed to surround us.

Oh, no.

We looked at each other in disbelief. Blinked.

"Maybe she'll go back to sleep," I said, my hands paused on my zipper.

"Maybe."

But the crying continued, and the spell was broken.

What the hell were we doing, anyway?

As we stared at each other, it dawned on us what we'd been about to do. What we'd done.

"Um," Emme started.

"Oops," I finished.

"Yeah. We should maybe—"

"Right."

Quickly and silently, we put ourselves back together. Emme pulled down her skirt as I put on my shirt. She scooped up her bra from the floor while I zipped and buttoned my pants. Paisley continued to howl.

"I'll get her," I said, heading for the stairs.

"Okay."

My heart was still pounding as I went up. Holy shit. Holy *shit*. I'd kissed Emme. I'd given her an orgasm with my tongue. I'd nearly fucked her.

How had that even happened? One second I'd been standing there watching her do the dishes, thinking about how pretty she looked, what a good friend she was, how much I appreciated her, and the next my mouth was closing over hers.

That was the last thing I remembered.

Inside my bedroom, I carefully took Paisley from the sleeper and cradled her in my arms. She was restless and fidgety, her arms moving all over the place, but her eyes were closed, leading me to believe I could get her back to sleep. It had only been an hour or so since her last feeding anyway. If I was going to get her on some kind of regular schedule, which all the books suggested, I had to be a little more disciplined about it. There was a pacifier in the sleeper, and I grabbed it, figuring I would give it another try. Holding her stomach against my chest so I could keep one of her arms in place, I fit the pacifier in her mouth and gently held it there, praying she would get the hang of it and like it. She tried to spit it out at first, but then began to suck on it. I thought for sure she would get mad there was no food in it, but she didn't. She kept it in her mouth and stayed quiet, and gradually I felt her little body relax.

I, however, was pretty fucking wound up. My erection had mostly gone away, thankfully, but it was crazy how badly I wanted to go back downstairs and finish what we'd started.

No, I told myself. *Out of the question. You shouldn't have even done what you did. Do you not have a big enough life crisis right now? Do you want to add another one? You don't do relationships, and that's ALL she does. It's what she wants and deserves. So keep your tongue in your mouth and your pants zipped before you add a whole new set of expectations to your plate and become the latest name on a very long list of assholes who let her down.*

I took a few more minutes to let that sink in and catch my breath. Then, moving slowly and carefully, I placed my daughter back in bed, waited a moment to make sure she remained asleep, and went back downstairs.

Emme was in the kitchen, finishing the dishes. She'd put her hair in a ponytail, and I recalled the way it had felt like spun silk in my hands. I wanted to touch it again. I wanted to touch *her* again. So I crossed my arms and leaned back against the counter, five feet away from her, the island between us. "You know, if that whole event planning thing doesn't work out, you'd be a kickass housekeeper. I'd hire you."

She smiled at me over one shoulder, eyes narrowed. "You couldn't afford me."

"Ha."

"You get her back to sleep?"

"I did. Got her to take the pacifier."

"Good job." She turned off the water and dried her hands. Then she turned around. "So."

Fuck, she was cute in my shirt. "So."

She twisted her hands together and glanced over at the couch. "Guess I was a little loud," she said sheepishly.

"I didn't mind."

"Honestly, I don't think I've ever been that loud."

Oh, Jesus, Emme. Don't tell me that. "Good."

"I'm sorry you didn't get to—you didn't—" She made a little bursting motion with her fingers.

I had to laugh. "What is that? An orgasm?"

"Yes," she said, giggling too, although her cheeks went a little pink.

"Well, don't be sorry. I quite enjoyed myself. And actually, it's probably better that we were interrupted before we took it too far."

"Definitely. I mean, what were we thinking?" Her eyes were wide.

"I'm not sure there was a whole lot of *thinking* going on."

She laughed. "Probably none at all."

"Let's call it a momentary lapse in sanity. Forget it happened."

Her smile was relieved. "Let's."

"Friends?"

She nodded. "Friends."

But we stood there looking at each other across the kitchen for a moment longer, and I found myself wishing that somehow we could be more. That there was a state of closeness that existed between friendship and commitment. Something more than platonic but less than romantic. Did such a thing exist?

No. And she wouldn't want it if it did.

"Well, I should go," she said. "It's late."

I followed her out of the kitchen and watched her drape her blouse and jacket over her arm. "Oh, your shirt!" she said, turning to me with a worried expression.

"Keep it," I told her. "Looks better on you."

She smiled at me and stepped into her heels. "I'll wash it and bring it back."

Actually, I kind of liked the idea of her lying around in

it, maybe sleeping in it with nothing underneath, but that was probably the kind of thing you didn't say to a friend. And you definitely didn't imagine yourself smelling it once she gave it back. "Okay."

She walked to the door and opened it herself, which totally violated my sense of chivalry, but I thought it might be smarter to keep some distance between us. "Night," she said, glancing back over her shoulder.

"Night," I echoed, remembering her hand in mine as we'd lain next to each other in bed last night.

The door shut behind her with a soft click, and I breathed a huge sigh of relief.

I needed a break from her. The more time we spent together, the easier she made my life, the harder it was to suppress these stupid urges I had whenever she was around. Urges that could ruin our friendship and destroy her opinion of me. If I was really the man I was pretending to be—no, the man I *wanted* to be, strong and able and independent, I'd be able to get through a few days without her.

I vowed to do it, starting tomorrow.

SEVEN

EMME

My head was spinning. I couldn't believe what we'd done. What we'd almost done. Was there a full moon or something? A strange disturbance in the electromagnetic spectrum? An unusual alignment of the planets? I'd read my horoscope earlier, and it hadn't mentioned anything *remotely* interesting—something about keeping my distance from issues that trigger my feelings of imprisonment, which I didn't even have.

I didn't recall letting myself into my apartment, going upstairs, or getting undressed for bed. It was only when I stood in front of the mirror, wearing only his white T-shirt over my underwear, toothbrush in one hand, toothpaste in the other, that I caught my reflection and realized where I was. But I had no idea how long I'd even been standing there. All I could think about was Nate.

Don't obsess. It was a mistake, it meant nothing, and you need to forget it.

And I would. I really would.

But not just yet.

It was too fresh in my mind, every detail still vivid and thrilling.

The torture of his lips so close to mine, not yet touching them. The booming in my chest as I waited to see what would happen. The will-he-or-won't-he agony that stole my breath and rendered me unable to move even one little finger.

And then...

Closing my eyes, I swooned, remembering how it had felt when he'd finally given in to it.

The pressure of his fingers at the back of my neck. The warmth of his mouth closing over mine. That first shocking stroke of his tongue between my lips, the barest hint of chocolate flavoring the kiss.

And then...

I opened my eyes and leaned forward on the vanity, lifting my chin and staring at my neck.

His mouth moving down my throat. His hands in my hair. The heat coming off his body as he'd loomed over me, tall and strong and masculine.

And then...

His fingers beneath my thighs. My body being lifted. My legs twining around him.

I set my toothbrush down and put a hand over my stomach, which was flipping wildly.

His weight on me.

His hands beneath my shirt.

His mouth on my breasts.

His tongue on my—

Oh my God, oh my God, oh my God.

Nothing had ever felt so good in my entire life. Where the hell did he learn all those tricks? Why didn't other guys I'd been with know them? How was it possible I'd never been with anybody who knew how to make me come like that, like my entire body was being gloriously ripped apart at the seams?

I clapped both hands over my lips, remembering how loud I'd been. Color seeped into my face. How embarrassing! He was probably used to women who were way more sultry and sophisticated during sex. Women who moaned and purred instead of screaming like a teenage girl on the Dragster at Cedar Point.

Then again, he hadn't seemed to mind. I remembered the feel of his cock through his jeans when he'd lain on top of me, thick and long and hard. He'd been as turned on as I was. For a moment, I let myself wonder what would have happened if Paisley hadn't woken up. Would we have gone further? Would we have gone all the way?

My stomach whooshed. My pelvic muscles clenched. My breath stopped.

Stop. Stop it right there. It would have been a huge mistake. You guys are friends, and nothing ruins a friendship like sex.

Forcing the thought of sex with Nate from my mind, I finished my teeth, washed my face, took my birth control pill, and switched off the light. Crawling beneath the covers, I lay on my back and stared at the ceiling. Suddenly I wasn't the least bit sleepy. My whole body was tingling. I wondered if Nate was still up. I wondered what he was thinking. I wondered if things would be awkward between us tomorrow and hoped they wouldn't be. I squeezed my eyes shut and tried to sleep.

But automatically, my mind wandered back to that moment Nate's hands froze as he unzipped his pants. Here, alone in my bed, I let him keep going. Let him shove down his jeans. Let him slide inside me and begin to move.

Then I stopped—what would it be like to have sex with Nate Pearson? Was he gentle or rough? Was he quiet or loud? Did he close his eyes, mutter incoherent curse words, and use his dick like a hammer, like a lot of guys did, making sex feel strangely impersonal, like it was something being done to you and not with you? Or did he *look* at you, use his whole body, talk to you, make you feel connected to him, share the dizzying climb and the rapturous fall?

Sighing, I opened my eyes again.

Probably I was idealizing him. Idealizing sex, even. I always wanted it to be something more than it was. I always wanted it to mean more than it did. In my head, I could still hear him call me a little girl in a fantasy world, even if he'd tried to say otherwise earlier tonight. But it seemed to me if you let someone into your body, if you let him see you and hear you and touch you at your most uninhibited and vulnerable, it was only natural to *feel* something in your heart for that person you didn't feel for anyone else. It shouldn't be something you did on a whim with someone who had no interest in your heart whatsoever. If that was childish of me to believe, so be it.

It was a good thing we'd stopped.

SUNDAY MORNING I woke up around nine, and I felt so energized that I decided to get in some exercise before meeting my sisters for our standing eleven o'clock Sunday brunch date. Since a peek out the window told me it was pouring rain, I decided against a walk or jog, threw on a sports bra and some leggings, and dug out the yoga mat Maren had given me for Christmas. It had been at the back of my closet and had some pretty good-sized dust bunnies clinging to it, but I cleaned it off and spread it out on my bedroom floor.

Once I was sitting on it, however, I realized I actually didn't *know* any yoga on my own. Wasn't there something called a downward dog? Or was it a warrior dog? Maybe a downward child? I guessed my way through a few haphazard poses, then gave up and did some old-fashioned jumping jacks, squats, push-ups (albeit from my knees), and crunches. For good measure, I did a few side stretches and runner's lunges before hitting the shower, congratulating myself on a well-rounded workout.

I dressed in jeans and a sweater, blow-dried my hair, braided it, and put on minimal makeup. Before I left, I checked my messages, since it was Maren's turn to pick the place and my phone had died last night before she'd texted the spot. Sure enough, there was a message from her saying **Rose's at 11**, **see you there**, which made me happy because I *loved* the little diner on East Jefferson. Best pancakes ever.

I had a few other messages—one from Coco asking if I'd have lunch with her and Mia tomorrow, which was normally my day off, and one from my cousin Mia, telling me she would be in town this week and wanted to see me. Ignoring the tug of disappointment I felt that Nate hadn't texted to tell me how the night had gone, I resisted the urge to message him and ask. I responded to Coco, saying yes, of course, and asked where and when I should meet them, and texted Mia back that I'd see her tomorrow, adding a bunch of smiley faces. It would be good to see her—it had been a few months, and spending time with her always inspired me. She had everything: adoring husband, three beautiful children, a gorgeous home, a successful business. We shared blood, so I figured if she could accomplish all that by age thirty-six, there was still hope for me.

I drove to Rose's, parked in the lot next to the small free-standing building, and hurried inside through the drizzle. The diner was crowded, as usual, but my sisters were already there and had a table. I made my way to the back of the restaurant and shrugged out of my coat before taking the seat next to Maren and across from Stella. "Hi. Sorry I'm a little late. I worked out this morning." Statements like these always made me feel like a better person.

"You did?" Maren sounded more surprised than I thought was necessary. "Where?"

"At home. I used the yoga mat you got me for Christmas."

She beamed, her face radiant. If there were anything that could convince me to eat, drink, and live cleaner, it would be Maren's skin. She was *always* radiant. I was constantly asking her what she used on her skin to make it so bright, and she always claimed it was plain old coconut oil. Stella and I were convinced she had to be lying, although she is the worst liar in the world and wouldn't have spent the money on expensive skincare or cosmetics anyway. Stella and I, on the other hand, were product junkies, and could happily blow a hundred bucks at Ulta with no regrets.

"I'm so glad you're using it," she said. "I was afraid it would sit neglected at the back of your closet."

I didn't tell her that's exactly where it had been before I'd dug it out. "It was very useful. Thanks." Before she could ask me about what I'd done, I addressed Stella. "Did you run this morning?"

She nodded. The most athletic of the three of us, she wore a track jacket and her hair pulled back. "Yep."

"In this awful weather?" Maren asked, gesturing toward the windows.

Stella shrugged and picked up her coffee. "You get used to it. It's not bad if you're dressed right."

Her answer didn't surprise me. Not only was our older sister a total creature of habit, she actually *enjoyed* running enough to do it in the rain, if you can believe that. She ran marathons in cities all over the country. I thought running was repetitive and miserable even in beautiful weather, so her dedication made little sense to me.

The waitress came by, and I asked for some coffee. A moment, later, she came back with my cup and we put in our orders—eggs and veggies for Stella, granola and fruit for Maren, pancakes and bacon for me.

"So how are you, Em?" Maren inquired, lifting her cup of tea to her lips. "When I talked to you on Friday, you were pretty upset."

For a moment, I couldn't even think of what she meant, and then I remembered the wedding invitation. It seemed like ages ago! Had I really cared so much I nearly set my apartment on fire?

"About what?" Stella asked.

"Stupid Richard and Lucy invited me to their wedding," I said.

Her eyes widened. "Seriously? Are you going to go?"

"No. Do you think I'm crazy?"

Neither of my sisters answered that.

"I wouldn't go either," Maren said. "I don't blame you for being upset."

I sipped my coffee. "I'm not even that upset about it anymore. I don't know why it had me so riled up."

"Bad day?" Stella suggested.

"Not really."

"Jealousy?"

I snorted. "I don't care about that asshole anymore. She can have him. Those two deserve each other. I think it was more the idea that they assumed I'd want to attend their stupid wedding after what they did."

"Yeah, that's pretty ballsy," she admitted.

"And it pisses me off that those two fell in love so fast and so easily when it's so hard for the rest of us, you know? Well, for me, anyway."

"And for me," added Maren. She'd recently broken up with someone she'd met at the studio because he smoked too much pot and didn't seem to have any ambition whatsoever.

Stella actually had a sort-of boyfriend, this psychologist she'd met at a workshop last year. He was nice enough, and attractive in a distinguished professor with glasses and elbow patches sort of way, but he never stopped talking about his fucking bees. He kept them in his yard and he was *obsessed*. Maren and I did not understand how Stella took it. His name was Walter, but we called him—wait for it— Buzz, and we were always making little buzzing noises or bee jokes. Kind of mean, but what are sisters for?

"Hang in there, both of you. You did the right thing to break up with that guy," she said to Maren. "And you deserve a lot better than Richard, Emme. He was a classic narcissist."

"Thanks. How's Buzz?" I hid my smile behind my coffee cup and felt Maren kick me beneath the table.

"He's fine, but do you have to call him that? There's a lot more to him than his beekeeping."

"You should tell him that."

She sat up taller. "It's very good for the environment, you know."

"I do know. Because he's told me multiple times."

"Bzzz," agreed Maren.

"Be nice," said Stella. "He's a good guy, smart and successful, and he treats me well. At this point in my life, I'll take it."

I rolled my eyes. "Stella, you're thirty-two, not eighty."

"Still."

I could tell she was getting testy. "Okay, okay. Sorry. Did either of you guys go out last night?"

"Not me," said Maren.

"Walter and I went to dinner and saw a film down at the DIA, then came back to my house."

"Did he finally sting you?" I couldn't resist, even though I knew the answer. Stella and Buzz did not have sex. This made my sister and her relationship even more baffling to Maren and me. If you were going to date a boring guy, wouldn't you at least want him to have a big dick or something?

She sighed and set down her cup, staring into it. "No, he didn't. I told you, it's not like that with us."

"I still don't get that," said Maren before I could. "What's the point of having a boyfriend if you don't have sex? Are you even attracted to him?"

"Yes, but our attraction is based more on mutual respect and admiration than on physical chemistry. We have a lot in common and enjoy spending time together. That's enough for me right now. Not every relationship needs sex to feel complete."

"Okay, as long as you are happy, we're happy for you." I wanted to cut her off before she went into therapist speak and started to lecture us about equating sex with love and intimacy. Well, mostly me. I wasn't sure what Maren's problem with guys was. She didn't seem to date assholes, but she never picked winners either. Stella was convinced she was still hung up on her high school ex, and sometimes I thought she might be right, although Maren always denied it.

"Thank you," said Stella. "What about you? How was your weekend?"

"Fine. Friday night, I hung out with Nate, and last night I had a wedding. Then I hung out with Nate again afterward."

"Nate the guy across the hall?" Stella's tone was surprised. "I thought you were just friends."

"We are just friends. I didn't stay the night or anything. I only went to help him out."

"With what?" Maren asked.

I paused to take a sip of coffee and consider how much I should tell them. I didn't want to betray Nate's confidence, but he wasn't going to be able to keep his daughter a secret forever, and I knew I could trust my sisters. We had our differences, but our bond was solid. "Okay, you can't say a word about this to anyone yet, but he found out he has a baby daughter."

Maren gasped. "When?"

"Late Friday night when I was there, the mother left her outside Nate's door with a letter saying she was his." I summarized the contents of the letter and described Nate's reaction.

"He *fainted*?" Stella asked.

I nodded. "Went down like a giant elm. Although he denies it."

"Of course he does."

At that point our meals arrived, and I waited until the server had left to go on, telling them about the first night I'd spent in his apartment.

"You slept over? Did anything happen?"

I picked up the little pitcher of maple syrup and soaked my stack of pancakes. "No. He only asked me to stay to help with her. Honestly, he is clueless when it comes to babies."

"What single guy isn't?" Maren popped a strawberry in her mouth.

Digging into my breakfast, I told them about the phone call with Rachel.

"Holy shit," remarked Stella. "I can't believe a mother would abandon her child to a stranger for a month. For any length of time at all. I wonder what's going on there."

"No idea," I said, my mouth full of fluffy, maple-soaked deliciousness. "She's lucky Nate is a good guy."

"Is he, though?" Stella cocked her head to one side. "You've told me some stories. I wouldn't think he's the dad type."

"I wouldn't have either," Maren added, "based on what you've said about him."

"He wasn't," I agreed. "But he doesn't really have a choice now, and he's trying really hard. You should see him with her. It's so sweet." In my mind I could still see him hold her up so he could smell her freshly washed hair. My belly fluttered.

"You're not doing all the work?" Stella sounded suspicious.

"Not at all!" I felt defensive about Nate. "I mean, I had to show him how to do everything, because he's never had any experience with a baby, but he's getting the hang of things. He feeds her and changes her and burps her and rocks her to sleep, and we gave her a bath together last night. Right in the kitchen sink, and afterward he took her and dried her off and got her ready for bed. So damn sweet."

My sisters exchanged an amused glance. "You mentioned that."

"What?" I demanded. "What's that look for?"

"Be careful, Em," Stella said. "Don't let him take advantage of you."

"What do you mean?"

Maren chimed in. "She means don't let him think he's got a sexy nanny living across the hall at his beck and call."

"He doesn't think that," I said, annoyed. "I *volunteered* to help him. And we didn't have sex! We're just friends."

"Okay, don't get angry. I just know how you get and I don't want to see you hurt."

"How I *get*?" I set my fork down too, my appetite diminished.

"Yes," Stella said in her I-am-a-therapist-so-I-know-more-about-your-feelings-than-you-do voice. "When you get a crush on someone, you go kamikaze immediately. And your crushes are never on guys who want that."

"I don't have a crush on him," I lied, staring at my plate. "We only messed around a little. Jeez. I'm sorry I told you."

Stella sighed. "No, no. Don't be sorry—*I'm* sorry. I didn't mean to upset you, Emme, I only want you to be careful. I've seen you fall for the wrong guy, hard and fast, plenty of times."

"I'm not falling for anybody," I said, hoping it was true, "*Nobody* is falling, so you can stop worrying. Nobody is even having sex. Although if we did decide to have sex, it would be nobody's business but our own. After all, if you and Buzz can have dating without sex, why couldn't Nate and I have sex without dating? Everybody should be free to do what they want."

"You're right," said Stella in a voice so calm it irked me. "You're right and I'm sorry. Different relationships work for different reasons, and I hope you and Nate have one that works for you. If it's sexual without being romantic and you're okay with it, then great."

"We only want you to be happy," said Maren, rubbing my shoulder.

"Thank you." I picked up my fork again and stabbed through my stack of pancakes, but I really didn't want any more.

Would I really be okay having sex without romance? On the ride home, I thought about it. The truth was, I wasn't sure. I'd never wanted to be that kind of person before. Maybe that was my trouble. Maybe it wasn't men who disappointed me; maybe I was setting *myself* up for disappointment every time by expecting too much.

Maybe, as Nate had put it, sometimes a fuck really was just a fuck.

After all, it was mostly about anatomy, right? Intercourse. Penetration. Insert Part A into Slot B. Why, I wondered, had I always been so convinced there had to be *emotions* involved? Couldn't you do it because it felt good? Because it relieved tension? Because it made you feel sexy and desirable and wanted? Look how good I'd felt in my skin this morning after that orgasm last night—good enough to wake up early and do yoga, for goodness sake! When was the last time I'd done *that* on a Sunday morning?

Maybe all this time, it was those women leaving Nate's apartment in the morning who'd had it right, and smug, self-important little me who'd had it wrong.

But how could I be sure?

EIGHT

NATE

Sunday morning, I woke up determined to do what I'd promised myself and stay away from Emme. I wouldn't text her with updates. I wouldn't call her for advice. I wouldn't invite her over to help. I needed to do things on my own, even if I was going on less than five hours of sleep and craved nothing but caffeine and sugar.

During Paisley's morning nap, I emailed my boss and told her I needed time off for a family emergency. She replied very quickly that she hoped things were all right and that it shouldn't be a problem to cover my caseload for the week. But she requested I come in on Monday morning, if at all possible, to get things in place. I told her I would let her know by the end of the day if I couldn't get there, then worried all afternoon about how I was going to make it happen. Did I take Paisley with me? I imagined myself walking through the lobby doors of the firm's building wearing a suit, tie, and the baby sling and wanted to die. But as I had no one to watch her yet, I didn't know if I'd have a choice. I figured I could ask Emme and that she'd probably say yes since Monday was her day off, but I didn't want to.

After Paisley woke up and drank her bottle, I took her to the grocery store, which turned out to be a much bigger ordeal than I had anticipated, and I had anticipated a pretty fucking big ordeal. First, the carts at the grocery store didn't have those built in seats for infants like the carts at Babies"R"Us, and I struggled to balance her car seat in the front compartment where little kids were supposed to sit. After a few minutes of grappling and sweating and muttering curse words under my breath, I was rescued by a merciful woman who took pity on me. "Here," she said. "Let me show you how to do it."

When Paisley's car seat was secure, I thanked her. "I'm new at this dad thing," I said apologetically. "Still learning how to do everything."

Things went okay for the next twenty minutes or so, but it was taking me forever to shop because I couldn't leave the cart and run to grab something I'd forgotten two aisles back —and I kept forgetting *everything* (sleep deprivation is no joke). It's not like I could say to Paisley, *stay right here, I'll be right back,* and dash over to the produce section again. I had to bring her with me every time.

Then, of course, she decided to shit herself right in the middle of the canned vegetable aisle. Her face turned a shade of red that rivaled the crushed tomatoes, and she grunted like a four-hundred-pound deadweight lifter. Other shoppers, who previously had all stopped to tell me how cute she was, now seemed to avoid us. When she was finished, the stench surrounded us like a toxic cloud everywhere we went. It was so bad I ended up cutting the shopping trip short and running for the checkout without even hitting the dairy aisle, even though I was out of eggs and milk. Then, as we were waiting to be rung up, she decided to start screaming over absolutely nothing and wouldn't stop.

"Sorry," I said to the cashier. And the customer ahead of me. And the customer behind me. And the woman one lane over. And anyone I passed on my way out to the parking lot.

I put her in the car first and then loaded the grocery bags into my trunk. It was on the way home that I wondered how I was supposed to get her and all of the grocery bags up to my apartment without the big cart. "How the hell do people do this?" I muttered out loud.

Her answer was a fresh round of wailing. I didn't blame her.

In the end, I made the first trip up to my apartment carrying as many grocery bags as I could in one hand and her car seat in the other. Then I put her in the stroller, wheeled her down to the parking garage, and loaded up. Bags were hanging off my arms and bulging out the bottom of the stroller, but I managed to get everything in one trip.

The one good thing that day was that I managed to bathe her all by myself without doing harm to either one of us or making too big a mess in the kitchen. In fact, she actually seemed to enjoy getting her hair washed, and when she was dry and dressed in a clean sleeper, I sat her on my lap and brushed her hair for the first time. I couldn't get it to lie completely flat, but it looked pretty fucking cute. She seemed to like that too, although she kept trying to grab the brush out of my hand. When I was done with her hair, I let her play with it, and she immediately tried to eat the thing. I watched her gnaw on the handle for a couple minutes, then I took out my phone and snapped a picture of her —my first.

The realization hit me that I was probably going to take thousands of photos of her in my lifetime, but this was the very first one. It choked me up a little, although I would never admit it to anyone.

Of course, the next thing I wanted to do was send the picture to someone, because what good was it to have a cute kid if you couldn't show her off? Emme was my first thought, not just because she was the only one of my friends who knew about Paisley, but because I genuinely wanted her to see the photo. Was it breaking my vow to text it to her? It's not like I was asking for help or anything.

Paternal pride overruled my stubbornness, and I decided to send it.

First bath on my own. We survived. I think she likes my mad hairstyling skills.

I sent the message and the photo, hoping for a quick and friendly reply. It took less than 30 seconds.

Emme: OMG! She is the cutest thing ever. Great job on the bath. Things going okay today?

I had to text with one hand, so it took me a couple minutes to write back.

Me: Yes. Grocery store was a bit hairy and smelly, but all is well. How are you?

Emme: Oh dear. Hairy and smelly? I'm fine. Cleaning my apartment and making spaghetti sauce and meatballs.

Homemade spaghetti sauce and meatballs. Jesus Christ, that sounded good. My stomach groaned with envy. Since Paisley had arrived, I was surviving on shit like chocolate-covered potato chips, dry cereal (since I'd run out of milk), raisins, lunchmeat, and cocktail olives. I hadn't even had the time or energy to make a proper sandwich. But I didn't want her to know that.

Me: Sounds good. Enjoy your dinner.

She didn't text back. I set my phone aside and exhaled. It sucked not being able to be honest with her. She and I had never had to bullshit each other, and I didn't like it. What I really wanted to say was, *How about you bring that spaghetti over here and hold the baby while I pour you a drink?*

But if she came over, I had a feeling I knew what would happen. I didn't trust myself.

WHILE PAISLEY TOOK her afternoon nap in the swing, I made a few work phone calls and did laundry. I was folding some of Paisley's things—they were so tiny in my big hands, it was ridiculous—when I wondered if I would have to move to a bigger place.

Fuck. I didn't want to move. I loved this apartment. Everything about it said *me*. Except...I hardly even knew who that was at this point. Did the old me still exist? Did being a father supersede every other part of my identity? Did I have a right to live where I wanted to live without worrying if it was right for a kid? How often would she even visit? What was my life going to look like moving forward? Could I shift back and forth from old Nate to single dad Nate at will? Be one thing when she was with me and another when she wasn't?

The walls started to close in on me, and I sank onto the couch, eyes closed. My stomach hurt. My brain hurt. How was I ever going to get used to the fact that nothing in my life would ever be the same? I didn't want these problems. I didn't want to move. I didn't want to be a father.

Then I thought of Emme. What had she said to me Friday night?

If you were really the alpha male you pretend to be, you'd take responsibility for this like a grown-ass man and not fall apart like the ridiculous boy I see in front of me.

Frowning, I got to my feet again. I wasn't fucking pretending. And I wouldn't fall apart.

After I had stacked Paisley's clothing beneath the changing table and put away my own laundry, I decided to make the call to my mother. Telling her would not be fun, but the longer I avoided it, the more cowardly I felt. I needed to do something that would make me feel strong. Show someone I was accepting responsibility like a man.

Then I could tell Emme about it.

I glanced at Paisley, who was sleeping peacefully in the swing, picked up my phone and made the call. My mother didn't answer, so I left a message asking her to call me back, which, of course, she did after Paisley woke up and was just getting started on her nightly crying jag.

"Hi, Mom," I said, shifting the screaming baby to my left arm so I could hold the phone to my ear with the right.

"Nate? Is that you?"

"Yes, it's me."

"Hello? Hello?"

I rolled my eyes and spoke louder. "Hello, Mom. It's me. Can you hear me?"

"Sort of. Where on earth are you?"

"I'm at home."

"Well, what's all that noise? Is your television on? Can you turn it off? I'm having trouble hearing you."

"It's not my television. It's a baby, and I can't turn it off. Sorry, I wish I could."

She was silent a moment. "Did you say a baby? What's a baby doing at your apartment? Whose baby?"

I took a deep breath. "It's *my* baby, Mom."

More silence on my mother's end. I imagined her taking the phone away from her ear to stare at it.

"I'm sorry, what?"

I spoke loud and clear. "I said, it's *my* baby."

"You have a *baby*?"

"Yes. She's eight weeks old, and her name is Paisley."

"Eight weeks old? I don't understand. You've had a baby for eight weeks and you're only telling me about it now? Oh my God. Oh my God, I have to sit down. I feel faint."

Stay calm. "No, Mom. She's eight weeks old, but I just found out about her two days ago." I waited for a reply, but didn't hear anything for a minute, and then there was the telltale crackle of a brown paper bag as she breathed in and out of it. "Mom? Are you okay?" More crackling. "Look, I know this is a shock. It was for me, too. I promise, I had no idea she even existed."

The crackling paused. "How is that possible? You didn't know you...got someone pregnant?"

"No, I didn't."

"I don't understand. Was it your girlfriend or something? Why wouldn't she tell you?"

"It wasn't my girlfriend. I don't have a girlfriend."

"Who on earth was it?"

"Just someone I know."

"Well, what's her name, for God's sake?"

"Rachel."

"Rachel what?"

I winced. I *really* needed to find out her last name. "I don't know."

"Merciful Jesus, Nate! Is she a prostitute?" More crackling.

"No! Jesus, Mom. She was just a woman I knew, okay? Let's leave it at that."

"So where is this woman now?"

"I don't know that, either. She left the baby with me and said she needed some time away."

"So how do you know it's even yours?"

Even though I knew the question was fair, and I'd had it too, it made me angry. "Because I do, all right? She's mine, and I'm keeping her."

She started up with the wheezing and the paper bag again, and I gave her a minute to calm down. My mother was the kind of person who could make a mountain out of a molehill, and I'd just put her at the foot of Everest.

"Mom? You there?" Paisley had accepted the pacifier and was finally quiet—for now, anyway—and the crackling noise had stopped.

"Yes. I'm here."

"Would you like to meet Paisley? I could drive up this week. I took some time off from work."

"Oh, dear. Oh, dear, I don't know what to say." Her voice was nervous and timid, like I'd asked her if she'd like to meet the Queen of England instead of her granddaughter.

"Say yes. She's really cute, and I'll bring her in the early part of the day, so she's not so fussy. Evenings are when she's at her worst."

"You were, too," she said, surprising me.

"I was?" We didn't talk about the past in my family.

"Yes. You'd cry and cry, no matter what Daddy and I did to soothe you. And we tried everything—cereal in your bottle, gripe water, whiskey on your gums."

"Whiskey? You tried to get me drunk so I'd pass out and stop crying?" I joked.

She laughed, a thing so rare I'd nearly forgotten what it sounded like. It made my throat tighten a little. "It was only a drop, I promise," she said. "But that's how things were back then."

"No wonder I developed a taste for a good bottle of rye." I looked down at Paisley and tried to imagine a parent thinking it was okay—and a great idea!—to rub booze on her gums. "But I think I'll skip the whiskey for now. She seems to like the pacifier, and she loves to be rocked to sleep."

"It's been a long time since I've held a baby," she said quietly. "I always thought I'd have grandchildren, but things turned out so differently than I'd planned."

"I know, Mom. Believe me. I know."

By the time we hung up, there was a tentative plan in place for me to drive up to Grand Rapids with Paisley next Saturday morning, depending on how my mother was feeling. I would give her a call that morning, and if she was up for a visit, we'd go.

I was tempted to call Emme and let her know how the conversation with my mother had gone, but she was probably eating dinner by now. I didn't want to bother her. But part of me couldn't stop thinking about inviting her over to spend the evening hanging out with me, eating spaghetti and meatballs, maybe watching a movie after we got Paisley to bed. It was torture. After a while, I swore the aroma from the sauce was drifting from her kitchen across the hall into my apartment. Paisley was fussy and wouldn't stop. I was hungry and lonely and wondering what the fuck had happened to my charmed life when there was a knock on the door.

As I walked over to answer it, I hoped it was her and prayed that it wasn't. I knew I wouldn't have the strength to send her away.

When I opened the door, there she stood, looking like an angel and holding two grocery bags in her hands. "Hi," she said. "I wasn't sure if you'd eaten yet, but I ended up making a lot of food and thought you might want some."

"I could kiss you." I meant it as a joke, but also, I was serious.

She grinned and wiggled a finger at me. "Ah, ah, ah. That's against the rules. We're friends, remember?" But there was a glint of mischief in her eye that hadn't been there last night. It thrilled and terrified me at the same time.

"Come on in," I said. "I haven't eaten. I'm starving, but Paisley here doesn't care."

"Paisley, what's wrong?" Emme stopped to kiss my daughter on her forehead. "Mmm, you smell nice. And you look so cute with your hair done. What is there to cry about?"

I followed Emme over to the kitchen, where she set the bags on the island and turned to me. "Do you want me to make you a plate now or put everything in the fridge for later?"

"Have you eaten already?" I asked, bouncing Paisley in my arms.

"No, but I don't have to eat here. I can hold her while you eat and then go home for my dinner."

"No, don't do that. Stay. Eat with me. She's been up for a while—maybe we can get her down and have a quiet dinner. Watch a movie or something." *It's not really breaking the promise*, I reasoned. *She came here, I didn't call her.*

"You're sure you're not too tired?" She started taking things out of the bags—plastic containers full of pasta and sauce and meatballs and salad. "You look exhausted."

"Thanks," I said, my mouth watering at the sight of a bag of frozen garlic bread. "But I think that's just how I look now. I'm fine."

She laughed and turned on the oven to preheat. "Sorry this is frozen. I'm not much of a baker. More of a cook."

"I'm in no position to complain, and it all looks amazing to me. My stomach has been growling all day."

"Aww. Poor thing." She patted my arm as she went by me to get to the cupboards where I kept bowls and plates. "I'll make it better."

"Can I make you a drink?" I asked. Actually at that moment, what I wanted to ask her was to move in with me, marry me, never leave me. But a drink was probably a better idea.

"Sure."

"Glass of wine?"

"Perfect."

I pulled a bottle of red from the beverage fridge and set it on the counter, but since I had Paisley in my arms it was Emme who opened it, took two glasses down from the cabinet, and poured. While she did that, I grabbed the little baby brush from the couch where I'd left it.

"I told my mother about her," I said, taking a seat at one of the barstools at the counter separating the kitchen from the living room. I balanced Paisley on one leg and gave her the brush, which she stuck right into her mouth. At least it quieted her down.

"You did?" Emme glanced at me over one shoulder as she stuck the pasta in the microwave. "How did it go? Was she upset?"

"She was, but pretty much anything upsets my mother. I'm hoping once the shock wears off she'll be glad to have a grandchild to fuss over. It would give her something good to focus on, I think."

"And your dad is gone?"

"Yeah. He died a few years back. Right before I moved in here, actually."

"I'm sorry." She stopped moving around and met my eyes. "Were you close?"

"Not very, but your dad is your dad." I was weirdly tempted to talk more about my family, which was *never* the case, but the words stuck in my throat. I'd burdened her enough with my shit lately, anyway.

"This is where having supportive sisters comes in handy, I guess. Too bad you don't have one of those."

"Yeah." *Or a brother*, I thought, wishing for the millionth time Adam was still alive. He'd be thirty now, like Emme. And he'd probably have just as big a heart. Much better for her than I would be.

"Want to borrow one of mine?" She flashed a smile at me as she stuck the bread in the oven. "I've got two, and one of them annoyed the crap out of me this morning. I'd loan her out for cheap, maybe even free."

I laughed a little. "Which one, the therapist or the yoga teacher?"

"The therapist. Which might do you some good, actually. Have you thought about that at all? To help you deal with everything?"

"I haven't thought about anything but sleep and baby poop for two days, with the occasional break for a work-related panic attack." *And, of course, occasionally picturing you naked.*

"I get it. Well, something to think about anyway. We all went when my parents divorced and my dad came out as gay." She shrugged. "I think it helped."

"That does sound like a lot to deal with as a kid."

"Well, we were older. In our teens."

"Still had to affect you."

She waved a hand in the air dismissively. "I don't know. Maybe. Anyway, my parents are both much happier now. Did your parents stay together?"

"Yes and no." I shifted Paisley to my other leg. "They never formally divorced, but after..." I stopped, unwilling to open up that much. Some wounds had to stay closed.

"After what?" she prompted, placing salad into bowls.

"There was just a point at which my parents must have decided they couldn't live together anymore. Or didn't want to. Who knows?" I focused on Paisley's little hands gripping the brush. "I was a teenager by then too. Neither of them talked to me."

"And no siblings, right?"

I swallowed hard. "No siblings."

WHILE EMME FINISHED GETTING dinner ready, I fed Paisley her nighttime bottle upstairs in my room where it was dark and quiet, then rocked her to sleep. It took me about twenty minutes, but she stayed down when I placed her in the sleeper. I kissed my fingertips, pressed them to her head, and silently made her a promise in the dark. *I'll be better than he was.*

I'd loved my dad, but I'd loved him because he'd been my father, not because of the *kind* of father he had been. While I didn't blame him, because the circumstances had been so far out of his control, the grief too unfathomable, I never wanted Paisley to suffer because I didn't put her first —above myself, and above anyone else.

And I never wanted Emme to suffer, either, which would surely be the case if she pinned her romantic hopes on me.

But when dinner was done, and the wine was gone, and the movie credits for Casino Royale (my thanks for her bringing dinner) were rolling, I didn't get up and turn on the lights like I should have. I stayed right where I was, lying on my back at one end of the couch with my legs stretched out toward Emme, who was on the other end, her legs stretched toward me. My feet were tucked between her and the back of the couch, but hers barely came to my stomach.

She yawned. "It's late."

I turned off the television, leaving us in darkness. "After midnight."

"What time will she wake up again?"

Closing my eyes, I brought my hands behind my head. "Who knows? Probably soon."

"Why don't you stay down here and sleep? I'll go upstairs, and when she wakes up, I'll take care of her. I don't have to get up early or anything, but tonight is probably the last night I can help you out for a while because of work."

God, she was too good to be true. Affection for her flooded through me, and I opened my eyes. It was dark, but I could see her perfectly. And I wanted her desperately.

It made me weak.

"You think I could sleep down here knowing you were in my bed?"

Stillness. Silence. "You couldn't?"

I shook my head. "Nope."

"I thought we said last night—"

"I know what we said. And we were right."

"So you...you still think it would be a mistake."

"Yep. Doesn't mean I don't want to do it."

"Nate—"

"Doesn't mean I've stopped thinking about it all night."

"Oh, God."

"Doesn't mean I could keep my hands off you if you stayed the night. In fact, I know I couldn't."

"So...so I should go?" She was confused, and I didn't blame her.

"Hell yes, you should go."

She nodded slowly, swinging her feet to the floor.

"But I want you to stay."

"Nate," she whispered. "Tell me what to do."

I reached for her. "Come here."

NINE

EMME

I didn't even hesitate.

When his arms opened, inviting me into his embrace, I went, stretching out above him, my body flush against his. He was warm and firm beneath me, and as our lips met I could feel our hearts galloping madly toward each other, as if they were driven by force.

We kissed with all the passion we'd been holding back. With hands wandering over clothing and then underneath. With tongues that sought to know the secrets of each other's mouths—the taste, the texture, the shape. With bodies that began to move, to writhe and flex, as our patience grew thin. Clothing was discarded. My sweater and bra. His T-shirt and Henley. My leggings. His jeans. My panties, already damp with desire. By then we were desperate for one another, and frantically hoping we wouldn't wake the baby.

"Give me ten seconds," he whispered between kisses.

I sat up and watched him hurry through the dark into the downstairs bathroom, returning a moment later already ripping the condom wrapper off. When he got close enough, I put my hands on his boxer briefs and pulled them down. His erection, tall and thick, sprang free. "Let me," I said. He handed me the condom and I rolled it on. My stomach was full of butterflies flying frantically in every direction.

"Lie back." He took me by the shoulders and guided me down, stepping free from his underwear and lowering his head between my thighs. I braced myself for the first, shocking sweep of his tongue, but he paused first. "Quiet this time, Calamity. I don't want any interruptions."

I nodded, and while I can't say I was quiet exactly—he was just so *good with his tongue*—I was at least less noisy. As I came down from the high, breathing hard, my body loose and liquid, we both listened.

Silence.

"Thank God," Nate said, positioning himself above me, the tip of his cock teasing my warm, wet center. But as he slid inside, he stifled his own loud groan. "Fuck. I don't know if *I* can be quiet."

I couldn't do anything—not moan, not sigh, not whisper —I couldn't even breathe as he buried himself slowly and deeply within me, stretching my body to fit his.

"Are you okay?" he whispered.

My fingernails dug into his shoulders.

"I'll go slow." He began to move in deep, gentle, undulating rolls that made his entire body seem to ripple over mine, like swells in the middle of the ocean.

Gradually, the discomfort subsided and I slid my palms down his back, opened my thighs even wider, answered the rhythm of his hips with my own.

I buried my face in his neck and inhaled, the masculine scent of him driving me higher. I swirled my tongue at the base of his throat, needing to taste his skin. He moaned again, the sound rumbling in his chest. "Nate," I whispered, wanting to feel his name in my mouth.

"Oh, God." He propped himself up on his hands above my shoulders and our eyes locked. "You need to come again for me now." His hips moved faster, the base of his cock rubbing my clit in quick, short strokes, the friction creating a fresh hum in my lower body.

But I'd never come twice during sex before—ever. "I don't know if I can," I fretted, worried I was letting him down. "I've never—"

"You've never been with me before. Come on. Let go. Let me take you there." His voice, deep and determined, quiet but intense, compelled my body to obey, as if it didn't give a fuck what my mind had to say about it, *this was happening.*

"That's it," he whispered as my eyes fluttered closed and the muscles in my body went stiff, as if every function and feeling other than pleasure was put on hold, even breathing. "Yes. Come for me. Let me feel it..." He fucked me harder and faster, chasing his own release as he moved through mine.

And then I was lost to it, to a world that was only the two of us. To the sound of his breath and the smell of his skin and the throb of his body inside me. To the fiery stars behind my eyes, to the heat coming off of our bodies. To the notion that finally, finally, I was the one in his arms. I was the one he wanted. I was the one he adored.

I was still floating in a sea of bliss when I felt his lips on my forehead. My eyes opened. "Did we wake her?"

"I don't know. My heart is pounding too loud to hear anything but you."

"Mine too." I moved my hands into the valley of his

lower back, pressing my palms to his skin. Suddenly I was sad I hadn't really gotten to see him naked. *Next time.*

Wait, would there be a next time? What was this? It had happened so fast, I hadn't really had a chance to think. Hadn't I been about to leave? I was pretty sure I had been, and then I'd heard those two little words that had plunged straight into my heart.

Come here.

And he hadn't said it playfully or facetiously. It wasn't a game. He'd just told me we'd been right to stop last night, and that I should go...

But he'd wanted me to stay.

Hearing him say that meant everything. It was the missing piece from last night. This was no momentary lapse in sanity. This was no oops. It didn't just *happen*. We'd talked about it. We'd tried to resist it. We'd failed.

But it didn't feel like a mistake, or an end to our friendship. It felt like a beginning. Of what, I wasn't sure. I only knew that I didn't want to walk away.

"Nate?"

"Hmm?" His lips were still resting on my head.

"Are we still friends?"

"I hope so."

"Me too."

"Then it's settled." He lifted himself from me. "I'll be right back, okay?"

"Okay."

While he was in the bathroom, I found my underwear and bra on the floor and put them on. I was pulling up my leggings when he came out, and I wished I could tell him not to get dressed so I could get my fill of his naked body, but I bit my tongue. It was magnificent, though. Even in the dark, I could see the sculpted curves of his arms, the lines on his stomach, the muscle tone in his legs. He threw on his underwear and jeans while I tugged my sweater over my head. Then he sat on the couch again. "I can't believe she's not up. It's a miracle."

"You should have been sleeping." I smoothed my hair and looked around for my shoes.

"Fuck sleeping. Hey. Come here for a second." He reached out and took my hand, pulling me onto his lap. "Are we okay?"

"Yes," I said, and I meant it. "I mean, I don't really know what we're doing, but I'm okay with that."

He nodded. "What made you come over tonight?"

"Truth? I just wanted to be with you. I'd been thinking of you all day."

"Same." He wrapped his arms around me. "When you called and said you were cooking spaghetti and meatballs, I was dying to ask you to come over with some."

"Why didn't you?"

He exhaled. "Because I'd promised myself I wouldn't call you today. I wanted to prove that I could get through one fucking day without your help. And...and I wasn't—I'm not—comfortable feeling like I need someone."

"That's silly. Everyone needs someone sometimes."

"Not me. Not until now."

My toes tingled, I was so happy. "It's okay. I'll keep it a secret."

He laughed a little. "Thanks. Anyway, when you showed up with food and that smile and two helping hands and adult conversation...I'd never been so glad to see anyone, ever. And I'm not sorry about what we did."

"Good. Me either."

"But I'm worried."

"About what?"

"About disappointing you. I can't...be what *you* need. I'm already overwhelmed trying to be what Paisley needs."

"But you know what's crazy? Somehow, that is exactly what I need—to see you, in all your alpha male I-don't-show-my-feelings glory, stepping into the role of father and showing you care. You're reaffirming my faith in the male species, Nate." I patted him on the back, and he laughed. "And you're good to me," I went on. "I feel good when I'm with you. I don't care what we call this. You don't have to be my boyfriend. And I don't need any promises, other than that you'll keep talking to me like this. Openly and honestly."

"I'll try." Exhaling, he rested his forehead on mine. "I don't want to fuck up, but I'm not good at this. Be patient with me?"

"Of course." I started to get up, and Nate held me in place.

Then he took my head in his hands and planted a kiss on my lips. Then another. "Thank you."

"You're welcome." I got to my feet. "Now get some sleep. Maybe I'll see you tomorrow."

He stood too. "Oh, God. That reminds me. I hate to even ask, but is there any way you could watch her for a couple hours in the morning? I have to be at the office to hand off some files, and I'm trying to avoid having to bring her."

"Sure, no problem. Will you be back by noon? I have to be at Coco's around twelve-thirty."

"Definitely."

"What time in the morning?" I asked, stifling a yawn as I pulled on my Uggs.

He cringed. "I hate to say it, because it's so late now, but eight?"

"I'll be here."

He walked me to the door, opened it up, and kissed me one last time. "You're the best."

I shrugged. "It's the least I can do after you saved me from burning down the building."

"Jesus, I'd forgotten about that." He laughed, shaking his head. "Only you. Goodnight, Calamity."

I smiled. "Night."

LATER, as I lay beneath the covers, I kept trying to poke and prod at my psyche, wondering if I was really okay with the sort of friends-with-benefits arrangement Nate and I had alluded to, or if I was lying to myself only so I could be with him. But no matter how many emotional rocks I turned over, I surprised myself by feeling okay. After all, the sex hadn't been meaningless. It hadn't felt cheap or gratuitous or impersonal. We hadn't used each other like anatomically correct robots performing a mechanical act.

In short, I hadn't felt like Slot B receiving Part A.

Had he thrown himself at my feet to declare his undying love? No. But that was okay. When it was over, I'd felt closer to him than I had before, and that was enough. And I liked that he'd been up front about his insecurities and his fear of disappointing me. Actual feelings! That felt like a huge step in a different direction. A new direction.

I'd move in a new direction, too. I certainly didn't need to repeat my usual song and dance routine, the one where I hurled myself body, heart, and soul into a new relationship and expected the guy to do the same. It had backfired every time.

This time, I vowed, would be different.

I would be understanding. I would be patient. I would slow down and enjoy the ride, wherever it took us.

But I really, really hoped it took us somewhere together.

MONDAY MORNING, my alarm went off at 6:45 AM, and I smiled upon awakening, even though I'd only gotten about five hours of sleep. It was the happiest I'd felt in a long time.

While I was in the shower, I thought about texting Nate to see if he wanted me to bring him some breakfast. Our building had a little coffee shop downstairs that I usually hit on my way to work, and it carried doughnuts and muffins and other things, too. I hurried through my routine, and dried off, then wrapped my head in a towel and sat on my bed.

Me: Can I bring you anything from the shop downstairs?

Nate: Yes. I'd like a case of Red Bull, 6 lines of cocaine, and a Pixie Stick.

Me: Will you settle for a doughnut?

Nate: I guess, if you don't have any cocaine.

Me: I'm fresh out. But I will bring you some coffee.

Nate: Thanks.

Smiling, I set my phone aside and got dressed, throwing on jeans and a long-sleeved gray shirt that drooped off one shoulder. Beneath it I wore a black lace bralette that would peek out. Sexy but not too sexy. Comfy but not sloppy. I wore my hair down because Nate seemed to like it that way, brushed my teeth, and put on only a little makeup.

Down in the lobby shop, I grabbed the coffee and

doughnuts, and on a whim also purchased a magazine whose cover advertised an article titled "Five Tips for Breaking Your Bad Relationship Patterns." It might have been total nonsense, but I figured I had nothing to lose and everything to gain by doing things differently this time around.

A few minutes later, I knocked on his door, a drinks carrier in one hand and a paper bag containing doughnuts and the magazine in the other. He opened it, and my breath caught. I don't know why. I'd seen him in a suit and tie a thousand times. But it was different today. For once, I didn't feel the least bit angry that he looked so damn good—I felt excited.

"Hi. You look nice."

"Thanks." He shut the door behind me and reached for one of the coffee cups. "Oh my God, I need this."

"It's all yours." I set the bag and carrier on the table, sort of disappointed he hadn't kissed me hello. "How was the night?"

He took a few gulps of coffee before answering. "Fair. She woke up after you left and then again at the asscrack of dawn, but I think there was a four-hour stretch of sleep somewhere during the night. That was kind of amazing."

"Ever think you'd be so happy to get a four-hour stretch of sleep?"

"Never. She's napping right now, upstairs in my room. The monitor is on." He picked up a leather messenger bag by the door and slung it over his shoulder. "I should head out. Call me if you need to. I'll be back by 11:30."

"Wait, don't you want your doughnut?"

He opened the door and glanced at his watch. "I don't really have time. Save it for me?"

"Okay." I went to give him a hug, but it was kind of

awkward because he didn't hug me back. Granted, his hands were full—one held the coffee and the other was holding the door open—but he didn't even lean into me or move at all. He just stood there. I gave his waist a quick squeeze and stepped back, but it was like hugging a tree trunk. "Bye."

"Bye." Halfway into the hallway, he looked back at me. "Oh, thanks for doing this. I owe you."

"It's no problem. See you later."

The door closed, and he was gone.

I stood there for a moment in the silence, wondering why he seemed so cool and distant this morning—nothing like the guy who'd kissed me goodnight at the door last night, let alone the guy who'd ripped off my clothes and given me two orgasms on the couch, or even the guy who spoke softly and seriously about being worried he'd let me down because he wasn't good at this. I'd felt special to him last night. This morning, I felt like a babysitter with a weird, inappropriate crush.

Sighing, I opened the bag of doughnuts and took out an apple fritter. I ate it standing at the big window overlooking the city, and decided I was being silly. He was probably just tired and distracted. Of course he was—he was going on four hours of sleep. He'd probably be different when he got home and could relax.

When Paisley woke up, I decided to take her for a walk after her bottle. I packed a little bag with some emergency supplies, bundled her up in the coat and leggings she'd arrived in, and strapped her into the stroller. Double checking to make sure I had Nate's key with me, I locked the door when we left and texted Nate on the elevator ride down to the lobby.

Taking Paisley for a walk. Don't worry, I have a key!

He didn't text back.

Outside, I pushed the stroller four blocks up one side of the street, crossed over, and came back down the other. I didn't see anyone I knew, but occasionally a stranger would peek into the stroller and smile. *She's adorable,* they'd say. *She has your chin,* one woman told me. *Daddy must have dark hair,* said another, looking back and forth from me to Paisley. Rather than tell them she wasn't mine, I smiled and said, *Thank you* and *Does she really?* and *Yes, he does.* I told myself it was easier to simply accept the compliments than explain whose baby she was, but secretly some part of me *liked* that people thought she was mine and Nate's. It was stupid, of course. They didn't know who Nate was. But in my mind, I allowed the fantasy to entertain me for a little while, unhealthy as it may have been.

Sometimes, a girl's gotta have some dessert.

After the walk, I fed her again and put her down for her nap. Ten minutes later, I was sitting on the couch reading the Five Tips article when Nate came in.

"Hi," I said, setting the magazine aside. "How did it go?"

"Fine." He set his bag down, took off his suit coat, and tossed it onto a chair.

I waited for him to go on. When he didn't, I asked, "Did you tell your boss?"

"Yeah."

"Was she surprised?"

He rubbed his face with two hands. "To say the least. But she was very understanding. Apparently there's some sort of provision for paternity leave at our firm, which I had no clue about, of course. But it allows me time off and keeps my job safe."

"That's good." I leaned forward, resting my elbows on my knees. "Will you take off the whole month?"

"I haven't decided yet."

"I think it's a good idea. You need time to bond with her."

"I guess." He took his phone out of his pocket and started checking his messages.

Something was off. I could feel it.

"Is everything okay?"

"Fine." He frowned at his screen.

"You seem kind of upset."

"I'm not."

"Okaaaay." I stood, hugging my magazine to my stomach. "Well, maybe I'll see you later?"

He yawned. "Maybe. Guess I'll change out of this suit before she wakes up."

I waited for a moment, hoping he'd at least give me a hug or kiss on the cheek—*something* to acknowledge the change in our status. It had changed, hadn't it? Or had last night been only a dream?

But he didn't touch me. In fact, he didn't even look at me.

"Thanks again for watching her," he said, heading for the stairs. "I appreciate it."

"It's okay." The apple fritter balled up in my stomach. "I'll...talk to you later."

He said nothing and disappeared into his bedroom, and I let myself out.

It happened, I thought, my stomach churning. *I'm one of those girls.*

TEN

NATE

Upstairs, I glanced at Paisley, who was still asleep, then fell back onto my bed, loosened my tie, and closed my eyes.

I'd never been so fucking tired.

Not as a kid, when I'd lain awake in bed, worrying all night about my brother, praying for a cure, a reprieve, a miracle. Not in college, when I'd pledged a fraternity and the active members kept us up twenty-four hours a day mopping floors, collecting beer cans, and doing their fucking laundry. Not in law school, when I'd study all night for days on end before an exam, then crash for twelve hours afterward.

But it wasn't only physical exhaustion. I was worn the fuck out mentally and emotionally too. Word of my situation had buzzed through the office fast. Everyone had been shocked, both that I had a daughter and that I was taking responsibility for her. That kind of pissed me off—did they think I would be so callous as to turn away my own child? A ton of people had burst out laughing. *You? With a daughter?* A few people offered congratulations and advice, but more common were things like, *Oh man. Wouldn't want to be you.* Or, *You know your life is over, right?* A few (male) colleagues expressed sympathy, saying shit like, "Dude, bitch had no right to do that to you," which only made me angrier. An older attorney at the firm told me, "Welcome to fatherhood, eighteen years of sleep deprivation, feeling like a failure, taking the blame, and going broke. Least you don't have to worry about all the damage your divorce will do."

My God, by the time I left there, I was totally demoralized. My nerve endings were beyond frayed. I felt like my life was coming apart at the seams, and there was nothing I could do to keep it together, or even keep it recognizable.

Paisley was one thing—how did fathers handle the constant pressure and doubt? Every second of the day, I was responsible for her. If anything happened, it was on me. As the days went by, I felt more confident with the routine, but Christ. When I thought ahead to eighteen years of this, I wanted to crawl in a hole and die. For fuck's sake, I'd be over FIFTY when she graduated from high school. FIFTY, worried about my teenage daughter out drinking or getting into someone's car who had. FIFTY, waiting for her to get home after she'd broken her curfew. FIFTY, panicking about her hanging out with guys like me who'd only been interested in one thing at sixteen. Was it too early to think about sending her to a convent as soon as she hit puberty?

Fucking puberty. That was another thing. How was I supposed to handle that? What if Rachel was a total flake and never came back for her? For fuck's sake, she hadn't even *called* since Saturday morning! What kind of mother could she be? The more I thought about it, the angrier I got that she'd simply abandoned my child in some random hallway. She could have knocked. She could have asked me for help. She could have done any number of things that wouldn't have put Paisley in danger. Even if she did come back, how would I know that my daughter would be safe with her?

Then there were the practical matters. If I was going to support a child, I had to work. That meant I needed a regular babysitter, in addition to finding a new place to live.

There were also legal matters. I'd filled out the Affidavit of Parentage the state of Michigan required in order to claim paternity, but I needed Rachel's information and signature. Then we'd have to work out a custody agreement.

There would be financial matters to deal with, too—child support. Health insurance. College fund. My will and trust. And I still had to face bringing Paisley home to meet my mother next weekend.

And Emme. I'd meant everything I'd said to her last night, but I was so damn terrified. Throughout the night, whether it was Paisley keeping me up or my anxiety, I just kept thinking of all the ways I could blow it with Emme.

Like today, I could tell she'd been looking for some display of affection from me, some sign that she was more to me than just the nanny—and she *was*, my God, she was—but I hadn't been able to give it to her. Even after what we'd done last night, something in me wouldn't allow it. I'd stood there like a fucking telephone pole when she'd tried to hug me. Why was I such a dick? Was I afraid of giving her too much hope? Was I trying to lower her expectations even further? Was I too entrenched in my emotional foxhole, the one I'd dug so many years ago and refused to climb out of?

Because the crazy thing was, I'd *wanted* to kiss her. Hold her for a moment. Feel like myself again, the way I'd felt during sex last night. I'd wanted to pull her in close, smell her hair and her skin, so I'd have the memory of it throughout the day. I'd wanted to tell her what was wrong when she asked, wanted to admit how upset I'd been by the reactions of people at work. I'd wanted to say *Yes, come back later, have dinner with me again, lie with me again, and this time, don't leave. Let me hold you in my arms as we fall asleep. Let me breathe you in all night. And whatever you do, don't let me push you away, because I'm going to try.*

What the actual fuck was *wrong* with me?

I couldn't even think. I fell asleep right there on my back, fully clothed, shoes on, feet on the floor arms outstretched, and dreamt I was being buried alive.

ELEVEN

EMME

Back in my apartment, I changed out of my jeans and shirt and put on black pants, a blush-colored blouse that tied around the neck, and low heels. We were actually just going to have lunch at her house, but I still wanted to appear professional. I'd learned a lot from both Mia and Coco, including that personal appearances matter, especially in our business.

Not that Nate had noticed much about my appearance this morning.

Annoyed, I frowned at my reflection as I wound my hair into a bun. Was I being unreasonable? Needy? Impatient? Had I been wrong about myself last night?

Maybe. But I didn't think so. And I couldn't shake the sense of resentment brewing as I drove over to Coco's. My expectations were pretty low, but they weren't nonexistent. I didn't need to be the center of his universe, but I'd at least like to feel like a part of the sky.

Coco and her husband, Nick, lived in a big, beautiful old home in Indian Village, one of Detroit's historic neighborhoods. They claimed it had been a giant mess when they bought it, and that something was always going wrong with it, but to my eye it looked perfect. Big flowerbeds waiting to be planted out front, huge rooms with high ceilings and crown moldings, gorgeous original wood floors that creaked when you walked on them, reminding you this house had a history. They had bumped out the back of the house in order to put on an addition with a big modern kitchen and family room, and since the house had been built on a double lot they'd still had enough room to put in a pool and patio with a built-in grill. Nick was a chef and owned several restaurants in the city, as well as the apartment building Nate and I lived in, which was how I managed to afford such a beautiful loft. They gave me a great deal on the rent.

I knocked on the big wooden front door about 12:15, and Nick answered it. Like Nate, Nick was tall, dark, and handsome, although in an entirely different way. Nick was clean-shaven, with olive skin and deep brown eyes, and his arms were sleeved with tattoos. I'd attended several pool parties here at their house and knew that he had them on his back and chest too. Once I asked him if he had a favorite, and he pointed to the one on his left pec, which was a heart with an arrow through it and said Coco at the top. "It was my first one," he'd told me, "and will always be my favorite." Coco had rolled her eyes, but she'd kissed his cheek, and I could tell she was happy about it. I was sort of in love with them as a couple. Not in a creepy way—but for me, they were the gold standard of a relationship, and Nick was the ultimate husband. All man, but not afraid to let his feelings show.

"Hey, Emme. Come on in." He stepped back so I could enter, and immediately two small, dark-haired boys rushed into the front hall, circling his feet and mine like excited puppies. "Knock it off, you two," he scolded. "Mommy already told you to go play upstairs."

The two boys dutifully headed up the stairs, the littler one grabbing the back of the bigger one's shirt so he could scoot past him and beat him to the top. I smiled and slipped off my coat. "No school today?"

Nick took my coat and hung it up in the front hall closet. "Gianni's still at school. Those two monkeys had preschool this morning. I picked them up at eleven and fed them quickly so they'd stay out of your way. Come on back, girls are in the kitchen." He lowered his voice. "I'll warn you —Coco's a little grumpy."

I nodded, figuring at nine months pregnant, that was her right. "Got it."

I followed him down the hall into the kitchen, a beautiful open space with white cupboards, marble countertops, tons of copper cookware hanging over the island cooktop, and a big farmhouse sink. It smelled absolutely divine, like lemon and garlic and sautéed chicken. My mouth began to water.

Coco was sitting at the kitchen table, her bare feet propped on an adjacent chair. Her long dark hair was heaped in a nest at the top of her head, and she wore what looked like one of Nick's black Burger bar T-shirts, her pregnant stomach bulging at the front, distorting the logo, and a pair of gray sweatpants. That's how I knew for sure she must be really uncomfortable, because she *never* wore sweatpants. Ever.

Mia jumped out of the chair across from Coco's. "Hi!" she squealed, running at me with her arms open. She was on the short side, like me, but dark-haired, and dressed much more casually in jeans and a V-neck T-shirt that said Abelard Vineyards on the front.

"Hi," I said, hugging her hard. "It's so good to see you. You look great."

"So do you. Come sit." She tugged on my hand, leading me over to the table.

I took the chair next to Mia's and set my bag on the floor. "How are you feeling?" I asked Coco.

She scowled. "Like I swallowed a mean alien shaped like a beach ball with arms and legs he's determined to beat me with from the inside out."

"He?" I looked from her to Mia and back to her again. As far as I knew, Coco and Nick hadn't wanted to learn the sex before birth. "You know for sure it's another boy?"

"No," said Nick firmly from behind us. "We don't."

"Why wouldn't it be a boy?" Coco asked, throwing her hands up. "I had three boys in a row. I think that's the only kind of baby we know how to make." She narrowed her eyes. "Either that or my grandmother put some sort of hex on me."

Mia laughed. "Well, you never know. Maybe this one will surprise you."

"Lunch in five minutes, ladies." Nick went over to the fridge and opened it. "Emme, can I get you something to drink? We have water, sparkling water, iced tea, Diet Coke, white wine, red wine, sparkling —"

"Oooh, try the sparkling." Mia lifted her wine glass to her lips. "I brought it."

"Wiiiiiiine," Coco moaned. "God, I miss wine. How long until I can have some again?"

"Babe, you could be sipping champagne tonight if you'd just pop that baby out," Nick answered cheerfully.

Coco put two hands on her belly. "Are you listening? Time to come out. Mama needs a glass of wine."

"I'll try the sparkling, thanks," I said to Nick. "Are you having any contractions?" I asked Coco.

She nodded. "A ton. In fact, I'm thinking this baby is coming sooner rather than later. Are you okay to handle everything at work this week?"

"Absolutely," I said, taking the glass of wine Nick handed me.

"Good. Amy can help you out, and Mia said she'd be willing to work too, if you need her."

"Definitely. I'm here until Thursday," Mia said.

Amy was Coco's assistant, and she had taken on a lot of extra work since Lucy quit. In fact, she'd done so well that we hadn't even replaced the Traitor. "I'll probably be fine with Amy, but it would be fun to work together," I said to Mia.

She smiled. "I think so too. In fact, speaking of working together, I wanted to ask you about something." Both of us sat back as Nick came over with two plates and set them in front of us.

"Here you go, ladies. Chicken Piccata, some veggies, a little gnocchi..."

"Looks delicious," I said, inhaling the aroma. "Thank you."

"You're welcome." He winked at me before going back to make a plate for his wife, and I thought again how lucky Coco was.

"So what's up?" I asked Mia, picking up my fork.

"What would you say to moving up north this summer and helping me start a new branch of Devine Events? We do so many special events at Abelard—tons of weddings— and I often get calls to design events for other spaces. I could really use someone to help."

"What about Skylar?" I asked, naming Mia's assistant.

"She had twins last fall and is taking a year off. I've been trying to get along without her, but I really can't. Not during summertime."

"What about Devine Events here?" I looked at Coco.

"I told Mia that I would need you for at least the next two months to get me through the newborn days and to help train Amy. She's good, but she's no Emme Devine." She smiled at me as Nick set a plate in front of her.

"Thanks." My heart fluttered happily at the compliment. I was confident at my job, but it was always nice to hear praise from someone you admired.

"And that's totally fine," Mia said. "I can deal with things for two months. June is when it really picks up, anyway. And it's beautiful up there in the summer. You'll love it."

"You should go," Coco encouraged. "Something different. Get out of the rut."

I stuck a bite of chicken piccata in my mouth and wondered if she was referring to a professional rut or a personal rut. Seemed like a bad sign that I wasn't sure.

"And if you don't want to stay after summer is over, you can come back down to Detroit." Mia picked up her wine glass. "Skylar will be ready to come back by then, and she could help me hire someone new. But if you like it and want to stay, great."

I thought about it as I took another bite. I had loved it up there when I went to visit Mia last summer. Old Mission Peninsula, where Abelard was located, was beautiful—rolling hills, gorgeous fields and orchards, picturesque views of the water. And Traverse City, right at the foot of the peninsula, had a nice small-town feel without being too small, great beaches, and plenty of shopping. Both places would offer lots of unique settings for events, and I was sure

I'd enjoy the work. But it would mean leaving life here behind...leaving Nate behind, and last night it had felt like we were right on the cusp of something good. Moving five hours away in two months would probably put an end to whatever it was. Seemed like it was going to be tough enough living right across the hall.

"Can I have some time to think about it?" I asked.

"Of course." Mia gestured broadly with her hand. "Take a couple weeks. A month, even."

"Thanks."

Suddenly, from above our heads came the sound of loud thumping.

Coco sighed. "Nick, the boys are jumping on the bed again. Can you please get them off?"

"I'm on it," he said. "Enjoy lunch, ladies. There's plenty more if you'd like." He left us alone, and we finished our plates, then went for seconds. We talked about Devine Events, the winery, the possibilities for different kinds of events there and other locations up north, and by the time we were done eating, I was actually really torn about making the move. It would be something different, and maybe a change of scenery was what I needed. I simply wanted to give this thing with Nate some time, a few weeks maybe, to see if it went anywhere. If it didn't, I'd tell Mia I was taking the job.

After lunch, Mia and I were too full for dessert, but Coco asked us to bring her a spoon and the carton of Blue Moon from the freezer. I got them for her while Mia refilled our wine glasses.

"I can't fucking get enough of this stuff. It's obscene." Coco stuck her spoon in the carton and scooped out a big blob of ice cream. "So Emme, with the MGM event Thursday—" She stopped talking, a quizzical look on her face and dropped her spoon into the carton. "Either I just wet my pants, or my water broke. Either thing is totally possible."

Mia and I stared at her. "Are you serious?" I asked.

Coco nodded, putting the spoon in the carton. "Can one of you get Nick?"

"I will." I jumped up and ran to the stairs. "Nick?" I called from the landing. "Coco needs you."

He came flying down three steps at a time a second later. "What is it?" His expression was concerned.

"She thinks her water broke," I said breathlessly, following him into the kitchen.

Nick went right to her side and took her by the arm. "What can I do, baby?"

"Help me up."

Nick took one arm and Mia the other as she struggled to her feet. The back of her pants were wet, and she groaned as she walked slowly to the bathroom.

"Don't ever get pregnant, Emme," Coco said over her shoulder as Nick led her to the bathroom off the hall. "See what happens? You can't even tell when you pee your pants anymore. And your husband knows all about it. Romance is dead!" she yelled as she disappeared inside the bathroom and shut the door.

Mia rolled her eyes, and Nick looked at me. "Ignore her. She always gets this way. Having a baby is wonderful. You should have ten of them."

"Wonderful for you, maybe!" Coco yelled through the closed door. "For me it's going to be twelve hours of labor and getting this beach ball alien out!"

Nick's face lit up with a grin. "Does that mean it *was* your water breaking?"

"Yes." The toilet flushed, the sink ran, and she came

out. "Help me upstairs," she said to him. "I have to change and grab my bag. Sorry girls. I have to cut the lunch date short."

"How dare you go into labor before I finish my wine," Mia joked.

"Don't worry about us," I told her.

"Oh, no. My parents are still in Mexico," Coco said to Nick. "I *told* them not to take that trip so close to my due date! There's no one to watch the kids!"

"Hello. I'm here," Mia said, putting a hand on her chest. "I can handle them."

"I can stay and help, too," I offered.

She gave us both a grateful look. "You guys are amazing. Can someone grab Gianni from school at three-thirty?"

"Done," I said.

"And feed them something for dinner?" she went on as Nick led her toward the stairs.

"Do not worry about a thing, babe," Mia said. "Just get that baby out so you can have some wine with us this week!"

By the time Nick and Coco came back downstairs, the boys at their heels, Mia and I had put the lunch dishes in the dishwasher, stuck the ice cream back in the freezer, and put the leftovers in the fridge.

"Stay here," Nick told his wife, leading her to the side door. "I'm going to back the car out." Even though this was their fourth child, I could see he was worried about his wife, who was wincing as she walked, her eyes shut. He bolted out and ran to the garage. A moment later, his SUV eased into view, and Mia held the door open with one arm, giving Coco a quick hug with the other. "Love you," she said. "Good luck."

Nick jumped out to help his wife around to the passenger side, and after closing her door, he hustled around to the driver's side again. "I'll keep you posted," he said, waving to us and the boys, who were jumping up and down on either side of me, yelling, "Bye, Mommy! Bye, Daddy! Bring us home a baby! But not a girl!"

Mia and I laughed. "It doesn't work that way, sorry to break it to you," she told them. "How about I put a movie on for you guys? And get you a snack?"

They were up for that, and as soon as we got them set up in the family room off the kitchen, Mia pulled the wine bottle from the fridge and poured the last of it into our glasses. "Can you stay a little while?" she asked. "I still want to catch up."

"Sure." I sank back into my chair. "How are Lucas and the kids?"

She lit up, as she always did when talking about her family, and pulled out her phone to show me photos of the beautiful French-style country home they'd built on the peninsula right next to their vineyards, of the tasting room and gardens where they held events, and a wedding they'd held there over last Christmas. She scrolled through a few more. "Oh, this was last summer." It was a family photo in which she held their youngest, a boy named Gabe, in her arms, and Lucas held the hands of their two older children, Henri and Ellie. Behind them, the hilltop rows of grapevines disappeared into the sunset.

"God, this looks like a postcard." I shook my head. "You have the perfect family. The perfect life."

She smiled. "Thanks. Sometimes it feels that way, sometimes it doesn't. But I'm very lucky. Now tell me about you. How are your parents? Your sisters?"

I filled her in on everyone, even Stella's relationship with Buzz, which made her laugh. "Well, different relationships work for different reasons," she said. "*I* couldn't live without sex, but maybe that's just me."

"I don't think I could either," I confessed, thinking about last night. My stomach muscles tightened up.

"Are you seeing anyone now?" she asked. "Last time we talked, you were getting over that Richard guy."

"Ugh." I made a face. "He's long gone. As for now..." I wasn't sure how to answer her question. "Maybe."

She tilted her head. "Maybe?"

"It's sort of complicated."

"Talk to me," she said, tipping up her wine glass.

Taking a deep breath, I told her about Nate, the baby, and what had happened between us over the weekend. "So it's *really* new," I said. "But I really like him. And I think he likes me." At least, I'd thought so last night.

"Got it. Is he the reason you're hesitant to move away for the summer?"

"Yes," I admitted, spinning my empty glass by the stem. "But he probably shouldn't be. It's not like we're anything serious."

She poked my shoulder. "Give it a chance, Em. It's been one night."

"I know, but...I've known him a while. And he's been very up front with me that he's not a relationship kind of guy and doesn't really believe in happily ever after and all that."

Mia nodded knowingly. "I once knew a guy like that. Want to know where he is now? At home with our three kids."

"Nate's not like Lucas at all, though. Or like Nick. Those guys are not afraid of showing their feelings."

"They weren't those guys when we met them." Mia rubbed

my arm. "I don't know Nate, so I can't say for sure, but I do know what it's like to feel the way you do and worry he'll never feel the same. Hang in there, give him some time to realize what he has. Concentrate on other things. Let him miss you."

"Is that what you did?"

She thought for a moment. "Lucas and I lived an ocean apart for *months* after we first met, so missing each other came with the territory. But I'll tell you what I did have to learn to do—stop obsessing over what the future would bring and learn to enjoy the present."

I sighed. "You sound like Maren. She's always telling me I should learn to be more mindful. She thinks it would help me achieve more inner peace and harmony." I wiggled my fingers and made a heart pattern in the air between us.

Mia laughed. "God, I love Maren. Who knows, maybe she's right! Certainly more inner peace and harmony never hurt anybody."

I thanked her for the advice and the job offer, and we moved on to other topics. At three-thirty, I stayed with the little ones while she ran to pick up Gianni from school and a little later, I helped her get dinner together for the three of them. Nick had texted that there was no baby yet, but Coco was definitely in labor and he'd let us know as soon as he had news.

I got home around six and contemplated meditation or some yoga in the interest of being more mindful, but decided to put on my pajamas, do some laundry, and catch up on This Is Us instead (going through half a box of tissues because I cannot watch that show without crying). For dinner, I warmed up leftover spaghetti and wondered if Nate was doing the same. I was almost tempted to text him and see if he wanted help or company, but decided not to. He'd really been kind of an ass this morning.

And I'd gone to him last night. It was his turn. Even *he* should be able to figure that out.

While I was getting ready for bed, Nick texted that Coco had delivered a baby girl they'd named Francis, after Nick's great-grandmother, and would call Frannie. Baby was fine, Coco was fine, and everyone was enjoying some champagne. It made me smile—they had every reason to celebrate. A once-in-a-lifetime love, four beautiful children, nothing but happily ever after ahead of them.

How did some people get so *lucky*? I wondered as I lay awake in the dark. In this massive world full of billions of people, how did some manage to find that *one* person they were meant to be with? How did they get all the pieces to fall so perfectly into place? Was it a matter of geography? Because Coco and Nick had gone to the same college. He saw her walk by on campus one day and knew she was the one. So there was *timing* involved, too. What if she'd been late for class that day? What if he'd been looking in the other direction?

I thought about Mia and Lucas. They had met in Paris when Mia happened to go into a bar where he was working one night. What if she had chosen a different bar? What if he hadn't been working that night? What if it hadn't been raining and she hadn't gone into a bar at all? What if she'd kept walking? If any one of the circumstances had been altered the slightest bit, one of the pieces might not have fit, and their paths would never have crossed. Their story would have gone untold.

I considered Stella's decision to be with a man whose company she enjoyed, even though there didn't seem to be a physical spark between them. Was she settling because she'd gotten tired of waiting around, or was she making the best of it? Logically, I could see where having a companion like Walter would be better than spending night after night alone. But it just seemed so unfair.

Why did lightning strike for some people, and not for others? Why did some of us pick the wrong people over and over again, and others got it right the first time? Why were we told as kids to listen to our *hearts* when things like geography or timing or luck seemed to matter so much more?

What did our hearts know, anyway?

TWELVE

NATE

Emme didn't call, text, or stop by again on Monday.

I didn't hear from her all day Tuesday, either.

Or Wednesday.

At first, I felt guilty because I figured it was my fault for acting like nothing was different between us on Monday morning after everything that had happened Sunday night. Her feelings were probably hurt. Or maybe she was confused. I knew I should reach out, apologize, explain myself, but for some reason, I couldn't bring myself to pick up the phone or go across the hall and knock on her door. And maybe I was wrong, anyway. Maybe she was totally fine and simply busy at work. After all, she had told me she would be really busy this week.

But I missed her. Not just her help with Paisley, but her company. Her face. Her laugh. The way she made me feel. We'd spent so much time together over the last several days, it was hard to believe that before Paisley arrived, we might have gone a week or so without even seeing each other in the hall. There were probably entire days that passed where

I didn't think about her once. Now that seemed impossible. I couldn't get her out of my head.

After a while, I started to get angry with her. Was she punishing me? Was she purposely ignoring me in order to make a point? Was she sending some sort of message that said *I don't want anything if I can't have it all?* Was this some passive-aggressive way to let me know I had already succeeded in disappointing her in less than twenty-four hours?

Wasn't *she* the one who had said she wanted to be open and honest? This seemed like a juvenile game to me, and I wouldn't play it. If she was upset about something, she should tell me, not expect me to read her mind, goddammit! This was exactly why I hadn't wanted to get involved with her in the first place. She was too emotional. She didn't understand me. And clearly she'd lied about having no expectations. In the meantime, I was tired, crabby, and lonely, trapped in my apartment with no one but a baby for company and hardly getting any sleep.

By Wednesday night, I couldn't take it anymore. When I heard her voice in the hallway around 10 PM, I raced over to my door and put my ear against it.

"Absolutely, it went great," she was saying. "Don't worry about anything, just get some rest. Are you glad to be home?" A pause. Keys jingling. "Good. And how's Frannie doing? I saw the picture, she's so cute! All that hair!"

Coco must have had the baby, I thought. *Sounds like it was a girl.* I heard her key turn in the lock.

"Well, I can't wait to come see you both. You let me know when you're ready for visitors." Another pause, followed by laughter. "I bet they are. Sounds good. Okay, take care of yourself. Bye."

After that, I heard the door to her apartment open and

close. I straightened up, trying to think of some reason to go over there and see her. A concrete reason, not an emotional one. My eyes scanned the room, but nothing jumped out at me. A moment later, Paisley, who had been napping in the swing, woke up and started to cry. It was while I was in the kitchen making her bottle that it hit me—her plastic containers, the ones she had brought the spaghetti and meatballs in. I'd eaten all the leftovers from them yesterday and washed them out. I could return them. That was a good reason, wasn't it?

After feeding Paisley, I put her in the sling, gathered up the containers, and went across the hall. I knocked on the door, my stomach jittering like I was a teenager picking up his first date. Quickly, I ran a hand through my hair and checked my breath. I was fairly certain I'd showered and brushed my teeth sometime today, but I definitely hadn't done anything extra. Did my clothes match? Were there stains on my shirt? Had I put shoes on? Yes, no, yes. *Fuck.* I was nervous. I heard footsteps inside her apartment, and my chest tightened up. But when she opened the door, I played it cool.

Well, as cool as a guy could wearing a baby on his chest and carrying a bunch of GladWare.

"Hey," I said casually. "I brought your containers back."

"Oh. Thanks." Her expression was blank, at least while she was looking at me. When her eyes dropped to Paisley, she smiled. "Hi there, peanut. You doing okay?"

I couldn't see Paisley's face, but she wasn't crying, and she kicked her feet and wiggled her arms like she was happy to see Emme. I was too, but I didn't let on. "We're fine," I answered, as if she'd asked how both of us were doing. "How are you?"

She straightened up and gave me the blank expression again. "Fine. I just got home from work."

I nodded, taking in her black blouse, pencil skirt and heels. Her curves looked delectable—breasts, hips, calves. "You look nice."

"Thank you. Want me to take those?" She reached for the containers in my hands, but I didn't want to give them to her, because then she could turn around and go inside with them and I would be forced to go home and spend another evening all by myself.

"I'll bring them in," I offered, and without being invited, sort of side-stepped past her into her apartment. "Should I put them in the kitchen?"

She sighed heavily and shut the door. "Okay."

I set them on the counter and noticed she had just opened a bottle of Abelard Pinot Noir. One empty glass stood next to the bottle. "Your cousin's winery, right? They make some great wines. Have you ever tried their Riesling?"

"No." She walked toward me slowly, her arms crossed over her chest. "I'm not much of a Riesling girl."

I nodded. The silence that followed was awkward. The apology I owed her was stuck in the back of my throat, I couldn't think of anything else to say, and she did not appear inclined to rescue me. Could I blame her?

But a moment later she came into the kitchen and took another glass down. "Would you like some?" Her voice held no enthusiasm whatsoever.

It was a fairly lackluster invitation, but I took it. "Okay. Thanks."

She poured wine for both of us and handed one glass to me. Then without saying anything, she leaned back against the counter and took a long drink from hers. I was trying to think of something to say when she spoke up.

"I saw my cousin on Monday, and she offered me a job up north."

"Are you going to take it?"

"I haven't decided yet."

Immediately there was a pit in my stomach. I didn't want her to take a job somewhere else, but I couldn't say that. "You should. That's a great area."

"It is."

I could tell from the look on her face she was hurt. God, I was a fuck-up. I'd come over here because I'd missed her laugh, and all I was doing was making her miserable. I tried again. "Last time we drank wine in your kitchen, there was a barbecued bunny on your counter."

She nodded.

"And more of a smile on your face."

"Sorry. Guess it's been a long day." She crossed her legs at the ankle and held one arm across her stomach. The message was clear.

Damn. She's tough. I set my wine glass down without drinking from it. "Emme, come on."

"What?"

"Stop trying to freeze me out."

Her jaw dropped. "*I'm* trying to freeze *you* out?"

"Yes. It's obvious."

Then she laughed, but it wasn't the kind I'd been waiting for. "That's a good one, Nate, since *you're* the one who acted like a total stranger Monday morning."

"I did not act like a total stranger," I said defensively, although I knew exactly what she meant. "I acted like a *friend*, which is what we are."

She rolled her eyes. "Okay, whatever. If you want to pretend like nothing happened between us, go right ahead. But we had a conversation about it, and—"

"During which you said you'd be patient with me," I interrupted.

"And during which *you* said you'd be open and honest with me."

"I said I'd *try*," I shot back. "I *told* you, I'm bad at this. I don't get it."

She came off the counter and stood up taller. "That's bullshit, Nate. You're not bad at this because you don't get it. You're bad at this because you won't let yourself be good. Because you don't want anybody to need you."

My temper flared. How dare she throw my own words back in my face! This was why you shouldn't reveal your weaknesses to people—they used them against you. I was so mad, I couldn't find the words to defend myself. That *never* happened to me.

Emme, however, had plenty of words. "Well, I don't need you. And I don't need this in my life. So you got what you wanted."

This is not what I wanted! I felt like screaming. But I just stood there, my hands clenched into fists, my face and neck boiling hot, my jaw locked. Paisley began to cry.

Without saying anything else, I turned around and stormed out. Her door had slammed behind me when I realized I'd forgotten to bring a key and was locked out of my apartment. Fuck!

I drummed my head with the heels of my hands while Paisley cried and squirmed in the sling. Now I had to knock on her door and ask for her help, *again*, when I'd just been a dick to her, *again*. What was the matter with me? I braced myself with one arm against my door and took a few deep breaths. With the other hand I rubbed Paisley's tummy through the front of the sling. "I'm sorry, kid. This is not your fault."

It wasn't Emme's fault either. I couldn't lash out at her because I was angry at the direction my life had taken and felt ill-equipped to deal with it. Nor could I blame her for getting so close to me that she saw through my crap. I'd let her get this close. I wanted her even closer. It was just so fucking *hard* to let someone in after all this time.

But I didn't like who I'd been in there. I could do better.

Turning around, I closed my eyes for a second, took one more deep breath, then knocked on her door.

She didn't answer right away, and when she finally did, I could tell she'd been crying. Her eyes were bloodshot, her mascara was smudged, and her nose was red. I felt horrible.

"I'm sorry," I said. "You were right. I was a dick on Monday morning, and I knew it. I've been missing you for two days but I was too stubborn to admit it and apologize. Returning the containers was only an excuse to see you."

She sniffed.

"Can you forgive me? Please?"

It took her a moment, but she nodded slowly, her arms crossing over her chest again. "Fine. Is that all you want? Forgiveness?"

I swallowed hard. I could say yes. I could walk away from this right now. And she could take that job up north and meet some great guy in the wine business who'd treat her right. But when I pictured her in someone else's arms, I felt sick. "No. That's not all I want."

She waited, listening.

"I want another chance with you. I want to try harder. And I don't want you to take that job up north."

"Nate," she said, her voice shaky. "Don't say these things if you don't mean them."

"I mean them." I looked her right in the eye. "Please, Emme. Give me another chance. I can do better."

"You have to let me in," she said, tearing up again. "I can be patient, I can be your friend, I can forgive. But you have to let me in. Talk to me. Trust me."

"I will," I promised, wishing I could hug her right now. Between us, Paisley cried louder. "From now on, I will."

Emme sniffed and smiled. "Poor thing. You should get her to bed."

"I know, but..." I hung my head. "I locked myself out."

"You *what?*"

"I forgot my key."

She burst out laughing, wiping her eyes. "Oh my God. This is a first. Hold on, let me get your key." Then she cocked her head. "Wait a minute. That's not why you apologized, is it? Just so you could get your key?"

I held up both hands. "No. I swear to God, I meant the apology and I would have done it anyway. Forgetting my key just sort of...sped it up."

"Ha. Serves you right."

A minute later, she let us into my apartment and lingered in the doorway. "Need help with her?" she asked.

"No, I've got her," I said, lifting Paisley from the sling. "I'll try to get her back to sleep. But I'd love it if you'd stay."

The smile I'd been waiting for lit up her face. "Let me change out of my work clothes and come back, okay?"

"Of course." I took off the sling and tossed it onto a chair. "But first, come here." Holding Paisley off to one side, I opened my other arm to Emme. She snuggled into my side, laying her head on my shoulder and wrapping her arms around my waist. I kissed the top of her head. "I'm sorry," I said again. "I was an idiot."

"You were," she agreed. "But you're going through a lot of stuff right now, and none of it is easy. I'm here for you."

"Thanks." I closed my eyes, wondering how long she'd last.

PAISLEY FELL ASLEEP RELATIVELY QUICKLY, after only about fifteen minutes of pacing and rocking. I put her in her sleeper and went downstairs, surprised to find Emme sitting on one of the chrome and leather chairs, wearing a pink T-shirt and plaid pajama pants. Her feet were bare, she'd let her hair down, and her makeup was off.

"I let myself in," she said, rising. "Hope that was okay."

"Of course." I turned out all the lights but for one lamp, so I could see her beautiful face, and went to her, taking her head in my hands. "I wish I could take you somewhere. I'm sorry we're always stuck in this apartment having to be quiet. We can't even be in my bed."

"Shh." She ran her hands up my chest and rose up on her toes to press her lips to mine. "I don't care where we are. I just want to be close to you." As her fingers worked their way down the buttons on my shirt, I reached beneath hers, sliding my hands over her soft, warm skin, closing my palms over her breasts, teasing her tight little nipples with my thumbs. My cock grew hard and thick inside my jeans.

She shoved my shirt off my shoulders, and I let it drop to the floor and whisked my T-shirt over my head. Immediately she brought her mouth to my chest, kissing her way down to one nipple, circling and stroking it with her tongue. Her left hand moved to my crotch and rubbed the erection bulging against the denim.

My knees nearly buckled. "Fuck, that feels good." I reached one hand between her legs and caressed her softly through the flannel.

She moaned and brought her hands to the button and zipper of my jeans. After pushing them to my knees, she grabbed me by the hips, turned my back toward the chair she'd been sitting in, and pushed me down. Then she knelt in front of me.

"Oh, God," I said as she lifted her shirt over her head. Her ivory skin glowed, her perfect breasts made my mouth water, and her mischievous expression had my cock twitching.

She piled her long blond waves onto the top of her head as she swayed over my lap. "Hold my hair?" she asked playfully.

I replaced her hands with mine, thinking I needed at least two more pairs to touch every place on her body I wanted to touch right now. But a moment later, I was mesmerized by the sight of her fingers reaching for my cock, wrapping around it, moving up and down the shaft, swirling over the tip. She brought her lips closer to it, and I held my breath, my jaw clenched tight, fighting the instinct to use my hands on her head to push her mouth onto me. All I could think of was how good it was going to feel to slide my cock past those luscious pouty lips into the warm, wet heaven of her mouth.

But she made me wait. She went slow, licking up the sides of my cock from bottom to top, circling her tongue around the tip, rubbing her lips gently over the most sensitive nerve endings in my body. Finally, she took the head in her mouth, sucking softly, her hands still wrapped around my length. My leg muscles tightened. My hips wanted to move. My breath was coming in short, quick bursts.

"Emme," I begged.

She looked up at me, and laughed softly as her tongue swept over my crown. "Want something?"

"Yes."

"Let me hear it. You promised to talk to me, remember?" Her breath was warm on my skin. She gave me one more lick, a long, circular stroke, like you do with a dripping ice cream cone on a hot day. "Tell me what you want."

I might have laughed in surprise if I hadn't been so wound up. She wanted me to talk dirty to her? No problem. "I want your mouth on my cock, and I want it now."

"So demanding," she teased, but she gave me what I wanted, opening her lips and sliding down about a third of the way before coming up and then doing it again.

"All the way," I said gruffly. "I want to feel my cock hit the back of your throat."

She went farther this time, about halfway, and stayed there, using her hands to pump up and down while she sucked. It felt so good I could have come in a heartbeat, but I still wanted to see her take it all.

"Deeper," I commanded, using my hands now to guide her—not too rough, but enough for me to assume some control. "Oh, fuck yeah, like that..." I watched more of my cock disappear into her mouth, felt the tip bottom out. She struggled for a moment, and I listened carefully to her sounds to make sure she could breathe. I didn't want to choke her.

Not yet, anyway.

But I couldn't stay in control for long, not the way she was sucking and stroking me, not the way her hands were working, not the way she kept glancing up at me with those big eyes, like she loved the way I tasted, couldn't get enough of my cock, wanted me to come just like that, hot and hard, right down the back of her throat. I was so fucking close— my hands were fisted tight in her hair, my dick was like steel, all the muscles in my lower body were humming.

Any other time, any other woman, maybe even any other night, I'd have done it.

But I wanted something else tonight.

I lifted her head off me.

"What's wrong?" she asked breathlessly.

"Nothing. I just don't want this to end yet." I stood, pulling her to her feet, and doing away with her pajama pants and underwear. I ditched my jeans too, but not before grabbing a condom from my wallet. "And you're too fucking good. I wasn't going to last."

"Good," she said, laughing as I sat down again and pulled her onto my lap, her thighs straddling mine. She rolled the condom on like she'd done last time while I licked two fingers and reached between her legs, gliding my wet fingertips over her clit. Her mouth fell open. She grasped my shoulders and rocked her hips over my hand. I slipped my fingers easily inside her—she was already wet from blowing me, which was so fucking hot—and she moaned as she sank down lower, hungry for more. I brought her to orgasm just like that, spellbound as I watched her skin flush and her head fall back and her body shiver.

A moment later, I was easing her onto my cock, hoping I had the strength to last long enough to make her come again. But it felt so fucking good to be inside her, to watch her ride me with reckless abandon, to smell sex and summer on her skin.

When I was so close to the breaking point I knew it was a matter of seconds, not minutes, I flexed my hips and held her tight to my body, concentrating on finding that spot deep inside her that would make her lose control. I knew I had found it when I felt her hands tighten around my biceps, saw the stunned expression on her face, heard her sounds change from rapid gasps to a low, breathless murmur... *oh my God oh my God oh my God.*

She went stiff, her eyes closed, and her mouth formed a perfect O. It was all I needed. I gave myself over to pure animalistic greed, gripping her hips and moving my body and hers solely to serve my pleasure before erupting inside her, my cock surging again and again and again.

Afterward, I pulled her in close and held her still for a moment. Her arms came around me, and she cradled my head against her chest. And it was the weirdest fucking thing ever, but as my heart rate came down, my throat tightened up. What the hell was going on with me? For a few terrifying seconds, I thought I was going to embarrass myself and start blubbering like a fucking baby. I couldn't breathe.

My gut instinct was to get away from her. Get up. Get rid of the condom and say goodnight. My usual routine.

But I didn't do it. I stayed right there in her arms until the feeling passed, and my lungs were functioning normally again. My throat was clear.

It was Emme who got up first. "Be right back," she said, hurrying into the downstairs bathroom.

I went upstairs, cleaned up, threw on a pair of athletic pants, checked on Paisley, and came back down. Emme was back in her underwear and T-shirt, pulling on her pants. I sat on the couch. "Come here."

Smiling, she sat down and cuddled close, tossing her legs across my lap and laying her head on my chest.

"Are you tired?" I asked her.

"A little. You?"

"A lot. But I haven't talked to you in days and I want to hear your voice. Tell me about the job offer. And did Coco have the baby?"

While she talked, she rubbed my bare chest with her fingertips. She told me about the conversation with her cousin, about how Coco had gone into labor right there at the table, and about how she was pretty much running the business herself this week.

"No wonder Mia wants you up there," I said, giving her a squeeze. "You're a pro. And even though I'm selfish and I hope you'll say no, I understand that it's a great opportunity and I would support you if you decided to take it."

"Thanks." She looked up at me and smiled. "That means a lot to me. Now it's your turn. Tell me things."

Reminding myself that it was okay to appear less than perfect in her eyes, that she actually *wanted* that, I opened up about Monday's visit to the office and how it had affected me. "It's hard enough dealing with my own negative feelings about suddenly being a father," I admitted. "Hearing other people's made it ten times worse."

She was furious. "Why would people say those things to you? How can people be so horrible?"

"They were being honest, I guess."

"Fuck that. Honesty is not an excuse for rudeness. If you don't have something nice to say..."

I kissed the top of her head. "You're so cute."

We sat in silence for a moment, then she tilted her face toward mine, a smile on her lips. "Did you really think I wouldn't see through that whole 'returning your containers' thing?"

I grinned sheepishly. "Yeah, I guess that was sort of transparent."

"It was *totally* transparent. If I hadn't been so upset with you, I would have laughed."

I brushed the hair back from her face. "You know I'm

probably still going to fuck up from time to time. Say stupid shit. Act like a dick. Try to push you away."

She nodded. "Yes."

"Don't let me." I held her closer, pressed my lips to her forehead. "Don't let me."

THIRTEEN

EMME

Four days later I met my sisters for Sunday brunch at
PARC in Campus Martius downtown.

"Good morning," I chirped as I slid onto the booth along
the wall next to Stella. Across the table, Maren gave me
a smile.

"Morning," she said. "You look nice. Is that a new
blouse?"

"Thanks. It is new, actually." Nate had bought it for me
yesterday during our shopping excursion at Partridge
Creek. His mother had canceled their planned visit last
minute, something about not feeling up to having guests,
and even though he'd pretended not to be upset about it, I
could tell that he was. I suggested the afternoon shopping
trip as a way to get him and Paisley out of the apartment
and into the sunshine. It had been a gorgeous couple of days
—warm and sunny, temperatures in the mid sixties even
though the official start of spring was still a few days away.

"It's really pretty," said Stella. "You don't normally wear
a lot of patterns."

The blouse was floral patterned silk chiffon, a rose print

on a sheer white background. Very springy and romantic. I lifted my shoulders. "Guess I'm branching out a little bit. Changing up my style."

"It's more than the blouse." Maren was studying me with a sister's critical eye. "There's something different about you. You're glowing."

"Am I?" I pretended to study the menu.

Stella leaned around me, trying to get a better look at my face. "Yes. What's going on with you?"

"Let me get something to drink and I'll tell you." I signaled a server and put in an order for a glass of champagne.

"Ooh, that sounds good. I'll join you," said Maren.

"Me too," said Stella.

While we waited for our drinks, I looked at the menu for real. I had never been here before, but everything sounded scrumptious. Or maybe it was just my good mood.

The server returned after a minute with our glasses of bubbly, promising to come back shortly to take our order.

"Okay, spill," Stella said as soon as we were alone again.

"Yes. Why are you glowing?" Maren asked.

"First, a toast. To spring!" I raised my glass. "A time of rebirth and awakening."

They exchanged a look as we clinked. "She's having sex with someone," said Stella.

"Good sex," added Maren.

I leaned forward dramatically. "*Amazing* sex," I clarified. "Four nights of the most amazing sex you can possibly imagine."

Maren groaned with envy. "Nate?"

"Yes." I took a sip of my champagne—it was delicious, possibly the best thing I had ever tasted.

"So tell us what happened," said Stella, shifting impatiently next to me in the booth. "When we saw you last Sunday, you were all *we're just friends* about it."

I laughed. "Well, that was true, but then I went over there later that night."

Maren was on the edge of her seat. "And?"

"And things got unexpectedly and very decidedly more than friendly." I leaned even closer to them and whispered. "I had two."

"Two?" Stella questioned, like she didn't quite believe it.

"Two."

"I've heard that's possible, but no one I know has ever verified it," Maren said.

I took another sip, delighted with the way the bubbles danced on my tongue. "Consider it verified."

"How did you even manage it with the baby and all?" Stella wondered.

"We were on the couch that time, and she was sleeping upstairs. I don't know how we didn't wake her up, but thankfully we didn't."

The server came back over, and we put in our orders—Stella went for shrimp and polenta, Maren ordered the omelette, and I chose the cinnamon roll bread pudding. I didn't even feel guilty about it. I'd worked out four times this week, and besides, I figured Nate and I were burning at least a couple hundred calories a night.

"Okay, keep going," Maren prodded.

"Okay, so after that first time, he got a little weird. I mean, not that night—that night he was fine and when I left, everything felt good between us. He basically admitted he felt something for me, but he's got this thing about needing people. He doesn't want to need anybody, and he doesn't want anybody to need him. I babysat for him the following morning, and I could tell something was wrong. He was kind of aloof and indifferent."

"Did you ask him why?" Stella looked curious.

"No, because I sort of knew why. He was scared."

"So what did you do?" Maren asked.

"Actually, nothing. I wasn't happy about it, but I figured there was no point in pursuing him if he wasn't interested in taking a chance with me, so I let it go. And we went almost three days without even talking or seeing each other."

"*You* let it go?" The look on Maren's face told me how surprised she was, and admittedly, in the past I probably would have gone over there to pick a fight or at least demand to know what I had done wrong.

"I did," I confirmed with a shrug. "I felt like it was his issue, and he needed to work it out on his own."

"Wow." She sat back, her expression thoughtful and a little impressed. "Very Zen of you, Emme. You didn't even call us to vent about it. The blouse really isn't the only thing that's new."

"Thank you." I wasn't going to mention that the biggest reason I didn't call them to vent was because I didn't want them to say I-told-you-so about Nate just using me as Nanny McFuck across the hall. "I'm really trying to do things differently with Nate. I've made so many mistakes in the past by either choosing the wrong guys, or expecting too much too soon, and blaming myself when they let me down. I don't want to do that this time."

"That's great," said Stella. "You sound very healthy."

"I feel it. I mean, I didn't for the few days we weren't speaking, but he showed up at my door Wednesday night with the baby in a sling on his chest and these plastic containers of mine in his hand, pretending he just wanted to return them." I laughed, shaking my head. "It was so obvious what he was doing." I told them about our argument and how I'd stood up for myself. "It was scary, because I knew I risked alienating him completely, but I was looking at him and I could see that he didn't believe the bullshit he was giving me. He was just scared and too stubborn to admit it." I shrugged. "So I called him out on it. I figured I had nothing to lose."

The server appeared with our plates and set them down in front of us. When she was gone, Stella patted my leg beneath the table. "I'm really proud of you. That took guts." She picked up her knife and fork and began cutting a piece of shrimp. "It's not easy to change your relationship habits, but I'm so glad to see you realize you deserve more."

I smiled. "Thanks. I felt proud of myself, too. Although when he turned around and stormed out, I burst into tears. That wasn't too Zen of me. But it only took him a few minutes to realize his mistake and knock on my door again." Picking up my spoon, I giggled. "Of course, it helped that he had locked himself out of his apartment."

Maren laughed. "See? The universe heard you and arranged everything."

"Or he was so distracted by his conflicting feelings, he simply forgot the key," said Stella wryly. "He's only human, after all."

"Not when it comes to sex," I said under my breath before digging my spoon into the bread pudding and licking it clean. "I'm convinced he has some kind of superpower when it comes to orgasms."

Both my sisters sighed loudly. "How are you not waking the baby?" Maren asked.

"Well, we *did* wake her Thursday night," I admitted. I had gone over to his apartment after my event at the MGM, even though it had been almost midnight. Not that we wasted any time—we were naked on his living room floor within ten minutes of my arrival, our clothing flung all over the room. When we were done (didn't take long), Nate had rug burns on his knees, I found my bra hanging off a lamp, and we'd been anything but quiet. It took Nate half an hour to get her back to sleep after that.

Friday night, we'd done it in the kitchen, me still in my work clothes and Nate behind me with his hand clamped over my mouth. I had a bruise on the front of my hip where it kept banging into the edge of the counter, but Nate had been completely unapologetic, claiming it was my fault for coming over in a little black dress and heels without my underwear on. However, when I'd shown him it was still there last night, he'd dropped to his knees and kissed it softly.

"So do you spend the night there?" Stella wondered.

"No," I said. "He always asks if I want to stay, but the baby sleeps in his room. I feel like three might be a little crowded in there, and I had to get up for work pretty early every day last week. Did I tell you Coco had her baby?"

They wanted to hear all about that, and about how Mia was doing as well.

"She's doing great," I said, licking some maple crème anglaise from my finger. "Actually, she offered me a job up there."

My sister stared at me.

"Really?" Stella said. "At the winery?"

I told them what her offer entailed, and that I was tempted by it but had asked for some time to think it over.

"It might be nice for a change, and I do like that area, but..." Swirling the last of my champagne around in the bottom of my glass, I shrugged. "This thing with Nate feels really good. I know it's only the beginning, and in the past my instincts have not been the greatest, but I'm hopeful. I really think he might be what I've been looking for."

They didn't say anything right away, which was a little disconcerting. Finally Stella spoke. "That's great, Emme. As long as you're being careful and keeping perspective on things, why not take time to think over the offer? I think that's smart to keep the option open awhile."

"Me too," echoed Maren.

"Thanks." Then I sighed. "The one thing I wish is that we were able to have, like, an actual date. Go out for dinner or something." I wrinkled my nose, dropping my eyes to the napkin in my lap. "But with the baby, it's hard. And I don't want to whine about it. He finally seems like he's getting used to the idea that he's a father, and that it's for life. Like, this is not a temporary thing that's going to go away once Paisley's mom decides to show up again."

"Has she been in touch?" Stella asked.

I shook my head. "Nope. Not since that one phone call."

"What's he going to do then?" Maren asked. "Will they share custody?"

"I assume so." I nodded, picking up my spoon and poking at my meal again, but I didn't really feel like eating anymore. The truth was, Nate was kind of evasive on the subject of joint custody or a more permanent arrangement for Paisley once the month was up. I'd asked him only yesterday if he was planning to get a bigger apartment or maybe even buy a house with a backyard somewhere, and he'd sort of grunted that he was thinking about it but hadn't really seemed too willing to discuss it.

I hadn't pressed the issue—it wasn't really my business, and I was learning with Nate that it was better to let him decide when it was time to open up about things rather than poking and prodding at him. He didn't respond well to pressure. But he was working on sharing more about himself with me. Yesterday as we'd walked around Partridge Creek, pushing Paisley in the stroller, he'd talked a little bit about his mom and her anxiety, her bouts of agoraphobia and obsessive-compulsive tendencies. It was the most he'd ever talked to me about such a personal subject, and I'd listened attentively, swallowing all the questions I had. I wanted him to feel like he could talk to me without being judged or analyzed or evaluated for relationship potential. It was not about that. It was about him feeling comfortable enough with himself to show me part of what he normally buried. It was about trust.

"You know, I could watch the baby for you," Maren offered. "If you've got a night off next week and you two want to have dinner, as long as I'm not teaching that night, I'd be happy to do it."

"I wouldn't mind either," Stella said. "If Maren has to teach on your night off, let me know. I'll do it. I love babies."

"Really?" Love and gratitude for my sisters flooded through me. "You would do that?"

"Of course," Maren said, and Stella nodded.

"You guys are the best. Let me check my schedule and get back with you," I told them excitedly. "And let me make sure it's okay with Nate, but I'm pretty sure he'll go for it."

Later that afternoon, I told him about their offer as we ambled along the Riverwalk with Paisley in the stroller. He stopped in his tracks.

"Are you serious? They really offered to do that?" He looked especially handsome with his hair all windblown and aviator sunglasses on.

"Yes. And they'd be really good with her. Stella was a nanny too, and Maren is basically a Disney princess. In fact, I've hired her out to do rich kids' birthday parties dressed up like Cinderella a bunch of times." I giggled at the memory. "And she's always a good sport about it. Although she makes good money every time, at least a few hundred bucks, so that helps."

Nate shook his head. "I cannot believe people actually pay that kind of money for someone to show up in a costume at a birthday party, especially for a kid."

"Oh, believe it," I told him. "I've done kids' parties that cost thousands and thousands of dollars. These people don't just want someone in a Cinderella getup from Target with an iPod. They want the gown and the castle, the pumpkin carriage, real white horses, elaborate decorations, a DJ with a stereo system, silver tea sets, cakes shaped like a glass slipper, fireworks, bounce houses, piñatas, a dance floor, face painters—"

He groaned. "Stop. Just stop right there. Before Paisley hears you and gets ideas."

I laughed. "Don't you want to give your daughter a princess party?"

"No. She can have a regular party with kids from the neighborhood like we did when we were kids, where you play musical chairs and pin the tail on the donkey, and eat a slice of homemade yellow cake with chocolate frosting on paper plates with plastic forks and ice cream melting all around it," said Nate.

"We?" I asked curiously. "I thought you didn't have any siblings."

"I meant you and me," he said quickly. "Kids from our generation."

"Ah. Well, I suspect you're going to want to spoil your daughter a little more than that. I bet she'll have you wrapped around her little finger, just like my sisters and I were with our dad. He never could say no to us."

Nate went quiet after that, so quiet that I was concerned I'd said something wrong. Was he thinking about his future with Paisley? Or his past? Was he picturing the suburban neighborhood where he grew up and wondering if he owed his daughter the same kind of upbringing? Downtown loft living was great for single people like us, but if you had kids, you had to think about things like safe outdoor places for them to play, schools, friends nearby. But rather than ask him about his plans again, I changed the subject. "So what do you think about letting my sisters babysit so we could go out one night this week? I looked at my schedule earlier and believe it or not, we don't have any events scheduled for this weekend."

"Really? That's nice."

I could tell he was still distracted, and tried not to be disappointed at our mismatched levels of excitement. "Well, you let me know."

We walked in silence for a few minutes, and I looked out over the Detroit River, holding my hair back from blowing in my face and wondering what he was thinking, why he'd suddenly gone mute. When we reached the foot of the Belle Isle bridge, I asked if he wanted to walk across or turn around.

He glanced into the stroller. "Turn around, I guess. She'll have to eat soon, and it's easier to feed her at home."

I nodded, and we started walking back. After another

ten minutes went by, I couldn't bear the silence any longer. "Is everything okay?"

"Yeah." But his expression remained serious, his jaw clenched.

"Because you seem a little upset," I went on, making an effort to sound friendly and not accusatory. "And I was just wondering if I said something wrong."

"You didn't."

"Oh. Okay, good."

More silence. I was about to lose my mind when he stopped walking. I got about four feet ahead of him and turned around.

"I'm sorry," he said. "You're right. I am upset about something, but it's nothing you need to worry about." He pushed the stroller and caught up to me. "And I would like to take you out this weekend. Could you ask your sisters if Friday night would be okay? I still want to try to visit my mom on Saturday."

"Of course," I said, relieved it wasn't me but concerned about whatever it was that was bothering him. "I'll text them right now." Pulling my phone from the pocket of my denim jacket, I messaged both sisters at once. Maren got back to me right away and said she'd be happy to do it, and Stella replied a few minutes later that she was supposed to attend a work function with Walter but would rather babysit with Maren, so she was going to try to get out of it.

"We're all set." I dropped my phone back into my pocket and grinned at Nate, hoping to cheer him up. "We have not one but *two* qualified babysitters anxious to give you some relief and us some adult time."

"Great," he said, giving me half a smile.

"What should we do?" I faced him and galloped side-ways a few steps, thrilled at the prospect of an evening out with him by my side, holding a restaurant door open for me, taking my hand as we walked through a crowded room, sitting across a candlelit table.

"Leave it to me." He sounded a little better, happier. "I'll take care of everything. I want to treat you."

My stomach fluttered. "I can't wait."

Friday night, my sisters knocked on my apartment door around six. I let them in, and they followed me upstairs to my bedroom so I could finish getting ready. Nate had made a reservation for seven o'clock, but he hadn't told me where. He'd said I could dress up or dress down, whatever I pleased. Since *he* was the one I wanted to please, I'd chosen a bright red dress that showed off my legs and had a deep V in the front. But other than that, it wasn't skimpy or provocative—it had long, blousy sleeves that cuffed at the wrist, a little belt around the waist, and a soft, flowing skirt. I'd noticed that Nate was turned on by things that were suggestive without being overly revealing. I liked that about him.

Now, what I wore beneath the dress was another matter entirely—a sexy bra and panties in cherry-colored lace.

"I love your dress," said Stella, following me up the stairs. "It looks amazing on you."

"Thanks. You can borrow it any time. It would look great on you too, with your runner's legs." I smiled at her over my shoulder.

"Thanks, but I don't really go anywhere that would

require a sexy little red dress," she said wistfully. "I wish I did."

"Make Buzz take you out dancing," said Maren as we reached the top of the stairs. "Go to Cliff Bell's and do the Charleston. It would be the bee's knees."

Stella smacked Maren on the arm as she and I snickered. "You guys should be grateful to Walter for letting me off the hook tonight."

"We are," I said, going into my bathroom to take one final look at my reflection. I'd curled my hair and let it swing loose around my shoulders. My makeup I kept minimal, a little blush, some black liquid eyeliner around my eyes, and red lips to match my dress. In my ears I wore tiny diamond earrings, and a cursive E hung from a delicate gold chain around my neck. After giving myself a couple sprays of perfume, I stepped into strappy nude heels and spun around for my sisters, who were sitting on my bed. "Well?"

"Ten." Maren was confident.

"Eleven," said Stella. "And I love how the shoes show off your red painted toes, but are your feet going to be cold?"

"Nate does a good job keeping me warm." I grabbed a small black clutch from my closet and tossed my lipstick in it.

"Things are still going well for you guys?" she asked.

"Totally," I said. There were times during this week where he'd gone a little silent and moody, but that could easily be blamed on sleep deprivation, the major changes in his life, and concerns about the future. Overall, he was the same Nate I'd always known—sexy, funny, charming, generous—just more human. I couldn't get enough of him.

"That's great," Maren said as they followed me down the stairs. "I'm dying to meet him."

"He's excited to meet you, too, and I'm ready, so let's do

it." I added a few more things—mints, some cash, my keys—before heading across the hall with my sisters, locking my door behind me.

Although I had a key to Nate's apartment, I always knocked. I didn't want to make any presumptions where his privacy was concerned, and besides, I always went a little breathless when he opened the door. I like that feeling, the rush of it, like cresting the top of the hill on a rollercoaster. Tonight was no exception.

"Hi," he said, quickly scanning all three of us but bringing his eyes right back to me. They drank me in from head to toe and back again. "Wow. You look stunning."

"Thank you. You look very handsome." He wore a charcoal suit with a white shirt, no tie. His hair was neatly combed, his scruff trimmed, and since I'd insisted on going straight home last night after one (lingering) good night kiss, his eyes were clear and bright after a good night's sleep. He'd texted this morning that even Paisley had gone six straight hours without waking up.

He kissed my cheek and stepped back, opening the door wide. "Come on in. I can't thank you enough for doing this," he said to my sisters, offering his hand. "I'm Nate, and over there in the swing is Paisley."

Stella and Maren shook his hand and gave him their names with a smile before making a beeline for the baby. Immediately they started cooing over her, remarking on all her dark hair, her big eyes, and the cute little sleeper that I bought for her last Saturday at Partridge Creek. On the chest it said *You got this, Dad* and was covered with arrows labeled *arm, arm, leg, leg, head,* and *snap here.*

"There are instructions for making her bottles on the kitchen counter next to the can of formula. Diapers and wipes and pajamas are over there on the changing table."

Nate gestured left, then right. "Extra pacifiers are upstairs on the nightstand, and I left my cell phone number on the coffee table. Call if you need anything or have any questions." He actually looked kind of nervous about leaving, which I found adorable.

"Don't worry about a thing," said Maren, pulling Paisley out of the swing. "Just go have fun."

"Thanks." Nate dropped his keys and his cell phone in his pocket. "She gets pretty fussy around nine or ten, but we shouldn't be too much later than that."

"You have no curfew." Stella gave us a wave. "Enjoy your night out."

Flashing my sisters a grateful smile, I took Nate's hand, sensing he needed some reassurance that it was okay to leave her. "Ready?"

Eye contact with me seemed to do the trick. "Definitely." He held the door open for me, and we walked out into the hall.

We waited silently for the elevator, and when it arrived he guided me into it with one hand on my lower back. It was empty, and as soon as the doors were shut behind us, he spun me to face him and grabbed me tight around the waist with one arm. "You. Are. Gorgeous."

The elevator began to descend, making me feel weightless. My heart beat faster. "Thank you."

He buried his face in my neck. Inhaling deeply, he squeezed me tighter. "Thank you. For suggesting this. For arranging it."

"Of course. You deserve a night out."

He opened his mouth and kissed his way down the side of my throat, making my arms and legs tingle. "Easy, easy," I admonished when I felt his hand brushing up my thigh. "We've got hours, don't we?"

"Yes. And I intend to make every second count." But he released me as the elevator slowed to a stop, and I straightened my dress before the doors opened into the parking garage beneath the building. Nate took my hand as we walked to his car, and opened the passenger door for me. Once I was seated, he closed it and walked around to the driver's side.

"So where are we going?" I asked as he started the engine. "You've kept it a secret all week."

Nate took my hand and kissed it before exiting the garage, but he said nothing.

I moaned with frustration as we eased into traffic, but secretly I loved that he wanted to surprise me. In a few minutes, we pulled up at the Detroit Foundation Hotel, a beautifully restored brick building that had been the Detroit Fire Department's headquarters in the 1920s, complete with three huge sets of double doors painted bright red across the front. Immediately, one valet opened my door and offered me a hand as I stepped onto the curb. Nate accepted a slip of paper from a second valet, told him we were hotel guests, then came around and took my arm.

"Hotel guests?" I whispered as we headed for the entrance. "Why did you say that?"

Again, Nate only smiled as he opened the door to the restaurant for me. "So many questions," he said, taking my arm again as we walked in together. "Don't you trust me to do this right?"

The hostess greeted Nate by name and told him his table was ready. I saw the way her eyes lingered on his handsome features and broad chest, and felt proud to be the one on his arm. "I trust you," I said, looking up at him as my pulse skittered out of control. It occurred to me that I couldn't recall the last time I had trusted any man this way.

Once we'd been left alone, I looked at him across the table and realized that for once in my romantic life, everything was falling into place exactly the way I had imagined it. The crowded room, the arm in mine, the candlelight glowing softly between us. Beyond that, there was the beat of my heart, the look in his eye, the feeling that somehow we were doing this right.

We were finding our way.

FOURTEEN

NATE

The evening was perfect so far, everything I wanted for Emme.

I couldn't take my eyes off her. She was luminous in the candlelight, her blue eyes on fire, her red lips beckoning. Every time she took a bite of something, I watched her mouth, thinking about all the ways she used it on me. I imagined that red lipstick smeared on my cock, and got so hard I nearly asked for the check before the appetizer was gone. But it wasn't only her mouth turning me on.

Her hands distracted me too. I'd watch them wrap around her cocktail glass or slowly butter a piece of bread or pop an olive from her martini between her lips, and a memory would hit me from the last two weeks—her fists tightening in my hair, her nails raking down my back, her fingers clutching at my shoulders, my arms, my ass. My hardened flesh sliding against her palms as her tongue stroked my chest, the unabashed way her hands explored every part of me, her fingers seeking out hidden places that made my body tremble and my vision fade. I'd had the most intense orgasms of my entire life with her, and I'd never even taken her to bed. Not properly, anyway.

Tonight would change all that, even if it was only for a couple hours.

Not that it was all about sex with Emme and me. It wasn't. It never had been. In a way, that would have been *much* easier for me to deal with. But somehow, right from the start—actually before the start—I had known it would be different with her. She and I already had a connection, and it wasn't based on sex. So I couldn't start from there with her and simply keep it at the physical level, which for me was surface level. Things had never been just surface level with Emme. We'd cared about each other before we'd had sex. That was the difference.

That was the scary thing.

Because the sex only strengthened the original connection. Built it into something more. I felt something for her I had never felt for anyone. It was strange and foreign in a way, like it didn't really belong to me, yet it was deeply rooted inside me. Every night when she went back to her apartment, it felt like a loss. I was constantly thinking about when I would see her again, the things we would do, what I could say to make her laugh. She was so easy to be with, so understanding of my erratic moods and silences, so free with her thoughts and feelings, even as I struggled to open up about mine. And she never pushed me too hard.

She deserved more of me than I was giving, I knew that for certain.

But I had no idea where to start.

AFTER DINNER, I asked her if she'd like to have dessert up in our room.

Her face lit up. "We have a room?"

Twenty minutes later, I was unlocking the door to our temporary private oasis, and holding it open for her. Emme went straight to the window while I hung the Do Not Disturb sign and turned the lock.

"Oooh," she said, placing one palm on the glass. "Look at this view of the city."

I came up behind her and wrapped my arms around her waist. "I'm sure it's great, but I don't give a fuck about the city tonight. Or anyone or anything outside this room. And the only view I want to see encompasses every square inch of your naked body."

She laughed a little, low and deep at the back of her throat. "You might change your mind when you see what I'm wearing under this dress."

I groaned, moving her hair aside so I could kiss her neck, and she tilted her head. Her skin was warm and satin smooth under my tongue. My hands moved over her breasts, down her stomach and up the sides of her thighs before undoing the little belt at her waist. Then I worked my way up the buttons on her chest. When they were undone, she turned to face me, raising her arms. I lifted the dress from the hem up over her head and tossed it onto a chair near the window.

When I saw what she was wearing, my eyes nearly popped out of my head. My dick, already hard, twitched excitedly in my pants. "Oh my God. You're so fucking hot. Don't move, I need to turn a light on."

"I've got it." She went over to the lamp by the chair and switched it on, turning her skin from ivory to gold, her lingerie from black to red, and my desire from hot to molten. She walked toward me again in her heels. "Like it?"

All I could do was nod. She took my breath away.

She smiled as she reached me and twined her arms around my neck, pressing close. "Good. Now let's not waste any more time."

Fuck, it was hard not to rush—knowing we only had a couple hours made us anxious to take advantage of every minute. I swear to God she wanted me inside her for every one of them, she begged and pleaded, teased and tempted. She used her hands, her mouth, her voice, her breasts, her hips, her hair, even her little red-painted toes to drive me wild. I held off as long as I could, because I knew once I was buried within her, there would be no holding back. And as desperate as I was to give her what she wanted—what we both wanted—I was just as determined to savor every single moment. I wanted to slow down, commit everything to memory. The sight of her lying back against snow-white sheets. The feel of that lace against my lips. The sound of her uninhibited cry of abandon as I brought her to orgasm, first with my fingers, then with my tongue.

She protested the second one. "No, stop," she panted, trying to pull me up. "I want to come together. I feel so close to you when that happens."

"We will," I promised, kissing a path up her inner thigh.

"Not if you do it with your mouth next. I can't come three times."

"Want to bet?" I'd settled between her legs, ready to test her limits with my skill. For good measure, I'd used my hand again too, and she'd come within minutes, bucking wildly beneath me on the bed, her fingers clenching the sheets.

"Nate," she whimpered afterward, her skin warm and

damp, her breath short and quick. "Please. *Please*. I need to be that close to you."

I lifted my head from between her thighs, her taste lingering on my tongue, and moved up her body. I needed it too. Emotionally, maybe I couldn't give her all of me, but physically I'd give her everything and beyond. I wanted to do things for her and with her I'd never done before, and maybe it was because I felt guilty about closing off other parts of myself, but maybe, maybe this was the only language I spoke fluently. The only way I could convince her of what she meant to me.

I knew I should get up and get a condom, but I didn't. I paused right before entering her, and we locked eyes. She knew what I was asking.

"It's okay," she whispered. "It's what I want, too. And we're safe."

As insane as it sounds, I *felt* safe. Safe and strong and powerful. Protective and protected. And I realized, as I began to move inside her, our hands clasped above her head, her legs wrapped around me, what it truly meant to trust someone. After my childhood, I'd lost the ability to trust, and she'd brought it back.

Feelings for her overwhelmed me. With my eyes pinned on hers, I watched her spiral upward once more, watched her surrender to everything she felt and all the passion she evoked in me. I saw agony and pleasure intertwine on her face, felt her body tense beneath me, listened to her say my name, softly at first and then louder, louder, louder, until she was shouting and gasping and wrenching her hands free to pull me in deeper and deeper as she came and I held nothing back, gave her everything, everything, everything I had, felt it flowing from me into her, my body, my heart, my soul, my trust.

I fell on top of her, and rolled to my side, taking her with me. We kissed and clung to one another, my mind a mad jumble of unspoken thoughts I wanted to give voice to but couldn't. There were so many things I needed to tell her. But my head—it was spinning. Or was that the room? The world? The universe?

I needed something to anchor me in the chaos that had become my life. I needed to feel like I was going to be okay. Because this room, this private little corner of heaven, wasn't ours to keep. We had to turn the key in when we left, and we had to leave soon. And out there, nothing was certain. I didn't know who I was. I didn't know what I was doing. I didn't know who to become.

I didn't know how to let myself love someone.

But maybe it was time to try.

———————

"WHAT TIME IS IT?" she whispered. We were lying on our sides, facing each other on the bed, our legs still twined.

I picked up my head and looked at the digital clock on the nightstand behind her. "Almost eleven."

She sighed. "I don't want to go."

"I don't either."

"But we should."

"Yes."

She started to get up and I put a hand on her shoulder. "Wait one minute. There's something I want to tell you."

She stretched out again with her head on the pillow, her hands tucked beneath her cheek. "Okay."

For a moment, I panicked. How did you tell a girl you were falling in love with her? That she was part of what was changing your world—and you—for the better? That you might be an emotionally stunted, jaded divorce lawyer and completely inept as a dad and boyfriend, but there was a good reason for that and you were going to try harder to deserve her faith and trust?

No. That was no good.

I had to go back to the beginning.

I reached for one of her hands and took it in mine between us, just like she'd done to me the first night she'd slept over. My first night with Paisley. She hadn't abandoned me then, and I hoped she wouldn't now.

"I lied to you," I said.

She blinked, her expression blank. "What?"

"I lied to you. About not having any siblings. I had a brother."

"You did?"

I nodded, my throat closing. "His name was Adam."

"What happened?"

"He died when he was nine. Leukemia. I was twelve."

Her eyes grew shiny. "Oh, Nate."

"It pretty much destroyed me. It destroyed all of us." I wiped at my eyes with a thumb and forefinger.

"Of course it did. I don't know how you get over something like that."

"You don't."

"Were you close?" she asked softly.

I nodded, unable to speak.

"Best friends, probably. Like my sisters and me."

After a moment, I found my voice by thinking about pain other than mine. "We'd been a perfectly normal, happy family before that. And then afterward...my mother developed her obsessive fears about germs and crowds and touching things. She blamed them for Adam's death—of course, that wasn't the truth. What she really blamed was herself. But she couldn't handle that. She tried to externalize it. It was the only way to deal with her grief and guilt. Eventually she disappeared into her fears. The mother I'd known was gone."

Emme nodded and wiped her eyes. "What about your dad?"

"He drank his sorrow. Abandoned us emotionally if not physically. He died of heart disease three years ago but the man I remember as Dad was gone long before that."

"And you?" she asked, another tear slipping from the corner of her eye. "How did you cope? You lost everyone, didn't you?"

My throat seized up again. I focused on our joined hands. "I promised myself I would never love anyone that much again."

"Of course you did."

"I wanted to protect myself. I thought if I never loved anyone like that, I couldn't get hurt again. I wouldn't have to be afraid."

A few more tears trickled from her eyes.

"It's why I've never wanted to have a relationship. Why I've never wanted to get married. Why I never even considered being a father."

She nodded. "And now?"

"Now there's Paisley." I took a breath. "And I love her more every day. It's like my love for Adam was—pure and simple and effortless. Unconditional. I don't know what the fuck I'm doing as a father, but I love her and I'm trying."

"It's enough, Nate." She brushed my hair off my forehead. "You're doing more than a lot of guys would in your shoes."

"It's not enough. It'll never feel like enough. Because it

will never make up for the fact that I didn't want her." I squeezed my eyes shut. "I feel so fucking guilty about that."

"Stop." She propped her head up on her hand. "You don't have to feel guilty about that. You would have wanted her if you'd known."

I opened my eyes and stared at her.

"Okay, maybe not right away, but..." She grabbed my hand again. "You would have been excited eventually. Look at you now, after only two weeks. Can you imagine your life without her?"

"Frankly, yes. It's my old life. I fucking miss it. I mean, I don't want to give her up, but I miss it. I miss *me*, who I was —I wasn't afraid of anything. I was on top of the world. Now it's spinning out of control around me, and I'm a fucking mess."

"You aren't," she said fiercely. "Not to me, you aren't."

It made me smile a little. "No?"

"No." She sat all the way up. "You're brave. And strong. And sexy. Hearing you admit the truth and talk about your fears tonight makes me want you even more. You're a good man, Nate Pearson. Paisley is damn lucky to have you. And so am I."

I looked up at her. "You do have me."

A pause. "Do I?"

I sat up and took her face in my hands, praying to God— if there was one—she'd understand what I was saying to her. "You have me, Emme."

She turned her head so one cheek rested in my palm. "You have me, too."

I glanced at the clock, hoping against all odds the numbers hadn't changed, or even better, had gone backward. No luck—but... "Hey," I said. "Look what time it is."

She turned her head and gasped. "Eleven eleven!"

"Go ahead. Make your wish."

She looked at me again for a moment, squeezed her eyes shut like she was concentrating hard, then exhaled and opened them. "Your turn."

I sighed exaggeratedly. "Do I have to?"

"Yes. You know my rule!"

"Fine." I remembered the first wish I'd made at 11:11 PM, when we'd been in my kitchen exactly two weeks ago. That night I'd wished that the next person Emme fell in love with would love her back like she deserved and make her happy.

Now I looked at her hopeful, smiling, beautiful face and made it different.

I wish I could be the one.

FIFTEEN

EMME

"Did you have a good time?" Stella looked up from her phone from where she sat on the couch. Maren sat on the opposite end reading a magazine.

"Yes." I smiled blissfully. "Thank you so much."

"How was she?" Nate went over to the monitor on the kitchen counter and peered at the screen.

"An angel," said Maren, tucking the magazine into the shoulder bag at her feet. "She got a little fussy after you left and she found herself with two strangers, but she quieted down eventually and she took her bottle with no problem. We got her to sleep around ten or so."

"I can't thank you enough," Nate said as my sisters stood up and gathered up their things. He went into the kitchen for a moment and came out with two bottles of wine in his hands. "These are for you."

"That's so nice of you, but it's totally not necessary." Stella smiled at him as she slipped her sweater on.

"Please take them." Nate held the bottles out. "You have no idea how much I appreciate the favor."

It took a little more cajoling, but eventually each of my

sisters left with a bottle of wine tucked under her arm. When the door was closed behind them, he turned to me and pulled me into his arms. "Thank you so much for arranging for them to be here. I had such a good time tonight."

"Me too. Thank you for the perfect date." I wrapped my arms around his waist and lay my head on his shoulder.

"Your sisters are great."

"They are. I mean, they can drive me crazy, but I adore them."

"How do they drive you crazy?"

"Oh, the usual stuff. Stella is the oldest so she can be a bit of a know-it-all. Add to that she's a therapist, so she sometimes treats me like one of her patients and tries to analyze my behavior. It's so annoying. And Maren can drive me nuts with all her organic foods and meditation techniques and spiritual wellness. I get that clean living is good, but there are some things I like dirty." I giggled. "Like martinis and sex."

"Thank God for that." He kissed the top of my head. "Which one has the bee man for a boyfriend?"

"Stella. But I don't know that she'd actually call Walter her boyfriend. They don't even have sex."

"They don't?"

"No, it's totally weird to Maren and me, but they don't. And she says she's fine with that."

"What about him?"

I shrugged. "I assume he's fine with it too."

"I cannot imagine any guy being fine with a relationship where there is no sex. But maybe that's just me."

"Stella always goes for more intellectual types because she likes guys who are smart, but then there never seems to be that physical thing between them."

"I'm intellectual," said Nate. "I like sex."

I laughed. "But you don't like relationships."

"Well, I never have *before*."

I leaned back a little and looked up at him. "And now?"

"Now there's you." He touched his lips to mine. "Want to stay over tonight? At the risk of sounding like Walter, we don't have to have sex. I only want to be close to you."

My entire body warmed. "How am I supposed to say no to that? Just let me run home and get ready for bed. I'll come back over."

"Okay. You've got the key?"

I smiled. "I've got the key."

After one more kiss, I went to my apartment, changed out of my dress and into a little white camisole and some pajama pants, over which I threw a big fluffy pink robe. I took off my jewelry, washed my face, and brushed my teeth. My hair was mussed and considerably less voluminous than when I'd left home earlier, but I left it alone. We were only going to sleep, anyway. I hurried down the stairs and across the hall in my bare feet and let myself back into Nate's apartment, where I found him feeding Paisley on the couch. He still wore his dress pants, but only his undershirt on top and his feet were bare.

"She woke up, huh?" I dropped down beside him, cuddling close to his side and tucking my legs beneath me.

"Yeah, when I went up there to change. But it's good timing—maybe she'll give us a solid four or five hour stretch after this."

I kissed his shoulder. "I can do the next feeding so you can sleep through the night for a change."

"That's okay. I didn't invite you over to help me with her. And I don't mind doing it—kind of helps me feel like I'm making up for missing the first two months of her life."

Smiling, I looked at the baby in his arms. "You have certainly come a long way since the night you fainted at the sight of her."

"I didn't faint," he said stubbornly. "I...fell over in surprise."

"I think that's called fainting, babe."

"Not at all. There's a clear difference."

Laughing a little, I patted his leg. "Okay. Anyway, you've made lots of progress."

He was quiet for a minute as he watched her take the bottle. "Sometimes it still doesn't seem real. That I have a child. A daughter."

"It was *quite* a shock."

"I didn't think I could do this. Be a father."

"I know."

"And it wasn't just that I didn't know how to take care of her. I didn't think I could love her the way a father should love his child."

Chills ran down my arms, despite the fact that I was wrapped in my giant fleece robe. "And now?"

"Now I'm blown away by how quickly and completely I fell in love with her. I didn't think it was possible for me to feel that way at all, let alone so fast. It shocks me." He swallowed. "And scares me."

"I'm sure it does. Given what you told me earlier, it can't be easy to allow yourself to love like that without fear. You've been protecting yourself for so long. But Nate, all that time, you were also denying yourself the *joy* of loving someone. Yes, love makes you vulnerable to hurt, but it also makes you happy. Don't you think?"

"I guess."

It troubled me to think love was still something he feared. "Aren't you happy?"

He looked at me and gave me a little smile. "When I'm with you, I am."

My heart quickened. "Good. I like making you happy."

He gave me a kiss before looking down at Paisley again. "Life is just so different now, you know? What makes me happy has changed so much. I hardly recognize myself."

I put my arm around him and laid my head on his shoulder. "Well, I like the changes in you. I know you probably feel like a stranger to yourself, but I think this person who's capable of so much love was always there inside you. Waiting to be set free."

He laughed a little. "I'm picturing a little madman running around in my body throwing hearts everywhere."

I giggled. "Exactly. You finally let him out of Feelings Jail. He's been trapped there for years."

"Feelings Jail." Shaking his head, Nate set the empty bottle on the coffee table and stood up, moving Paisley to one shoulder. "You're insane."

"But I'm right, aren't I? Doesn't it feel better to allow yourself to love and be loved than to keep yourself isolated and closed off? Wasn't that ever lonely?"

"Yes," he admitted, rubbing Paisley's back. "Sometimes it was."

My jaw fell open. "Wow. I didn't actually think you were going to admit that."

"I wasn't going to, but the little feelings madman made me do it."

I took one of the cushions from behind me and whacked his legs with it. "Now you're just making fun of me."

He grinned. "I can't help it. Not everything about me has changed."

A few minutes later, we turned out all the lights and went upstairs to bed. It was almost like we were a little family, and the notion gave me a warm feeling deep in my belly. Maybe it would happen someday.

In his bedroom I took off my robe and pants and slipped between the covers. Then I watched as he cradled his daughter and put her to sleep, walking back and forth at the foot of the bed, bouncing her gently. She fussed at first, but eventually she kept the pacifier in her mouth and quieted down. After about five minutes, he was able to lay her in the sleeper.

He disappeared into his closet for a moment, and when he returned he wore only his boxer briefs. My stomach flipped at the sight of all his bare skin, at the memory of what it had felt like to be naked and pressed against him, at the thought that he'd been inside me without protection. Nothing between us. He got into bed, and I snuggled up next to him, my head on his chest. His arms wrapped around me.

We lay that way in silence for a few minutes, and I thought he might have fallen asleep, but then he spoke softly in the dark. "Come with me tomorrow."

At first I couldn't think what he meant. "What?"

"To my mom's house. I want you to come with me."

I propped myself up on his chest and looked down at him. "Are you sure?"

"Yes." He rubbed my upper arms. "Going there is always difficult. And you make everything better."

My toes wiggled. "Okay. I'll go with you."

"Thank you."

I lowered my lips to his and held them there a moment. "Thank you for asking me."

"You might not thank me after we get there. My mother is...odd."

"That's okay. I'm not going for her, I'm going for you. To support you."

He brushed my hair back from my face. "I don't deserve you."

"Maybe not. But you've got great hands and a big dick, and it's *super* convenient that you live right across the hall."

He laughed quietly. "I'm so glad you're here."

"Me too." I put my head down again and closed my eyes. "Night."

"Night."

I fell asleep to the gentle rise and fall of his chest and the soft stroke of his hand up and down my back.

"What was your favorite thing to do on a rainy day when you were a kid?" It was a few minutes after ten, and we were in the car on the way to his mom's house.

The good weather had passed and rain drummed down against the windshield, pooled beneath overpasses on the highway, and made the driving difficult. The windshield wipers in Nate's fancy car were working overtime, but I still had no idea how he could see. Not that I minded the slow drive. The interior of his car was warm and cozy, Paisley was napping in the back, and the extra time together was perfect for conversation. I was thrilled that he had asked me to come with him today and saw it as the perfect opportunity to learn more about him.

"Probably Legos. I had about a million of them."

"And what would you build?"

"Cities. My brother and I would build entire cities out

of Legos—skyscrapers and houses and garages for our matchbox cars. We had a huge room in the basement devoted to Legos. We used to play down there all the time on rainy days."

"What about when it was sunny?"

"If it wasn't raining, we were always outside. There were lots of kids in our neighborhood, and we'd have epic games of Peas and Carrots, which was basically hide and seek."

I laughed. "Why'd you call it Peas and Carrots?"

"I have no idea," he said, glancing over his shoulder as he changed lanes. "But we always did. And once you were hidden in your spot, you had to yell out *peas and carrots* to give the person who was it at least a *clue* where you are hiding, because the houses were so big and the yards were fair game, too. And the tree behind our house was always Goal." He was quiet for a moment, then he laughed. "Also, I was obsessed with Batman when I was young and always wore a cape like he did. I even slept in it."

"You did?"

"Yep. Wore it over my Batman pajamas."

"Please tell me you still have Batman pajamas."

He grinned and shook his head. "Sorry. But if you really want me to, I'll come to bed in a cape for you sometime."

I clapped my hands. "Oooooh, please do. Naked except for the cape. And I think you should wear the mask with the pointy ears too. So sexy."

He reached over and put a hand on my leg. "Anything for you, babe. Glad to know you have a superhero kink. I like it."

"What about your brother?" I asked. "Was he Robin to your Batman?"

Nate took his hand away. "Yes."

An uncomfortable silence followed, during which I was kicking myself for ruining the light mood. Nate's neck muscles were tense, his mouth a grim line. "I'm sorry," I said. "I didn't mean to upset you by bringing him up. I was only curious."

It took him a moment, but eventually the tension left his body, and his jaw unclenched. "It's okay. I'm just not used to talking about him." He put his hand on my leg again and surprised me by going on. "It's like there were two eras of my childhood. The Before years, which were idyllic, and the After years, which were agony. And no one ever talked about any of it. We buried the past just like we buried my brother."

A lump formed in my throat, and I took his hand in both of mine, hoping he would keep talking. He did, although not right away.

"I'm sure we all thought we were doing the right thing by suffering in silence, sparing each other the pain of talking about Adam and our life before leukemia, or even about our grief after he was gone. But it was so hard. I remember feeling torn between wanting to remember him out loud and wishing he had never existed in the first place. I felt a lot of guilt about that."

"God, that must have been so awful for you." I squeezed his hand.

"It was. And there was no one I could talk to about it. My mother was drowning in her own grief and guilt, my father turned to the bottle for solace, and my friends didn't know how to deal with such a huge loss—what twelve-year-old boy does?"

"You needed therapy," I said. "I can't believe no one suggested it."

He shrugged. "Someone might have, I don't remember.

But my parents were not in the right frame of mind to arrange it, and I probably would have refused to go, anyway. Talking about it wasn't going to bring my brother back."

"No, but it might have eased your guilty feelings a little bit. Helped you to process the loss and prevented you from being so afraid to care for someone again."

He shrugged. "Maybe."

"Do you want to talk about him now? About the Before years, I mean? I'd like to know about him." For a moment, I was afraid I'd gone too far, but then he started to talk.

"He loved baseball. And Swedish fish. And knock-knock jokes. He had a book full of them, and they were all terrible." He smiled. "I remember this one he used to trot out every time he met someone new. Knock knock."

"Who's there?" I said.

"I eat mop."

"I eat mop who?" As soon as the words were out, I realized what it sounded like I'd said, and burst out laughing. Nate did too, and the sound made my heart beat faster.

"Yeah, he used to love getting people with that one, especially girls."

"Well, he'd have gotten me, that's for sure." I giggled again. "And I'm going to get my sisters with it."

"Adam would be proud."

"What else did he like to do?"

"Whatever I was doing. He was forever tagging along after me. He used to sleep at the foot of my bed like a puppy. And when he got too big for that, he'd sleep on the floor in my room."

"Aww. I bet he idolized you."

"He did." He paused and swallowed hard. "He was a good kid. I miss him every day."

I kissed the back of his hand. "Thanks for telling me about him."

We listen to the radio for a while after that—we discovered we both loved This American Life on NPR—but it wasn't too long before Paisley woke up. Since we were still about an hour from Nate's mom's house, we decided to pull off the road and feed her. "Are you hungry?" asked Nate as we exited the highway. "Do you want to grab lunch?"

"Sure," I said. "Anyplace is fine with me."

We ended up at a Coney Island, and the hostess seated us in a big corner booth. I shrugged out of my jacket and fluffed my hair, which was damp from the rain. Nate set Paisley's car seat in the booth, sat down next to her, and unbuckled the straps. "Can you make the bottle for me?" he asked, handing me the diaper bag. "I should change her."

"Why don't I take her to the ladies room and change her? They'll probably have a changing table in there."

"Won't they have one in the men's room?"

I shrugged. "Not usually."

Nate's expression was angry. "That doesn't seem fair. They just assume a dad would never need to change a diaper?"

"I guess."

"That's bullshit." He stood up. "Give me the diaper bag."

I handed it to him, and he threw it over his shoulder and took off toward the bathrooms with Paisley crying in his arms.

Ten minutes later, he was back, his expression much more relaxed. "They had a family restroom with a table," he said as he slid into the booth. "I didn't even know there was such a thing."

"You learn something new every day." I turned my

menu to face him. "Here. Take a look at that while I make the bottle."

He glanced at it. "God, I need to get back in the gym. I have *not* been eating well."

"I might be able to watch her for you a few times next week so you can go work out if you want. Although with Coco still out, my schedule is pretty full. Hand me the diaper bag?"

He passed it over the table. "Yeah, I probably have to hire an actual babysitter or nanny. I can't be off work for much longer."

"I can help you find someone," I said as the server approached. "I think Coco mentioned an agency or website that she used to find a sitter one time. I'll ask her what it is."

We ordered burgers and fries and took turns eating and holding Paisley, since she continued to be fussy even after her bottle. At some point while I was holding her and trying to eat the last few bites of my burger, Nate pulled a twenty-dollar bill from his wallet, put it on the table, and stood up. "I'll take her so you can finish," he said. "I'm done. If she comes back, will you ask for the check?" He took Paisley from my arms and walked up front with her.

I quickly finished eating, and when the server came by to check on us, I asked her for the bill.

"Of course," she said. "Is your husband finished with his plate?" She gestured toward Nate's unfinished fries.

For a few seconds, I couldn't answer. I was too busy being pleased she had referred to Nate as my husband. "Yes. The baby was fussy so he took her up front, but he's done."

She smiled and picked up the plate, stacking it on top of mine. "Any man who takes a crying baby so his wife can finish her lunch is a keeper. I'll be right back with the check."

"Thanks, Sharon," I said, referring to the name on her name tag. I loved Sharon. Sharon was awesome.

By the time Nate returned to the table to put Paisley in her car seat, Sharon was setting the change on the table. "Good job, dad. You got her to quiet down. I was just telling your wife how lucky she is to have a man who helps with the baby."

Nate's eyebrows rose, and he gave me a surprised look. I bit my lip. I was kind of afraid he was going to tell her the truth and spoil my little fantasy, but he didn't. Actually, he looked more amused than anything. "Thanks," he said to Sharon. He carefully transferred Paisley to her car seat and buckled her up while I put my coat on, then we left the restaurant, hurrying across the parking lot in the rain.

When we were on the highway again, he glanced over at me. "My *wife*? Did I miss the part where we got married?"

I laughed. "Relax, you're still single."

"Oh, good. Because I can only handle one identity crisis at a time. I just discovered I'm a father. I can't discover I'm a husband all of a sudden, too." He shuddered.

I shifted in my seat to face him and crossed my arms. "Would it be so horrible, to be married to me?"

"No, darling. The man who marries you will be the luckiest man in the world, and I promise to represent you in the divorce and make sure we rake his stupid ass over the coals for fucking up a good thing. It *would*, however, be horrible to be married to *me*. I wouldn't put you through it."

I rolled my eyes and faced forward again, and he turned on NPR again. But I couldn't pay attention to the show. My mind kept drifting back to what he had said about getting married. It's not like I hadn't known his views on the subject before, but it hadn't been personal then. Now he wasn't only saying he had no interest in marriage, he was also saying he had no interest in marriage *to me*. Was I crazy to feel a little hurt by that?

Yes, said a voice in my head. *You have been dating for exactly two weeks. Get a grip. Stay in the moment.*

No, said my heart. *It's only natural to dream about a future with someone you love. It's impossible to stay in the moment all the time.*

Was I in love with Nate?

I glanced at his handsome profile and it gave me butterflies, but I hadn't really needed to look at him to know the answer.

Of course I was in love with Nate. I even thought he might be in love with me. What had he said last night? *You have me.* Maybe they weren't the usual three little words you dreamed of hearing from the one who'd captured your heart, but there was something about the way he said them that made them just as meaningful. *You have me.* I felt it in my bones. And I'd heard other guys say "I love you" before when they clearly hadn't meant it. It wasn't the words themselves that mattered. It was the sentiment.

But what did it mean to have him? Or to be his? What good did it do to belong to each other if you knew it was only temporary? How could you enjoy the moment if you were constantly aware that there would be no future? That your time together was running out? It made our entire relationship seem like sand in an hourglass.

Then again, maybe I was wrong. Maybe I just needed to be patient with Nate, like I'd promised to be. After all, look how far he'd come as a father. It wasn't that far-fetched to think he might change his mind about marriage in the future, was it? And it's not like I was in a rush. I just liked knowing it was a possibility. I liked anticipation. My favorite moments at the weddings I planned were always those right before the bride walked up the aisle. When she stood at the back of the church and looked toward the front where her future husband waited for her. When she took that first step, it wasn't only toward a man. It was toward a dream. It gave me chills every single time.

I wanted that for myself. ·

Time. That's all I needed to do, give it time. If Nate was really the one, and something in my gut told me he was, then he was worth waiting for.

I could be patient.

SIXTEEN

NATE

Something was off with me.

Or maybe it was off with Emme—she'd gone quiet after that whole marriage conversation. Was it that? Did it bother her that I had no intention of getting married? Were her feelings hurt? I hoped not. It wasn't personal—I was crazy about her, and I mean that in the truest sense of the word. There were times I actually thought I was losing my mind because I wanted her so badly. I was constantly thinking about her, always wondering what I could do to make her smile, and keeping my hands off her was nearly impossible. There was nothing I wouldn't do for her...

Except get married. I just couldn't.

So much about my life had spun off track. In the last couple weeks, I'd had to scrap every plan and dream I'd had for myself. I'd had to accept a completely new reality, map out an entirely different future. It made the ground feel slippery under my feet. Like nothing was certain. Was it too much to ask to hold on to some part of my former life, some piece of my former self?

And wasn't it enough that we were together now? That

I felt more for her than I ever had for any woman? That I, Nate Pearson, divorce attorney and commitment-phobe, was in a *relationship*? I'd told her things last night I'd never told anyone. She knew more about me, the real me, than any human being on the planet. I trusted her. And I was trying hard to be the kind of person she wanted me to be. Wasn't all that enough?

Not to mention the fact that I knew how unlikely it was that a marriage would last, and I'd seen firsthand how shitty divorces could be. They were soul crushing. Heartbreaking. Embarrassing. And *really* fucking expensive. Frankly, I had no idea why people still bothered to get married in the first place. It's not like you needed the certificate to have kids if you really wanted to. And I didn't want any more kids, anyway. One was plenty.

I glanced over at Emme, who was stone-faced as she stared out the windshield. She probably wanted kids of her own, maybe even two or three of them. And before that, she'd want the big wedding with five hundred guests and twenty-seven bridesmaids and five circus tents and a partridge in a pear tree and whatever other nonsense brides could dream up. I knew that about her. I had always known it.

But I wanted to be with her.

So now what? Did we need to talk about this? Did I owe it to her to make sure she knew how I felt? But what if that was a deal-breaker? What if she broke it off? The chocolate milkshake I'd drunk with my lunch seemed to curdle in my stomach.

I didn't like thinking about my life without her. I didn't want to go back to one-night stands with women whose names I could barely recall. And when I thought of her with someone else—my hands tightened on the steering wheel—I wanted to fucking put my fist through the windshield.

I couldn't lose her. I needed her.

Especially now, when I was turning onto my old street and my nerves were already tying themselves into knots. What would my mother's mental state be? How would she handle meeting her grandchild? Which version of her would greet us today, the angst-ridden agoraphobe who'd never recovered from the tragic loss of her younger son, or some semblance of the mother I'd once known, who baked amazing chocolate chip cookies and wore a perfume called Happy and laughed at all of Adam's terrible jokes?

I pulled into the driveway and put the car in park, but didn't turn off the engine.

Emme looked over at me. "You okay?"

"Yeah." I cleared my throat, which felt tight and scratchy all of a sudden. "Coming here is sometimes difficult."

"I get it."

Of course you do. My throat tightened even more. Why did I feel like I owed her an apology?

Maybe it was the house messing with me. I looked at it through the driver side window, a red brick center entrance colonial with black shutters and white trim. The hydrangea bushes on either side of the front door still had dead brown leaves, but I knew they would bloom bright pink and blue this summer. If I squinted, I could still see my mother cutting them back, my dad mowing the front lawn, my brother and I racing down the driveway on our bikes, our capes flying behind us.

My mother appeared in the living room window. She'd moved the curtain aside and was peering out intently, like a lonely old lady looking for some neighborhood gossip. I couldn't tell if she was wearing gloves or not.

I unbuckled my seatbelt. "Might as well go in."

Emme covered my hand with hers for a moment but didn't say anything, and I felt a rush of gratitude.

I looked at our hands. "I'm really glad you're here."

"Me too. Do I get to see your old bedroom? Are there, like, posters of Cindy Crawford on the walls?"

Laughing, I shook my head. "You'd be more likely to see nineties movie posters, but I'm pretty sure my mother has taken them all down."

A few minutes later we approached the front door, which opened before we even stepped onto the porch. My mother stood twisting her hands together, her expression a bit anxious, but at least she wasn't wearing gloves. She was dressed in jeans and a turtleneck sweater, and her hair was shorter than the last time I'd seen her, which had been about two months ago. It used to be dark and thick and she'd worn it long when I was a kid, but now it was much thinner, almost entirely gray, and barely covered her ears.

"You're here," she said, looking frantically from me to Emme to Paisley in her car seat, which I carried in one hand.

"Hi, Mom. We're here."

"I was getting worried. It's such a long drive, and there's that one stretch that's really long without any exits from the highway." She covered one hand with the other and switched repeatedly. They were pink and chapped from so much handwashing. "I always dread that part of the drive. Sometimes I dread it so much I have to turn around and come home."

"I know. But we were fine." I nodded toward Emme. "This is my friend Emme." And because I knew what her next question was going to be, I added, "She's not the baby's mother."

"Nice to meet you, Mrs. Pearson." Emme smiled warmly.

"Hello." My mother gave Emme a quick nod before looking at Paisley again. "And that's the baby?"

"This is Paisley. Can we come in?"

"Oh! Yes, of course," she said, almost like she was surprised, as if maybe she hadn't planned on actually inviting us into the house. She backed away from the door, and I gestured for Emme to go in before me. Once we all stood in the front hall and the door was closed behind us, my mother seemed to recover some of her manners. "Can I take your coat?" she asked Emme.

"Sure." Emme took off her denim jacket and handed it to my mom. "Thank you. You have a beautiful home."

"Thank you, dear." She hung the jacket in the front hall closet. "It's really too big for only one person, but I'm so used to it. I just don't think I would like a new house."

I set the car seat and diaper bag down on the floor and crouched down to unbuckle Paisley, who was starting to wake up. "Hey you," I said to her. "Want to meet your grandmother?"

"Oh my. Oh my goodness." My mother came a little closer. "She's so small."

I unsnapped Paisley's coat and carefully took her arms from her sleeves, then I scooped her up and stood so my mom could see her.

"Oh, look at her." She reached out almost like she might touch Paisley's foot but changed her mind. "I haven't been around a baby this young in a long time. She's so cute."

"She is." I felt proud of my daughter. "Would you like to hold her?"

"Oh, I don't know if I should." She shook her head as she backed away, repeatedly covering one hand with the other again. "I went to the salon a few days ago, and I'm telling you, everyone in there was sneezing and coughing and blowing their noses. I'm sure I picked up something terribly contagious. I wouldn't want to give it to her."

I thought about assuring her it was fine, but decided against it. If she wanted to hold her grandchild, she could. If she didn't, I wasn't going to force her. "Okay. Maybe later."

"Maybe if I put on my gloves," she began, but I cut her off.

"No, gloves aren't necessary, Mom. I'm sure your hands are clean, but you don't have to hold her. I'll hold her." I wandered into the living room, where framed school photos of my brother and me still hung on the hunter green walls. "Hey Emme, come look at these."

Emme followed me into the large, high-ceilinged room, her arms crossed over her chest. She laughed when she saw my senior picture, a big eight-by-ten in a mahogany frame. "Oh my God, I've never seen you totally clean-shaven before. Look at your baby face! And your spiky hair!"

I winced. "Yeah, I'm not sure who I was trying to be with that hair."

"Brad Pitt in *Fight Club?*" she suggested.

"Probably."

"Nate was always so vain about his hair." My mother, who had followed us into the room, continued to stare at Paisley in my arms and fidget. "It used to take him forever to get ready for school."

"Thanks, Mom."

Emme laughed. "Really?"

"Yes." My mother nodded and smiled. "It had to be just right or he'd be in a bad mood all day."

"Okay. That's enough." Part of me was glad my mother was doing well enough to keep the mood light, even if she was poking fun at me. Another part was surprised she even remembered any of my moods, bad or otherwise, or what had caused them. She had always seemed so focused on herself. Then again, I'd been a typical surly, sullen teenager in those days. I probably hadn't noticed that much about what was going on around me either.

"That's hilarious," Emme said, catching my eye and grinning delightedly.

"Can I get either of you something to drink?" my mother asked.

"No, thank you." Emme smiled and shook her head.

"I'll take a cup of coffee if you've got it," I said. "But don't go to any trouble."

"It's no trouble to make some. I'll be right back." She gave Paisley another lingering stare before heading into the kitchen.

"Your mom wants to hold Paisley so badly," Emme whispered. "I can tell."

"Me too. But I'm not playing her game about the germs. I don't want to argue with her, and I don't need to hear all her statistics about how dirty public places are or how easily viruses are spread."

"Why not let her wear the gloves if it will make her feel better?"

"Because it's ridiculous. She doesn't need to wear gloves in the house. I don't want to encourage that kind of behavior. Her therapist told her she had to stop doing it."

"I just feel so bad for her. It must be terrible to be so afraid all the time. So afraid that you can't even hold your own granddaughter. Can't you let her do it this once?"

"No. Look, I feel bad for her too. And I used to give in

to her all the time. When we ran out of milk and she wouldn't go to the store to get it because the dairy aisle is too far from the store exit, I went and got the milk. When she wanted to attend my high school graduation wearing gloves and a surgical mask because there weren't any windows in the auditorium so the air had to be full of contaminants, I said okay. When she was too scared to fly to North Carolina to see me graduate from college because she might have a panic attack on the plane, I told her it was fine. But I made a conscious decision a couple years ago to stop doing that. It wasn't helping her." I was probably being too hard on Emme, maybe even on my mother, but I'd been dealing with this for a long time, and I couldn't be in this house without bad memories knocking at my psyche.

Emme put a hand on my arm. "You're right. I'm sorry. It's good that you can be strong for her sake and not give in."

"I'm sorry too. I didn't mean to snap at you." I took a deep breath and exhaled. "This house comes with a lot of baggage for me. I don't always deal with it well."

She snuck a quick kiss on the lips. "You're doing great. And maybe your mom eventually won't be able to resist holding Paisley at some point while we're here. She's being so good right now, isn't she?"

"She is." I kissed the top of my daughter's head.

"And if not, there's always the next time." She turned back to the wall with all the pictures on it and pointed at one of Adam, the last one taken. "This is your brother?"

"Yes." As always when I looked at that picture, something in my chest caved. Nothing about the grin on his face or the gleam in his eye or the wayward lock of hair above his forehead indicated he had less than a year to live.

"Adorable." She glanced over at some of my earlier photos. "You guys looked a lot alike."

"Yes."

"And you know what?" She moved down the row of Adam's pictures, then went over to the fireplace and studied a couple of the baby pictures on the white-painted mantel. "I can totally see the family resemblance in Paisley."

My mother entered the room carrying a tray with two steaming cups on it as well as a small sugar bowl and a carton of half-and-half. "I brought you some too, dear. In case you wanted a little warm-up." She smiled at Emme and set the tray on the table in front of the burgundy sofa.

"Thank you. Actually, it smells delicious. I think I will have a cup." Emme went over to the sofa and sat down. "I was just saying to Nate that Paisley really resembles his side of the family."

My mother nodded. "I think so too. Nate had that same kind of hair when he was a baby. And her eyes are exactly like his."

Some of the tension in me began to ease. And then.

"But Nate, really you need to get a complete medical history from the mother's side of the family. You never know what conditions she could be predisposed to." My mother's eyes grew wide. "Cystic fibrosis, hemophilia, Huntington's, Parkinson's, Sickle Cell Disease, certain kinds of cancer—"

"Mom! Stop it! Paisley does not have any of those things!" I yelled.

"But you can't be too careful, Nate!" Her hands were working and working and working. "If we had known a little sooner that Adam might have been predisposed—"

"Mom." Fury was boiling in my veins like molten lava, but I tried to keep my temper in check. "Stop. Talking."

"I'm only trying to spare you what we went through! What if we'd been aware? I always think about that. What if we could have done something? What if there was an early treatment we missed out on because we didn't know any better?"

But I was done. Striding through the front hall, I threw the diaper bag over my shoulder and marched up the stairs. "I have to change her."

I took her into my old room, which looked very different now that it was a guest room—not that my mother had very many guests. The walls were now a butter yellow instead of dark blue, and the old gray carpet had been removed, the oak flooring underneath refurbished. My twin bed was still there, as were my desk and dresser, but the blackout shades were gone, replaced by curtains with a floral pattern.

I stared at the bed, remembering so many nights with my little brother asleep at my feet. He'd always wanted me to tell ghost stories, but then he'd get too scared to go back to his own bed—at least, that's the reason he gave at the time. But maybe he just wanted to be near me. I'd complained to my mother about it, whining about how it was *my* room and I didn't want to share it. Then after he was gone, there wasn't anything I wouldn't have given to have him back at the foot of my bed.

I lay Paisley on the bed's new daisy-patterned quilt, then pulled the changing pad from the diaper bag and slipped it beneath her. She didn't smell messy, but I'd learned that anything was possible during the diaper change.

Fuming silently, I went through the motions scarcely aware of what I was doing. How could my mother have said those things to me? How could she suggest that I might lose Paisley the way we lost Adam? Didn't she know how that loss haunted me still? Didn't she realize how it had affected me? Or see the things I had sacrificed in order to protect myself from that kind of suffering? Here she was throwing my fears in my face, reminding me how dangerous it was to love something as vulnerable as a child. My stomach churned.

Once Paisley was dressed again, I picked her up and held her close to my chest, tucking her head beneath my chin. "I'll never let anything happen to you," I promised her quietly. "Never."

But as soon as I uttered the words, I recognized their emptiness. How could I make that promise? What power did I have to protect her? I was no superhero. I was just a guy whose condom had failed. There was no honor or nobility in my journey to fatherhood. I hadn't even wanted it. What if I deserved to be punished for that? What if losing her was my life sentence?

I kissed the top of her head, letting my lips rest on her soft dark hair. I breathed in her clean baby sent. I squeezed her tighter, so tight she began to squirm and fuss.

I loosened my hold on her a little, but my mind continued to torture me. Staring at the bed where I'd spent so many nights praying and hoping for a miracle, certain that it would be delivered and then broken beyond repair when it wasn't, I remembered why I had lived my life alone up to this point. It wasn't only the child you loved who was vulnerable, it was *you*.

Where Paisley was concerned, I had no choice. I loved her because she was mine. But what about Emme? She was a choice, wasn't she? She was a wish I had made, a hope I had let break the surface. I'd been blinded by feelings for her, but now I saw my mistake.

What the fuck had I been thinking? Why had I let her in? Why had I given her pieces of me I could never get back? What was going to happen when she got tired of waiting around for me to change my mind about getting married or having a family and left me for someone who wanted the same things she did? It was bound to happen sooner or later. Why was I setting myself up for heartbreak, when I knew better than anyone that wishes don't come true?

"Hey. You okay?"

I turned to see Emme standing in the doorway. "I don't know."

She nodded and entered the room, tucking her hands in the pockets of her jeans. "That was kind of rough."

"Yeah."

Emme looked around the room. "Was this yours?"

"Once upon a time. But the walls were dark blue back then."

She smiled. "Like a bat cave."

"Yeah, I guess."

Her smile faded as she walked toward me, her eyes were full of concern. She wrapped her arms around my waist and laid her cheek against my arm. "I'm sorry, Nate. I don't know what to say."

"This isn't your fault." None of this was her fault, yet I kept wanting to apologize to her. Was it because I knew she was going to end up being hurt?

"Your mother is down there breathing into a paper bag."

"Jesus. Of course she is."

"What do you want to do?"

Get the fuck out of here. Turn back the clock. Get my life back on track. I took a breath. "Try again, I guess. Give it another hour or so. Is that okay with you?"

She kissed my shoulder. "Of course it is."

Before we went back downstairs, I went into Adam's room down the hall. It too had been repainted, from sky-blue to deep maroon. At some point, it had been converted into an office for my father and held a large desk, some bookshelves, and a leather chair in one corner. It smelled faintly of stale cigar smoke. I turned to Emme, waiting for me in the hallway. "Can I ask you to take Paisley downstairs? I need a minute to look for something."

"Sure." She reached for Paisley, smiling brightly at her. "I bet you're hungry, peanut. Want a snack?"

"Good idea," I told her. "Want to make her a bottle?"

She nodded and took the diaper bag from me too. "No problem. Maybe I can even recruit Grandma to help me."

After she left, I went over to the closet and opened the door. It held some suits of my father's zipped up in garment bags, a few dresses of my mother's from the days when they enjoyed an active social life, and tons of wrapping paper, ribbon, and bows in stacked plastic containers. No wonder my mother's gifts to me always smelled like mothballs. On the top shelf, I saw the box I was looking for. It was labeled BOYS.

I took it down and brought it over to the desk. A layer of dust covered the top, and I sent motes swirling when I lifted it off. Inside were relics from my childhood—I'd looked through this box many times and knew its contents. Our first pairs of shoes, bronzed, which we'd always thought was so weird but my mother claimed was a tradition in her family. Little velvet bags containing our baby teeth. Hats and gloves that had been knitted for us by relatives we'd never met. Childish drawings in crayon. School pictures. Adam's stuffed bear. My Batman cape. And there toward the bottom was the item I wanted—his joke book. I took it out and thumbed through it. Its pages were yellowed and it smelled musty, like a basement. Inside the front cover, he'd printed his name in blue ink. ***Adam Pearson.*** Beneath that, he'd written a note:

KEEP OUT! THIS MEANS YOU. This book is my personl proprty and the only other person alowd to read it is my brothr Nate Pearson.

Despite the tightness in my chest, I smiled. Not once had I ever wanted to read his stupid joke book. But it meant something to me now that he would have let me. *I should have been nicer. I should have laughed more. I should have appreciated being his big brother.*

I'd been planning to ask my mother if I could have the book, but holding it in my hands only made the pain in my heart worse. Setting it back in the box, I replaced the top and put it back on the shelf in the closet and shut the door. Fucking feelings. You had to bury them, or they'd suffocate you.

I'd forgotten that.

Downstairs, the scene in the living room surprised me. My mother sat on the couch holding Paisley while Emme, sitting right beside her, held the bottle as Paisley drank. Both of them looked up when I came into the room.

"I hope it's okay that I'm holding her," my mother said nervously, her eyes dropping back to her granddaughter's face. "I scrubbed my hands really well, and I'm not touching the bottle at all. So I don't think the germs will endanger her."

"It's fine."

I made eye contact with Emme. She smiled at me, her eyes shining, a beautiful, calming presence in this house full of ghosts, and my heart about exploded in my chest. My legs nearly gave out. My breath stopped.

Because I loved her. I *loved* her. For being here with me,

for understanding me, for making me feel like I wasn't alone.

Except I would end up alone, wouldn't I? When she was gone, when she'd given up on me, when she'd realized I couldn't give her everything she wanted and deserved.

You couldn't control everything in life, maybe not even your feelings, but you could control your actions. I had to walk away, or I had to push her away. The thought of doing either one made me sick to my stomach, but I told myself to be a fucking man and get over it. Harden my heart. Take control.

Make the choice.

SEVENTEEN

EMME

"So I know the beginning was a little difficult, but overall that went okay, don't you think?" I asked hopefully as we drove away from the house.

"I guess." He glanced in the rearview mirror at his daughter, who was sleeping peacefully, but even that didn't get rid of the worry lines creasing his forehead.

"At least your mom held her for a little while."

"Yeah."

"And she said maybe she would drive down in a couple weeks for another visit."

"I heard her." His tone said, *but I don't believe her.*

"And wasn't Paisley good today? I wonder if she's saving it all up for a meltdown tonight."

Nate frowned. "Probably."

"Well, no worries. I'll be there to help you. Maybe we can get takeout or something. Have a cocktail and watch a movie, just like the old days." I wiggled happily in my seat. "It's so nice to have a Saturday night off."

Nate didn't say anything.

"Hello? Does that sound like a plan?"

"What? Sure, whatever you want to do is fine with me."

Clearly, he was too distracted to look forward to an evening together, and maybe he needed time to process the visit home. It was obvious to me that all the memories there, both good and bad, affected him deeply, as did his mother's anxiety. If I'd thought he would talk to me about it, I would've asked him to. But even though he'd been more open with me over the last week—and especially last night— I didn't get the feeling he was in the mood for conversation right now. Seemed like he wanted to brood for a bit.

I didn't blame him for being upset. Painful memories aside, no parent wants to hear a list of all the harmful genetic conditions their child might be predisposed to, and it had to be even worse for Nate because of his brother. I'd seen the look on his face as his mother was talking, and at the word *cancer*, he'd gone completely white. He'd seemed a little better upstairs, but still on edge. Quiet and tense the rest of the afternoon.

But I wouldn't push. Instead, I reached over and put my hand on his leg, hoping he'd get the message—*I know that was hard for you, and I'm here if you need me.*

I don't even think he noticed it.

———

BY THE TIME we were in the elevator going up to our floor, I was starting to get concerned. Nate still hadn't spoken to me, other than answering my questions with short, vague responses, and his expression remained grim.

"You feeling okay?" I asked him.

"I'm fine."

But he wasn't.

The doors opened, and as we began to walk down the

hall, I tried again. "So what kind of food do you feel like having? We could—"

"What the hell are you doing here?"

I looked up at Nate in surprise and saw that his eyes were focused on something farther down the hall. I followed his line of vision and spotted a woman knocking on his door. She looked about my age. Dark ponytail. Blunt bangs. Jeans, boots, a light brown sweater.

"Who is that?" I asked, although in my gut I already knew.

Nate didn't answer, but he strode forward with huge, angry steps, carrying the car seat with one hand. I hurried to catch up.

"*Now* you decide to knock?" he demanded.

"Paisley!" After catching sight of the baby, the woman crouched down with her hands on her knees, smiling widely as Nate approached. "My baby girl! Mommy's missed you so much." She sniffed, her eyes tearing up.

"If you missed her so much, why haven't you called for two weeks?" Nate kept the car seat handle in his grip and angled away from Rachel, who moved around him trying to see her daughter.

"Because I needed the time alone to work on myself. I was in an intensive therapy program. And I wanted you to have time to get to know her."

By then, I'd caught up to them and probably should have gone inside my apartment to give them some privacy, but I felt rooted to the spot.

"What kind of program?" Nate demanded. "Are you an addict?"

"No!" She looked appalled, but softened her voice. "I have postpartum depression, Nate. I couldn't sleep or eat or find the energy to do anything. All I did was cry and feel like my life was over, and all my doctor did was prescribe sleeping pills, which didn't help. Now I'm finally getting real treatment. I have new medication that's actually working, and I'm going to therapy."

Hearing her story, I actually felt sorry for her, but Nate wouldn't bend. "We said one month. It's only been two weeks."

"Please, Nate, can't I just see her?" Rachel asked tearfully. She was pretty, with high cheekbones, a dimple in her chin, and straight white teeth. Self-consciously, I poked at my slightly crooked bottom teeth with the tip of my tongue. Dammit, why hadn't I worn my retainer more often?

"That's all you want? To see her?"

"Well, can't I hold her a little? I've missed her so much. You have no idea."

"*You* have no idea what it did to me learning I had a two-month-old baby. You should have told me."

She held up both hands in surrender. "You're right. I should have told you. Like I said in my note, I'd totally planned to give her up for adoption, but—"

"Without even asking me!" Nate yelled. "That was fucking *not* okay!"

"I know," Rachel said, weeping openly. "I'm sorry, Nate. I wasn't thinking straight. And we barely knew each other. I didn't plan on any of this."

"Me either." He glared at her. "You can come in for a few minutes and hold her, but then you have to leave."

"Um, I think I'll head home," I said quietly. "Nate, I'll see you later."

"No, Emme." Nate made eye contact with me for what felt like the first time in hours. "You don't have to go home. We have plans tonight, and we're not canceling them." He gave Rachel one last angry look before opening the door to his apartment.

I was torn between wanting to stay out of their business and fearing I'd miss something dramatic if I left. Also, and this is so stupid I'm ashamed I even thought it, I was kind of jealous. This beautiful, sad woman had a baby with Nate. He'd slept with her. He'd obviously found her attractive last year. What if she tried to seduce him or something? As soon as I had the thought, I felt guilty about it. I trusted Nate. But I still followed them into his apartment.

Nate set the car seat on the floor, and Rachel dropped her purse and hurried over to it. Kneeling down, she unstrapped her daughter and lifted her out, snuggling her close. Paisley woke up and started to fuss.

"She needs to be changed." Nate stood aside, arms folded across his chest, feet planted wide.

"I'll do it." Rachel stood up and looked around his apartment. "Wow, you've got a lot of baby stuff. Did you buy all this in the last two weeks?"

"No, I've always decorated my apartment this way." Nate rolled his eyes. "Of *course* I just bought it all. I had *nothing* here for her when you left her at my door. Not that you cared."

"I did care, Nate. I just couldn't think straight." She took Paisley over to the changing table, talking softly to her, asking her questions, telling her how much she missed her. By the look on Nate's face, I could tell he was getting angrier with every word. I went over and stood next to him.

"Hey," I whispered. "Are you sure you want me here?"

"Yes." He didn't take his eyes off them, almost like he didn't trust Rachel with his daughter.

When Paisley had been changed, Rachel picked her up and kissed her pudgy cheek. "She looks good."

"Of course she looks good," he snapped. "Did you think I wouldn't take care of my own child?"

"I meant it as a compliment. I wouldn't have left her with you if I thought you wouldn't take care of her."

"Thanks," he said flatly.

"Give me a break, will you? I came here to do you a favor."

He tilted his head. "What favor is that?"

Rachel stood a little taller. "You don't have to keep her for the full month. I came to take her back."

Nate moved fast. In two seconds he'd covered the ten feet between himself and Rachel and taken the baby from her arms. Rachel was so stunned she let it happen.

"No way," Nate said, circling around the couch to stand next to me again. "If that's what you came here for, you can forget about it. You're not taking her out of this apartment."

"Come on. You didn't even want her for a week, remember?" Rachel stuck her hands on her hips.

"Well, things have changed. And I have rights."

"Says who?" Rachel's tone turned antagonistic. "How do you even know she's really yours?"

My mouth fell open and I looked at Nate, expecting him to blow. But he didn't.

"I just do," he said calmly. "Want me to take a paternity test?"

"No." Rachel's shoulders slumped and she closed her eyes. "She's yours." A moment later she opened them, tears spilling over again. "But please let me have her back. She's everything to me. I feel so guilty for leaving her."

"No. After the month is up, we'll negotiate custody. You owe me this time with her." He paused. "Where do you live?"

Rachel wiped her eyes. "Battle Creek."

"What's your last name?"

"Brown."

"Did you give her my last name or yours?"

"Mine."

"What's her middle name?"

"Ann."

The authoritative way he was grilling her reminded me of a lawyer cross-examining a witness, or a detective questioning a suspect.

"I need your information and signature on the Affidavit of Parentage. Once paternity is established, I want my name on the birth certificate. And I want joint physical and legal custody."

"Fine, we'll work it out. But Nate, can I please hold her again?" asked Rachel. "Then I'll go. You can have the rest of your month, and I'll come back in two weeks. I thought you'd be glad to give her back early."

At first I didn't think Nate was going to give in, because he didn't move a muscle. But then he slowly walked toward her and allowed her to take the baby from his arms. "I'll be right down with the affidavit. You can fill out part of it now." He went directly to the stairs and headed up into his bedroom.

Rachel and I made eye contact for one brief, uncomfortable second before she looked down at Paisley again. "So are you his girlfriend?" she asked.

I didn't even know how to answer that question, not that it was any of her business.

"I think it's only fair to know who he's bringing around my child."

"I'm Emme. I live across the hall."

She looked up at me, eyebrows raised. "Interesting."

My temper sparked, and I reminded myself I wouldn't

be doing Nate any favors by causing trouble with the mother of his child. It was better if everyone got along.

"I didn't figure Nate for the type to have a girlfriend," she said.

"I guess you don't know him very well."

She shrugged. "Or he's got you fooled."

Channeling my inner Maren, I took a few deep breaths and searched for a peaceful place within myself. There had to be one in there somewhere.

"I'll admit, he's taken to this whole fatherhood thing much better than I thought he would." She looked around at all the baby gear. "I figured he'd be desperate to get rid of her by now."

"You figured wrong. He adores her."

Nate came down the stairs with papers in his hand. "I'll get a pen."

"I've got one," I said, glad to be useful in any capacity that sent this woman on her way. From my purse I dug out a Devine Events pen and handed it to him.

"Thanks." He went over to the counter separating the kitchen from the living room and set the pen and papers down. "You can do it right here," he said to Rachel. It was clear the matter was not up for discussion.

Rachel walked slowly to the counter. After reluctantly handing Paisley over to Nate, she filled out the paperwork. After a moment, she said to him, "We need a notary for the signatures."

"I know that." He paused. "How long are you in town? We have one at my firm. We could get it done on Monday."

"I can stay in town until then. I took a leave of absence from work."

"Fine." He walked to the door and opened it. "I'll text you a time and the address."

Biting her lip, she set the pen down. "Are you sure I can't take her with me? I'm not trying to keep her from you permanently."

"I'm sure. You'll see her on Monday. And then two weeks after that."

Rachel looked defeated, but she nodded. "Can I kiss her goodbye?"

"No."

"Nate," I said softly. Not because I liked Rachel or was remotely on her side, but because as a child of divorce I appreciated the effort to compromise where children were concerned.

He met my eyes, and for a moment I thought he was going to tell me this was none of my business—he'd have been right, too. But instead he closed his eyes and sighed. "Fine."

Once more, he handed Paisley over to her mother. The poor little thing was probably wondering what the heck was going on the way she was being passed like a basketball back and forth between them, although she wasn't fussing about it.

Rachel hugged and kissed her, promised to see her the day after tomorrow, and gave her back to Nate. Then she picked up her purse from the floor and walked out.

Nate shut the door behind her and stood facing it.

I felt like I'd been holding my breath for hours. "You okay?"

"Yeah."

"That was...a surprise."

"Yeah." He held his daughter close, kissed her head.

"Want me to get a bath going for her?" I asked.

"Sure. Thanks." All the life had gone out of his voice.

WE BATHED AND FED PAISLEY, ordered dinner in, and ate it sitting on the floor while she played on a blanket—although Nate didn't eat much, and he still wasn't very talkative. When Paisley started to get tired and crabby, Nate took her upstairs while I put the leftovers away and loaded the dishwasher. I kept telling myself not to read too much into Nate's mood, that it had nothing to do with me, but it was hard not to internalize it at least a little.

When he came down, he made us each a cocktail, and we spent the evening watching Bond on the couch like we used to. Only...it wasn't as much fun.

Nate was shutting down on me—I could sense it. He remained silent the entire time. He didn't laugh at any jokes or comment on Connery's superior Bondness or make any attempt to touch me. Half the time, he wasn't even looking at the screen. I'd look over and see him staring into space, his expression troubled. Something was really wrong.

When the movie was over, I turned off the television and scooted closer to him, slipping my arm through his and laying my head on his shoulder.

"Hey, neighbor. What's going on with you?"

"Sorry. I'm not very good company tonight."

He didn't answer the question. "You don't have to apologize. It's been kind of an emotional day. The visit home, and then Rachel showing up wanting to take the baby back."

"Yeah."

"Want to talk about it?"

"Not really."

"Okay. Well, I'm here if you do." I put my head down again, totally baffled. This was not the Nate I'd been with last night. It wasn't even the Nate from Coney Island earlier today. I tried to think of when he'd started putting the walls back up—was it at his mother's house? On the ride home?

And *why?*

"I want you to know, I was really proud of you today," I told him.

"For what?"

"For not giving up on your mother. For standing up to Rachel. For not letting Paisley go early."

"I didn't even consider it. In fact, when Rachel threatened to take her, something in me went a little caveman. I was *not* going to let her take my daughter away from me."

"Of course not." I loved the ferocity in his voice. And he looked so handsome sitting there, with that stubborn jaw set just so and his hair all tousled.

I put my hand on his thigh and spoke seductively. "Want some help working off all that tension?"

He looked at my hand and cleared his throat. "I'm not really in the mood."

Hurt, I pulled my hand away. "Oh. Okay."

"Sorry."

"That's okay. It's been a long day. You're probably tired."

"Yeah."

An awkward, awkward silence followed. What was going on? "I'll head home, I guess." I wanted him to argue. I wanted him to put his arms around me. I wanted him to tell me that last night wasn't just a dream, because at this point, I was beginning to think I'd imagined it.

What he said was, "Yeah, that's probably best. I think we could both use some space."

I froze. "What?"

"Some space. I think we've been...rushing things."

I stared at his profile. Was I hearing him right? "You want *space*?"

He ran a hand through his hair. "Yeah. I'm feeling a little crowded, okay? You probably are too."

"Crowded?" I parroted. This had to be a joke. Was he fucking kidding me with this? He felt *crowded*? After asking me to stay over last night, inviting me to come with him to his mom's house, and making me come in when Rachel was here when I'd offered to go home, *now* he felt fucking *crowded*?

With my face burning, I got off the couch, felt around in the dark for my sneakers and tugged them on. I needed to get home before I lost my temper or burst into tears.

How had this day gone so terribly wrong?

EIGHTEEN

NATE

Let her go.

She doesn't really want you. She wants some version of you that doesn't exist.

Let her find someone who can make her happy, someone who can make her his everything, someone who will give her the future she deserves, because you can't.

It had been hard enough to close myself off from her today, but it had taken every ounce of strength I had not to give in when she touched my leg and spoke low in my ear and offered to help me work off the tension. She had no idea how badly I wanted to do exactly that—throw her down on the couch and ravish her hot little body, give her all the love and attention I'd denied her today, take my pleasure in pleasing her, show her how grateful I was that she was here, that she was perfect, that she was mine.

But I couldn't. I had to let her go.

My hands balled into fists as she put on her shoes.

I'd feel better after she was gone, right? Just like I'd felt better after Rachel had gone. Less threatened. More in control. More like myself. It had felt so good to call the shots after she'd blindsided me—*again*—by showing up at my door and trying to take Paisley away. Maybe I'd been a little harsh, but fuck her for thinking she got to decide everything all the time. For thinking she could come and go with Paisley as she pleased. For treating me like I didn't matter, like what I wanted didn't matter. It had felt good to shut off my feelings, assert myself and take command of the situation. Tell her how things were going to go. Lay out *my* terms. It felt familiar.

That's all I wanted. To feel like myself again.

Emme walked to the door.

Don't look at her. Don't watch her go.

But I couldn't take my eyes off her.

She reached for the handle. And stopped. Turned around.

"No," she said, as if I'd asked her a question.

"What?"

"No. You don't get to be just another dick that blows me off without a good explanation. I'm worth more than that."

So much more. But I couldn't give in. "All I said was that I needed some space."

"That's bullshit. Something is going on with you, and you're not telling me what it is."

"That's ridiculous." I could have choked on my own self-loathing.

"No. It's not." She went over to the lamp and turned it on. "You look me in the eye and tell me nothing has changed since last night. Because the guy I was with last night is not the same person sitting on that couch right now."

"I don't know what you're talking about." I met her eyes for exactly two seconds and looked away.

"Yes, you do. You know exactly what I'm talking about. So what the fuck, Nate? Which version of you is real?"

My hands clenched my knees. My stomach churned. "Last night was me trying to be someone I'm not."

Silence. "Are you serious?"

I swallowed hard, gulping back all the words of apology threatening to escape my lips. "Yeah. I said what I thought you wanted to hear."

"Why?"

"I was trying to be what you wanted me to be."

"All I ever asked you to be was honest!"

"Guess I wasn't very good at it." Every word out of my mouth was despicable. I felt sick.

"Why'd you ask me to sleep over last night? Why'd you ask me to go with you to your mom's today?"

I shrugged. "Seemed like things I should ask you to do."

"Oh, my God. I cannot fucking believe this."

I risked a look at her, and she'd fisted her hands in her hair.

"I cannot fucking believe I fell for another one of you." Her eyes closed and she shook her head. "It's not possible."

Fuck. I did *not* want to be lumped in with all her other weasel exes who'd made her feel bad about herself. I wasn't dumping her—I was trying to get *her* to dump *me*.

I stood up. "Emme, I'm not saying we have to break things off completely."

She dropped her hands and gaped at me. "You can't mean that. *Now* who's living in a fantasy world?"

"You wanted me to be honest, so I'm being honest. Last night was more of an act than anything else. I wanted you to have a good time."

"Oh, my God." She put up a hand to silence me, but I went on.

"But that doesn't mean we have to stop hanging out completely. It just means I don't want a girlfriend. I really don't have time, with Paisley and everything."

"Don't you dare use your daughter as an excuse. This isn't about her."

I shrugged and crossed my arms over my chest like the stupid asshole I was while she gathered herself up.

"You know what, Nate? You were right about me. I trust too easily. I get carried away. I give up my heart without a fight. Congratulations on showing me the truth." She walked to the door and opened it before turning around again. "I get it now. Sometimes a fuck is just a fuck."

Then she was gone.

I COULDN'T SLEEP. Paisley was restless too, and I spent much of the night pacing the bedroom floor, trying to soothe her and trying to convince myself that I'd done the right thing in setting Emme free. I went over and over my reasons, and every single time I came to the same conclusion. Ultimately, it was never going to work. We were too different. We didn't want the same things. We would have hurt each other in the end.

But it felt fucking horrible.

I kept seeing her face when I told her I hadn't meant what I'd said Friday night. She'd been so devastated. It was such a shitty way to end things, to lie to her like that, but I'd been afraid that if I wasn't a complete dickhead, she'd have been understanding and granted me the space I requested.

Crowded. What a fucking joke. I never felt crowded by her. In fact, all I ever wanted to do was get closer.

I couldn't stop thinking about her.

How the hell was I going to get over her? Especially living right across the hall? Were we ever going to speak to each other again? God, I missed her already and she'd only been gone a few hours. And what if I saw her with a guy in the hall or something? Some douchebag who didn't deserve to touch her hair or hear her laugh or hold her hand, let alone see her naked or smell her skin or feel her legs wrapped around him?

Fuck that guy! I'd fucking tear him apart.

No one deserved those things. Not even me.

Especially not me.

I moved Paisley up to my shoulder, and noticed that she seemed a little warm. Immediately I pressed her cheek to mine. It was burning hot. An alarm bell went off in my head.

I turned on the nightstand lamp and saw that her face was flushed. Oh, fuck! What if she had a fever? What should I do?

My first instinct was to go get Emme, but then I remembered that I couldn't. Dammit! Grimacing, I grabbed my phone from the nightstand and called Rachel. No answer.

Fuck!

Should I take her to the emergency room? But what if they asked for information I didn't have? I didn't even know her fucking birth date, for God's sake! Or her social security number, her blood type, her weight, or anything else about her except her name. And I wasn't even legally her father yet. Would they let me give consent to treat her?

I couldn't worry about that—I had to take her. What if something was really wrong? I'd never forgive myself if anything happened to her while she was in my care.

"Shhhhh, it's okay," I murmured, for myself as much for her. My heart was pounding. "It's going to be okay."

I set her in the sleeper so I could quickly get dressed and put some shoes on. Downstairs, I got her into her jacket and car seat, grabbed my keys, and had just gone out the door when my phone vibrated. It was Rachel calling me back.

"Hello?"

"What's wrong?"

"I think she has a fever."

She gasped. "Oh no!"

"She was fine all day," I said quickly, as if I had to prove this wasn't my fault. "She ate and slept and was really good."

"Did you take her temperature?"

"No." That hadn't even occurred to me. I was too busy panicking.

"Do you have an infant thermometer?"

Did I? Had Emme put one in the basket at the baby store? Maybe she did. "Actually, yes. I think so. I'll look. You don't think I should take her right to the emergency room?"

"Depends on her fever. Take her temperature and tell me what it is. I'll either meet you at an Urgent Care or your apartment."

At that moment, Emme's apartment door opened and she appeared in her robe, pajama pants, and bare feet. My heart ached. Her eyes were puffy and bloodshot, and she looked as if she hadn't slept, either. I wanted to wrap my arms around her so badly.

"What's wrong?" she asked quietly, looking at Paisley. "Is she sick?"

"I think she has a fever," I said. "Do I have an infant thermometer?"

She nodded. "It's in a bin on one of the changing table shelves."

"I'll call you right back," I told Rachel.

"Hurry, please," she said.

We went into my apartment and Emme located the thermometer while I took Paisley out of her car seat. She wasn't crying anymore, but I could tell something was wrong. Her eyes were glassy, and she was listless and radiating heat. It gutted me that she felt pain I couldn't relieve.

"Here." Emme handed me something that looked like a toy. It was small and white with a long, skinny tip and had a digital screen on the front.

"How do I use it? Under the tongue?"

She shook her head. "It's a rectal thermometer."

"R-Rectal?" My voice cracked.

"Yes. You have to take it that way in babies this young. Want me to do it?"

Jesus Christ. Of course I did. But I couldn't bring myself to ask her. "No. I'll do it." I undressed Paisley, who began to cry again, like she knew something bad was coming. *She's going to hate me for this.* "Should I put her on the changing table?"

"Just turn her onto her belly on your lap," Emme instructed.

I laid Paisley across my thighs on her stomach and took the thermometer from Emme, noticing that she'd covered the tip with some kind of lubricant. Ten seconds later I was still staring at it. There was no way I could do this.

"Nate."

I looked up at Emme. "I can't do it. She trusts me not to hurt her."

She rolled her eyes and muttered something I didn't catch. "Give it to me."

I handed it over. She pressed a button and carefully inserted the tip. Paisley wiggled and protested, her little arms and legs flailing. Emme frowned as she tried to keep the thermometer in place. *Thank God she's here*, I kept thinking. Followed by, *I don't deserve it.*

The thermometer beeped a couple times and then a number popped onto the screen.

"Ninety nine point nine," Emme said.

"Should I take her to the ER?"

"I don't think you need to, but let me check something." Glancing around, she spotted my stack of baby books over on a side table. While she flipped through it, I took Paisley over to the changing table and put a new diaper on her, silently apologizing for the injustice she'd just suffered.

"No," Emme said, reading from the book. "In babies three months or younger, the American Academy of Pediatrics recommends taking a child to the doctor only if the fever is one hundred point four or higher. Call her doctor tomorrow." She set the book down. "But you do need to give her a fever reducer."

"Do I have one?"

"Yes. It's in the same bin under the table. Give me a second to clean off the thermometer and I'll find it for you."

She went into the kitchen and I finished dressing Paisley. When she came over to the table, she pulled a bin from beneath it, dropped the thermometer in and pulled out a red box that said Infants' Tylenol. "What does she weigh?"

Guilt slammed into me. "I don't know."

"You need to call Rachel."

I nodded. "Can you watch her for a second?"

"Yes." She picked her up and I went over to the couch, where I'd left my phone, and discovered Rachel had actually called twice in the last few minutes. I called her back.

"Nate? What took you so long? Is she okay?"

"She's okay. Her fever is ninety-nine point nine. We're giving her some Tylenol."

"We?"

"Emme is here." Our eyes met and Emme looked away fast. "How much does Paisley weigh?"

"She was eleven pounds, eight ounces at her last checkup."

"Eleven pounds, eight ounces," I told Emme.

"I'm coming over," Rachel said. "I'm already on my way."

I didn't want her here, but I didn't feel like I could say no, either. "Okay."

"Don't give her anything until I get there."

"Why not? She's got a fever and needs the medicine."

"Because I'm worried about the dosage. It's dangerous to give a baby too much."

"I'll read the dosage chart, Rachel. I'm not an idiot." But I felt like one. If Emme hadn't come over, I wouldn't have even known where the thermometer was, let alone how to use it. A thought ran through my mind—*I'm not cut out for this. And they both know it. Everyone knows it.*

"Just wait for me, please," Rachel demanded. "I'll be there in five minutes."

We hung up and I walked over to Emme and Paisley. "Rachel is on her way over. She doesn't want me to give her any medicine without her here."

"Are you going to wait?"

"I don't know."

Emme pressed her lips together, but didn't say anything. I picked up the Infants' Tylenol box and looked at the front. It had a picture of a woman holding a baby on it. It was always a woman with a baby, on everything. Dads might as well not even exist as far as marketing was concerned. I checked the back of the box. "It says one point two five milliliters for six to eleven pounds, and two point five for twelve to seventeen pounds. What if a baby is in between eleven and twelve pounds? How much do you give?"

"I'd go with the lesser amount to be safe."

The thought of making an unsafe decision for Paisley nauseated me. "I'll wait for Rachel."

"Fine." She kissed Paisley's forehead. "Feel better, peanut." Then she handed her to me. "I'm going home."

Please don't leave me. "Okay." I watched her walk to the door, my heart hammering. "Emme, wait."

"What?" She didn't even turn around, and I didn't blame her.

"Do you hate me?"

"No, Nate. I don't hate you. I hate what you did, but mostly I hate myself for falling for you. For believing your lies when I should have known better. I deserve this broken heart."

I swallowed hard, wishing she would be harder on me. Tell me I was an asshole. Call me a liar. Hit me if she wanted to. Hearing that she blamed herself made me feel even worse.

There were so many things I wanted to say to her. Simple things like *I'm sorry. Don't go. I need you.* And complicated things too, like *I'm ashamed to be such an inept father. Why does love have to hurt? You said you wouldn't let me push you away, but you did.*

But in the end, I said nothing, and she walked out.

RACHEL ARRIVED SHORTLY after Emme left, out of

breath and frantic to get her hands on Paisley, who'd fallen asleep in my arms. She woke up when Rachel reached for her and began to cry.

"Did you give her the medicine?" Rachel asked, holding her close.

I stared at her. "You told me to wait for you." She'd better not be mad at me for doing what she asked.

"I know, but you were so damn bossy earlier tonight I wasn't sure you would."

I went over to the changing table, angrily grabbed the box, and brought it over so she could see the dosage chart.

"Okay, let's go with one point two five milliliters. Open it up and grab the little dropper thing."

We managed to get Paisley to take the medicine, although she wasn't happy about it, and it took both of us to hold her still on the changing table and get the drops in her mouth.

"Good girl," Rachel said, scooping her up. "You'll feel better soon, angel." She cuddled Paisley against her chest and looked at me. "I'm sorry about earlier. I didn't mean to imply you weren't capable of giving it to her, I was just scared."

"I'm not sure I was capable of giving it to her. That took both of us."

"You'd have figured it out."

I shrugged. Only because Emme had been here. On my own, I was lost.

"It's not like I know what I'm doing either, Nate. I never planned on having kids, either. I liked my life just fine."

I didn't want to talk about life before. I didn't even want to think about it. "Do you want to feed her?" I asked Rachel, stifling a yawn.

"Sure."

In the kitchen, I made a bottle and grabbed a burp cloth, then handed them both to Rachel, who was sitting on the couch. I sat adjacent to them on a chair and tried to stay awake.

"You look exhausted," Rachel said.

"Because it's fucking four AM and I haven't slept at all." I hadn't meant to be a dick, but between the breakup with Emme and confronting my shortcomings as a father, my mood was shit.

"So she was up all night?"

"From about midnight on." I yawned again.

"Where's your girlfriend?"

"She's not my girlfriend," I snapped.

"*Sorry*," she said. "You mentioned her name earlier. I thought she was here, that's all."

"She went home. After rescuing me yet again." The words were out before I could stop them. My brain wasn't functioning right on so little sleep.

"Rescuing you?"

I rubbed my face with both hands and dropped them into my lap. "I didn't know where the thermometer was or how to use it. She did it for me."

"That was nice of her."

"Yeah."

"How long have you known her?"

"A few years."

"Earlier, she sort of made it sound like you two were a thing."

I frowned. "We were."

"You broke up *tonight*?"

"Look, I don't really want to talk about this, okay? It's none of your business and doesn't really matter anyway."

"Okay, okay. Relax. Jeez." She sat Paisley up to burp her. "I was only going to say she seemed nice."

"She is." And sweet and beautiful and sexy as fuck, and I was never going to hold her again. Had I even thanked her tonight? God, my level of assholery escalated with every passing minute.

"I didn't figure you for the type to have a girlfriend."

"I'm not."

"Then again, I didn't figure you for the type to be a good father either."

I'm not, I wanted to say. *I can't do it. I don't know why I thought I could.*

"And you are," she said.

"Thanks." But I wasn't. I was a fake.

"Are you okay, Nate?"

I closed my eyes. "I don't know. I can't even tell anymore."

"What's wrong?"

"I'm just...overwhelmed. And I'm not handling things very well."

"I understand." She paused. "Why don't I take Paisley home with me tonight?"

I didn't have it in me to argue. "Fine."

"This is really for the best," she said five minutes later, buckling Paisley into her car seat. "You need sleep, and babies really need their mommies when they're sick."

"Right," I said. My throat was tight.

"And we'll see you on Monday at your office."

"Right."

"And then I'll take her back to Battle Creek with me while you...figure things out. Okay?"

"Okay."

I went down to the parking garage with her to switch the base of the car seat from my SUV to her car. Paisley was asleep by then, and I could hardly look at her as Rachel buckled her in.

"Get some sleep," she said as she got behind the wheel. "We'll see you Monday."

I nodded, watched her drive away, and felt the weight of failure settle heavily on my shoulders.

I'd failed my daughter. I'd failed the only woman I'd ever loved. I'd failed myself.

But as I fell into bed a few minutes later, I told myself that they were both better off without me.

They were safe.

NINETEEN

EMME

After leaving Nate's the first time, I'd gone home, put on my pajamas and cried buckets into my pillow. I kept asking myself *how* over and over again.

How could he have done this to me? How could I have trusted him? How could he have fooled me so completely? How could I have been so dumb? How could he have said those things to me and not meant them? How could I have fallen in love with someone so duplicitous? Did I not have a single good instinct?

And *why* had he done this—what was the point? Had he only wanted my help with the baby all along? Had he only wanted to fuck me for a couple weeks? Had he honestly felt nothing for me all this time?

I didn't want to believe that. But what choice did I have?

Eventually, I'd given up on sleep and gone down to the couch. I was channel surfing, attempting in vain to find something to take my mind off my broken heart, when I'd heard Nate talking in the hall. Unable to help myself, I'd gone to the door and pressed my ear to it.

When I heard him say something about the emergency room, I'd opened the door without even thinking about it.

Everything after that, I'd done for Paisley. Not for Nate.

I was so *angry* with him. He'd done exactly what he'd said he wouldn't do—bullshit me. He'd pretended like he was better than all those other guys. He'd been good at it. He'd had me convinced I meant something to him.

He'd had me convinced we belonged together, and to each other. After everything he'd said to me, he turned out to be like everyone else. It *hurt*.

Maybe it had only been two weeks since we'd been dating, but we'd been friends for three years. He knew my insecurities, and it felt like he'd used them against me.

There was no excuse—not that he'd tried very hard to give me one.

I felt like such a fool.

After leaving his apartment the second time, I went home and collapsed into bed a second time. But I still couldn't sleep. I was worried about Paisley, heartbroken about Nate, and angry with myself. I'd tried so hard to do things right this time! I'd been patient and understanding. Yes, it had been hard to keep my feelings in check, but it's not like I could help that. Feelings weren't something I could control. And it wasn't as if I'd thrown myself at him and declared my undying love. I'd taken my cues from him and moved at his pace. It was Nate who'd come to me asking for a chance, Nate texting me to come over after work every night, Nate who'd said to me, *I don't deserve you.*

Well, I didn't deserve what he'd done to me—but it was hard not to feel like it was partly my fault.

AFTER GETTING ONLY a couple fitful hours of sleep, I didn't feel like getting ready and going out for brunch the next morning. I texted my sisters that I wasn't up for it, and they wanted to know what was wrong. I didn't feel like going into the whole thing via text, so I called Stella.

"Hey, what's going on?" she asked.

"Nate and I broke up last night." I lay back on my pillow and pulled up the blankets. Fresh tears threatened.

She gasped. "Oh, no! Why?"

"He said he felt crowded and wanted space. He said he didn't mean any of the things he'd said to me the night before."

"What? That makes no sense."

"I know, but it's what happened and I'm upset, with myself and with him. I hardly slept last night."

"Why don't Maren and I come over with breakfast?"

"I'm not that hungry."

"Bagels? Muffins? Doughnuts?"

"Whatever." Even doughnuts held little appeal.

"I'll pick up Maren and doughnuts and coffee. We should be there in about an hour."

"Okay." I hung up, and a few minutes later dragged myself into the bathroom for a shower. I turned the water on and while I waited for it to heat up, I made the mistake of looking in the mirror. My eyes, ringed beneath with dark circles, were bloodshot and dull. My eyelids puffy. My complexion sallow. I looked at my naked body and remembered how beautiful I'd felt in his arms, and wanted to cry all over again. Once I was in the shower, I let myself have one more good cry, and then I vowed to shed no more tears over Nate Pearson.

Afterward, I felt slightly more human, but I didn't have the energy to blow-dry my hair, so when I answered my sisters' knock, I was dressed in leggings and a sweater, but with my hair still damp. They each gave me a hug.

We sat down in the living room, Stella and I on the couch and Maren cross-legged on the floor.

"Stella told me what happened. Do you want to talk about it?" Maren asked. "You look so sad."

"I am sad." Even a cruller wasn't making me feel better, although I was eating it, anyway.

"So he asked for space out of the blue?" Stella questioned. "That really surprises me, after seeing you two together Friday night."

"You and me both," I said. "But he told me that was an act. That he was just saying the things he thought I wanted to hear. And I was the one who asked for total honesty at the start, so..." I shrugged.

"But do you think he was being honest?" Stella asked, setting her coffee cup on the table. "Or was he panicking and thinking, *Whoa, I better take a step back.*"

"That's a good point." Maren nodded. "Maybe he wasn't acting Friday night. Maybe he was acting last night."

I shook my head. "Stop. I can't even wrap my head around that. I didn't want any games this time around, you know? And what would he have to panic about? I wasn't pushing him. I wasn't asking for anything. And I sure as hell wasn't crowding him—if anything, *he* was the one taking us to the next level each time."

"That's what I mean," Stella said thoughtfully. "Maybe he scared himself."

"And then took it out on her?" Maren asked.

Stella nodded. "Right. Broke it off so he wouldn't have to deal with true feelings of intimacy, which he's admitted being uncomfortable with."

"But he *didn't* break it off," I said, reaching for another cruller, feeling like a broken heart justified two of them. "He was all, *Emme, this doesn't mean we have to stop seeing each other,* and I was like, *Uh, yeah, Nate, it does. You just told me you lied to me.*"

"Oh my God. He probably thought you'd still come over and have sex." Maren rolled her eyes.

"Or," said Stella, "He was forcing *you* to do the leaving, so that he wouldn't have to feel guilty about it. He could even blame you for the breakup."

"That's kind of messed up," Maren said.

"You know what? He is kind of messed up right now." I took a bite of my cruller and thought for a moment. "The whole fatherhood thing forced him to reevaluate his life. He's dealing with huge changes, in himself and in his future. Plus we went to his mom's house yesterday, and—" I shook my head—"it was emotional for him, because he lost his little brother to cancer when he was twelve. The house holds a lot of painful memories."

"That's sad, but it doesn't give him an excuse to be a jerk." Maren reached for her cup.

"No, but it might help explain it," said Stella. "All those changes might have snowballed in a way that made him feel really threatened all at once. And the house is a reminder of someone he loved and lost."

"Still," I said, "he was a total dick and he knows it." I told them about how I'd ended up going over to his apartment in the middle of the night. "And before I left, he asked me if I hated him, and I think he expected me to say yes."

"What did you say?" Maren asked.

"I told him the truth. That I don't hate him, I hate what he did. And I hate myself for falling for his act." My throat went dangerously tight, and I had to take a few deep breaths to prevent a meltdown.

Stella reached over and patted my leg. "Don't blame yourself, Emme. This is not your fault."

But I couldn't help feeling like it was.

We were silent a moment before Maren started giggling. "I'm sorry, but I keep imagining Nate's face when you handed him that rectal thermometer."

"Oh, he was *so* appalled." Despite everything, even I cracked a smile. "You'd have thought I asked him to eat the thing. It actually was kind of funny."

Later, when they were leaving, I said to Maren, "Your offer still good to help me find some peace and balance? I think I could use some."

"Of course," she said. "I think it's a great idea to use this opportunity to work on yourself. Turn your focus inward."

I nodded. "I'd like to break out of my harmful romantic patterns. I feel like I keep doing the same thing over and over again, like a hamster in one of those wheels. I need to do something different, change my approach or something. I really thought Nate was something special, that what we had was the real thing, but—" I lifted my shoulders as my eyes teared up—"I was wrong again."

"Listen, I have just the thing," she said. "Can you meet me at the studio at four?"

I had no work event scheduled that night, so it would work. "Yes. See you then."

Just the thing turned out to be a really difficult yoga class. I did my best to wrangle my feet behind my head and put my knees next to my ears and balance on my butt with my arms and legs in the air, but I was pretty much abysmal at all the poses except for Happy Baby, which actually made me laugh a little, it was so pathetic. Maybe that had been her plan all along?

Nope.

"You're not supposed to laugh in class," Maren whispered to me afterward. "People might think you are laughing at them."

"I was laughing at myself," I told her. "All those poses were so hard. I failed at all of them, and even on Happy Baby I had to try like three times to get my left foot in my hand. Aren't I allowed to laugh at myself? I either had to laugh or cry, and I figured crying would be more embarrassing."

Maren sighed. "Instead of laughing at yourself, why not focus on your breathing instead, what your muscles feel like, or what your body is capable of instead of thinking of it as failing?" She handed me a bottle of water from the fridge behind the desk. "Here, drink this. It's important to stay hydrated. You can bring it into the next class with you."

"The next class? I have to do another one?" I was already drenched in sweat and looking forward to a shower, my pajamas, and a glass of wine.

"I think this one is going to be very good for you."

"Good for me how? Is it another yoga class? Because I feel bad enough about myself as it is." And nothing was taking Nate off my mind.

"It's not a yoga class." She busied herself with something on the desk, and I immediately got suspicious.

"So what kind of class is it?"

"It's an affirmations session focusing on love and relationships," she said, needlessly straightening a stack of papers. "And it's going to be really good for you."

"Affirmations? Is that like meditation?"

"Sort of," she hedged, taking a long drink from her water bottle. "But affirmations are spoken out loud."

I gaped at her. "I have to speak out loud in there? No way."

"You said you wanted to break out of your harmful patterns, Emme. We can't rely only on our thoughts when we need to rewire ourselves like you're trying to do. We need to translate thoughts into words and words into actions in order to manifest our intentions."

"That sounds like a load of horseshit. I'm out of here." I looked around for the nearest exit, and she grabbed my arm.

"No! You don't want to be the hamster anymore, do you?"

"No," I admitted.

"Then stay. And trust me," she said, leading me into one of the smaller rooms off the lobby. "It's going to be great."

I had my doubts, but I followed her into the room anyway, figuring a hamster had nothing to lose.

Other than Maren and me, there were about ten other students plus the instructor, Harmony, in the room. Eight of them were women, and two were men. We all sat in a circle and the first thing Harmony wanted us to do was to voice one of the negative thoughts stuck in a loop in our brains. Most of the women said things like *I'm not pretty enough*, *I'm not thin enough*, or *I'll never find someone*. It was so depressing. Why did so many people do this to themselves? When it was Maren's turn, she said, "I don't really matter to the world. I feel insignificant."

I was so stunned by her statement that I didn't even realize it was my turn next. Everyone was waiting for me to speak, and she elbowed me in the side. "Emme," she whispered. "Go."

"Oh! Uh, I only fall in love with assholes." That hadn't been what I'd planned to say, but Maren had me flustered. Thankfully, everyone laughed, even Harmony and my sister. "Sorry," I said, holding up two hands. "I probably could have phrased that more elegantly. I'm failing at life today."

"The truth isn't always elegant," said Harmony. "And I like your honesty and self-awareness. Look at those things as triumphs."

After we all voiced our most nagging negative thoughts, Harmony explained that we needed to change the way we thought and felt about ourselves in order to change the frequency at which we were vibrating in the universe. I managed not to roll my eyes, but let Maren know with a giant sigh how I felt. She elbowed me again. "Just go with it, okay? For me, if not for yourself?"

"Fine. For you. But you owe me a real smoothie for this. Not one with kale in it."

"Deal."

So for the next twenty minutes, I listened to Harmony explain how positive affirmations could help us change our frequencies. She then gave each of us suggestions based on our individual needs. For Maren, she suggested something like *I am a positive contribution to this world.* For me, she suggested *I am deserving of a supportive, loving, awesome relationship.*

I kind of liked it.

"So? What did you think?" Maren asked as we sat sipping our smoothies.

"I thought the thing about our vibrations in the universe was a bunch of hooey, but the rest of it kind of made sense. I felt bad when everyone was voicing their negative thoughts."

She nodded. "Same."

"Do you really feel that way?" I asked her. "Like you don't really matter to the world?"

"Sometimes." She looked down at her smoothie. "I often

struggle with what I'm supposed to be doing with my life. When I was dancing, I felt like I really had purpose. I was creating something. But I've sort of been wandering since then."

"But you have a job you love, and you have peace and balance and inner homeogenius."

That made her smile. "Homeo*stasis*."

I smiled back, then I tilted my head. "It really surprises me that you feel that way."

Her cheeks went a little pink. "I do have all those things, and it feels really first world of me to complain that I don't have purpose in life when so many people in the world are suffering. I think that might be it—I'd like to do something outside myself, something bigger. I just don't know what."

"You'll figure it out, Maren," I said, putting a hand on hers. "You're destined for something great. I know it." It made me feel a little better actually, to think that someone as comfortable with herself as Maren seemed had her own brand of self-doubt. Not that I wanted my sister to feel bad, but something about knowing she occasionally did made me feel less alone.

Later on, when I was pouring myself a glass of wine and waiting for my frozen Lean Cuisine Enchilada Verde to cook, I tried out my positive affirmation. "I am deserving of a supportive, loving, awesome relationship," I said aloud. It felt a little weird, but I did it again anyway. "I am deserving of a supportive, loving, awesome relationship."

I repeated it again as I rinsed my dishes and put them in the dishwasher. And again as I brushed my teeth. And again as I lay in bed staring at the ceiling.

Did it make me feel less sad about Nate? No. I missed his voice and his smile and his arms around me so badly, it was a struggle not to break down and give my pillow another good soak.

However, I did start to believe it, and feel slightly better about my decision to stand up for myself and let him know that what he did was not okay. I deserved better in life, and it was up to me to go after it.

The next morning, I texted my cousin Mia that I'd thought about it long enough, and I'd decided to accept her offer.

TWENTY

NATE

I slept on and off the first half of Sunday, alternating naps
with periods of self-loathing and regret. There was a decent
amount of self-pity as well, which was sort of pathetic and
disgusting, but I kept telling myself that I'd done what I had
to, everyone was better off, and even though it hurt, I was
taking this pain for the greater good. I was a martyr.

Like I said. Pathetic.

I texted Rachel asking about Paisley, and she told me
she'd spoken to her pediatrician, who said to bring her in on
Tuesday for a check-up but as long as the fever stayed under
a hundred he wasn't too concerned. Rachel promised to text
me an update sometime this evening, and I messaged her
back with my firm's address, telling her I'd meet her there at
nine AM. I also emailed my boss and said I'd be back to
work earlier than expected.

After that, I forced myself out of bed and dragged my
ass to the gym. I did *not* want to be the guy who lays
around in bed feeling sorry for himself. I worked out hard,
and it felt good to punish my body. It took my mind off
the ache of missing Paisley and Emme. It also gave me

back a piece of my former self. I'd missed working out, missed spending time *by* myself *on* myself, missed feeling strong and capable and good at something. I watched myself in the mirror, sweat dripping from my skin, muscles flexing, body hard and tense, and I felt like me again. I probably spent two solid hours there. When I was done, I grabbed a shower and some food at the gym's cafe, still riding high.

Back at my apartment building however, the story changed.

In the hallway outside Emme's door, I listened carefully to see if I could hear anything inside, but it didn't sound as if she was home. Disappointed, I let myself into my apartment. It was probably a good thing that I needed to find a new place to live. Even if she didn't hate me, we were never going to be friends again like we were before. I fucking hated that.

I spent the rest of the evening doing laundry, cleaning up my apartment, and trying not to look at the baby furniture I'd bought. It seemed way too quiet, so I turned on CNN, but the news was depressing. I ended up turning it off and going to bed early.

Up in my bedroom, I lay in bed on my back, hands behind my head. The room seemed so empty. Why was that? I'd spent plenty of nights in bed alone. I liked my alone time. It was part of what I missed about my old life, wasn't it?

But I found myself looking at the little sleeper next to the bed and missing the daughter who'd turned my life upside down. Maybe I hadn't been the perfect dad right out of the gate, but I was the only father she had. Okay, trying to do an entire month all by myself had been a stupid move—especially since I had never even changed a diaper before—

but I'd learned a lot and I'd keep trying. Tomorrow, I'd ask Rachel if I could have her back over the weekend.

Although I *prayed* I'd never actually have to do that rectal thermometer thing.

When sleep continued to elude me, I couldn't help reaching for the pillow next to me and bringing it to my face. Inhaling deeply, I searched for any trace of the woman who'd made me so happy these last couple weeks. Who'd brought out a new side in me. Who'd made me love her.

And it was there—the scent of her hair.

I breathed in slowly, again and again, torturing myself with the memory of her until I couldn't stand it and threw the pillow to the floor. Wallowing was not going to help me get over this and move forward. I needed to refocus on the things that mattered, the things I could control: looking for a new apartment, arranging custody with Rachel, getting back to work, keeping fit.

Sooner or later my feelings would catch up.

———

ON MONDAY, Rachel and I filed the affidavit and I got to spend a little time with Paisley. I showed her off at the office, and even though I didn't like how everyone kept saying how *surprised* they were to see how good I was with her, I felt like a proud dad. When it was time for them to go, I walked with Rachel to her car.

"When can I see her again?" I asked once I'd buckled Paisley in and kissed her goodbye.

"This weekend?" she offered. "Assuming she's feeling good, I mean."

I nodded. "Should I drive to Battle Creek to pick her up?"

She thought for a second. "I could meet you halfway. That might be easier. Then one of us isn't driving three hours all the time."

"Okay. Let's plan on that. We can settle on a time this week."

"Sounds good." She paused. "I'm sorry again about how I handled the pregnancy and everything. I should have told you right away."

"Let's just move forward from here, okay? No sense in looking back."

She gave me a smile. "Good idea."

I opened the driver's side door for her, and she got behind the wheel. But before closing it, she said, "Hey, Nate?"

"Yeah?"

"I know you said it was none of my business, but I wanted to say again that I think Emme is really nice. And I could tell she has feelings for you."

I frowned and stared at the asphalt. Stuck my hands in my pockets.

"And Saturday night you seemed pretty miserable about the breakup. Is there any chance you could work it out?"

"I don't think so," I said with a shrug. "We don't want the same things."

"Okay, just thought I'd mention it. Have a good week."

I DIDN'T HAVE a good week. I had a shit week.

I did all the things I said I was going to do—let my landlord know I was looking to move out, contacted a real estate agent about finding a small house with a yard, went to the gym every night after work, and checked in with Rachel every day about Paisley. After work on Thursday, some of the single guys at the firm I used to hang around with asked me to go get a drink with them at Grey Ghost. We hung out at the bar for a while, talked up a group of women who were celebrating someone's thirtieth birthday, and ended up getting one big table with them for dinner. One of the women was clearly interested in me, a leggy brunette, and spent the entire evening trying to let me know she was up for a good time.

I wasn't even tempted. In fact, I was sort of repulsed.

All I could think about was that this was supposed to be fun, but it wasn't. It was my old life—slightly adjusted—but it didn't feel right. It was like trying to button a shirt you used to wear all the time but didn't fit you anymore. It was too tight, you couldn't breathe, and you realized you hated the pattern anyway.

I ended up throwing down some cash, making an excuse, and leaving the table early. It was a long walk to where I'd parked, but I didn't mind. Hands in my pockets, I took my time and tried to think about what I could do to feel good again, or at least less miserable. Clearly, the answer wasn't going back to work or spending more time at the gym.

When all my freedom had been abruptly taken away from me with Paisley's arrival, I'd lamented the loss of it, but getting it back again only reminded me what I'd started to dislike about it before—I was lonely. Back then, I'd been too stubborn to admit that maybe meaningless sex wasn't enough to satisfy the need to feel connected to another human being. And too scared to let myself feel anything for anyone beyond surface-level affection.

Then came Emme.

She was the first person who'd pushed me, with her irresistible combination of feisty and fragile, to go deeper. To let myself care. To let myself feel. Sex with her was better than it had ever been with anyone else *because* of that emotional connection. And the thought of having meaningless sex with someone else just for fun was abhorrent to me—I wouldn't even have been able to do it. And I didn't want to. I only wanted her.

My plan to forget her and embrace my old life wasn't working. I missed her. I needed her. I ached for her.

I made up my mind. When I got home, I'd knock on her door. Even if she slammed the door in my face two seconds later, it would be worth it.

I had to see her.

THIRTY MINUTES LATER, I stood in front of her door. My heart was beating way too fast. I straightened my hair and my tie. Checked my breath and my zipper. Took a deep breath.

Then I knocked.

And waited—nothing. I knocked again. No answer.

It was possible she was working tonight. She must have worked a lot all week, because I hadn't seen her once. Or else she was trying to avoid me, which was totally possible.

I was about to knock again when I heard her laugh. I turned toward the elevator and saw her walking down the hall, her phone at her ear. It was like I'd been punched in the stomach—I couldn't breathe.

"Yes, totally," she was saying. "That sounds perfect. I'll —" She'd spotted me and stopped walking. "Mia, can I call you back? Thanks. Bye." She lowered her phone. Her expression said *not amused.* "What are you doing?"

I have no fucking idea. "I'm...I'm locked out," I said.

"Oh." She tilted her head. "Where's Paisley?"

"With her mom. I let Rachel take her." Immediately I felt guilty about it. "She had that fever and I didn't know what I was doing..." I'd started to sweat. I wanted to take my suit coat off. "I thought she'd be better off with her mother."

Emme looked at me for a moment before speaking. "You gave up too soon."

"Emme—"

"Let me get your key," she said, turning her back to me to unlock her door. She opened the door and went inside without inviting me in.

I went in anyway.

Her apartment was dark and I shut the door behind me, cutting off the light from the hall.

"Hey." She spun to face me, backing up against the narrow console table to the right of the door. "What the hell are you—?"

I cut her off with a kiss, my hands clenching fistfuls of hair at the back of her head. My mouth opened over hers, my tongue slashing inside. She fought me at first, pushing against my chest with both hands. But her head slanted and her lips opened and her tongue reached for mine. I could feel the heat radiating off her body. Was it fury or desire?

I pulled my mouth off hers. Our breath mingled, quick and hot. "Do you hate me?" I whispered.

"Fuck you," she seethed. Then she slapped me. Hard.

I kissed her again, crushing my lips to hers. Her fingers slid into my hair, her nails raking against my scalp. I reached down and hiked up her skirt, slipping my hands up the back of her thighs and shoving down her underwear. "Do you hate me?"

"Fuck you." Her hands were at my belt. My zipper. My cock.

I lifted her up and set her on the table and she wrapped her legs around me. It felt familiar, fighting with her. Our kiss was a weapon, our mouths seeking to annihilate, consume, destroy.

I slid one finger inside her. Then two. She worked her hand up and down my cock, bit my bottom lip as I circled my thumb over her clit.

In the end it was she who decided, pulling me closer, placing me inside her.

I gave her an inch and stopped. She bit me again.

"You hate me," I said, wishing she would just admit it. I wanted to hear it.

She reached around and grabbed my ass, pulling me all the way inside her so quickly my knees nearly gave out. Her lips moved against mine. "Fuck. You."

I lost it all then—any ounce of control I still had left, which wasn't much. I fucked her like it was a vendetta, like I had vengeance in my blood, like I hated her as much as I loved her.

And I did love her. God help me, I loved her and wanted her and needed her. She was mine, she was mine— *that's* what I needed to prove. Her body answered to mine, her heart answered to mine, her soul answered to mine. We were together. We were one. We were inextricable.

We came together with the force of a nuclear blast. In fact, the only word I could think of as everything around us shattered was *destroyed*.

I was miserable without her. In pieces.

But what could I do?

When it was over, and reality sank in, I didn't know what to say. I pulled out of her and she slid off the table, tugging her skirt down as I zipped up my pants. She wouldn't look at me.

"Emme," I began.

She looked at me sharply. "Don't you dare apologize."

"I wasn't going to. I'm not sorry."

"Neither am I."

We glared at each other in the dark.

"I fucking miss you," I said. "I miss you so much."

She lifted her chin. "Good. Asshole."

"God, Emme. I know I can't make you happy. What am I supposed to do?"

"You don't know anything," she said. Then she sniffed, and a sob escaped her.

I took her head in my hands and rested my forehead against hers. We stayed that way for a moment, my heart desperately trying to break free from its cage, her entire body trembling, until she pushed me away.

"I took the job at the winery." Another weapon hurled at me.

My heart plummeted. "You did?"

"Yes. I'll get your key." She turned around and opened the drawer in the console table.

"Never mind," I told her, pulling open her apartment door. "I'm not locked out."

I HAD Paisley that weekend and wanted to knock on Emme's door a thousand times. To invite her over, to ask her to go for a walk, to tell her how much I missed her, how sorry I was. I loved having Paisley back with me, but it was so much better when I could share the experience with someone—the adorable moments, like when she started babbling at me and I swear she said Dada, and the less adorable moments, like when she shit herself so violently, it went up her back.

Up her *back*.

(I feel like there are reasons no one tells young people these things before they become parents. The world's population would probably decline dramatically.)

But I never had the nerve to reach out to Emme, and I took Paisley back again on Sunday as lonely as I'd ever been. The following week, my real estate agent took me to see four different houses, and I was dying to tell Emme about all of them. In fact, I wished she'd been with me every time, because I felt like she'd think of things I wouldn't, questions to ask and things to verify that were important for a family.

A family. Something I never thought I'd have. Or even want.

But as I walked through these houses, I kept picturing it —me and Paisley and Emme, always Emme. Planting flowers with Paisley as I mowed the lawn. Cooking with me in the kitchen. Sharing a bed with me.

After a while, I even started to picture another child. A sibling for Paisley. A little dark-haired boy with Emme's big heart and my sense of style.

A Connery man.

And then maybe there would be another little girl, a baby sister for Paisley to dote on. Another little angel with her mother's blond hair and blue eyes who loved to tell knock-knock jokes. I could see her. I could see it all. And it made me happy.

But how could I get there?

On Thursday I saw one house I liked more than all the others right off the bat, a two-story Dutch Colonial with three bedrooms and two baths built in 1926 but equipped with a brand new kitchen, a gorgeous old formal dining room, a fireplace, tons of windows, and a banister I could see kids sliding down as their mother yelled, "I told you not to slide down that banister again!"

It was perfect. It was terrifying. It was at my fingertips, just beyond reach.

I told my agent I needed to think about it for a few days.

Right after leaving that house, I went to the grocery store to pick up something for dinner. I was in the checkout line when I heard my name.

"Nate?"

I turned and saw Stella Devine behind me. "Hey," I said, wondering what Emme had told her sisters. "How are you?"

"Good." The smile she gave me was either genuine or really practiced. "How are you?"

"Okay."

"How's Paisley?"

"She's great. I pick her up for the weekend tomorrow."

"How nice."

There was an awkward pause. "I haven't seen Emme much lately," I said. "How is she?"

"I haven't seen her much either." She looked me right in the eye. "But honestly, I think she's pretty miserable."

I nodded, closing my eyes for a moment. "I am, too." Then I took a breath. "Stella, do you have time for coffee after this? I feel like I'm losing my mind. I need to ask you something."

She didn't answer right away, which made me feel like she was going to turn me down for sure and she was simply trying to think of a way to do it nicely. But she surprised me. "There's a Starbucks right across the street. Meet there?"

"Yes. Thank you."

Twenty minutes later we were sitting across from each other at a table for two in the back of the small, narrow coffee shop. Stella had taken the plastic top off her coffee and was blowing across its steaming surface, but I was ignoring mine. I hadn't planned this—what the hell had I been thinking? What was I going to say?

She must have sensed my discomfort as I struggled for words. "You wanted to ask me something?" she prompted.

"Emme told me she took that job up north," I blurted.

"Yes."

"Does she...does she really want to go?"

Stella lifted her shoulders. "Yes and no. She loves the city, but I think she likes the idea of a change. She hasn't been very happy lately."

I swallowed. "That's my fault. I hurt her."

"I know." She picked up her coffee and took a sip. "Why?"

"I don't know." I stared at a nick in the table's wooden surface.

"I think you do."

I looked up in surprise. Her tone was calm but eyes challenged me.

A moment later, she went on. "Usually when I have a patient who pushes away someone they care about, it's one or more of a few different things. They fear being rejected, they think they don't deserve love, or they just cannot stop thinking negatively about all the terrible what-ifs that could happen." She sipped again. "Any of that sound familiar?"

I laughed uncomfortably. "All of it?"

She gave me a gentle smile that reminded me so much of Emme my heart ached. "She mentioned you felt you needed space once you two had grown close."

Cringe. "Yeah, I said that to her, but it wasn't the truth. That was me trying to push her away."

"Because..."

"Because I panicked, I guess. I've avoided relationships my entire life because they never end happily, and they *always* end."

"Many do, but not all," she countered. "Relationships are a lot of work. They take a lot of compromise, trust, forgiveness, and communication."

I rubbed the back of my neck. "I don't know if I'm good at those things."

"Would you be willing to try? For Emme?"

"I'd do anything for Emme. But what if I can't give her what she wants? I have a daughter now, and she has to be my first priority. That's a huge change in my life and I'm scared to make another one. What if—?"

"Don't do that," Stella warned, setting her cup down. "No scary 'what ifs.' Stick to the present. So, you're a father —that's a big deal. Being a single parent will necessarily take up a lot of your time and energy, and not every woman would be okay coming in second all the time. I get that. But." She paused. "I think Emme understands."

"But is that fair to her? To ask her to be so understanding? She wants to get married eventually. What if I never do?"

She shrugged. "Again, that's a 'what if' you're using to shield yourself from intimacy."

I was beginning to see what Emme meant when she said it could be kind of annoying to have a sister who was also a therapist. But I also knew I needed to hear this. "Tell me what to do," I said. "I thought I'd feel better once she was gone and I could reclaim as much of my old life and my old self as possible, but I was wrong. I don't want to go back to who I was. It doesn't feel right anymore. Nothing feels right without her." I stopped to take a breath. "And now she's taken that job, and I'm worried I can't get her back. That I have nothing to offer her other than myself. Nothing to promise her."

Stella thought for a while before answering. "First, I think you can get her back. I'm not saying it won't take some work, because Emme is really hurt. She's determined to make changes in her life and the way she approaches relationships that will help her avoid having her heart broken again." She shrugged. "She's pretty much got your face in a red circle with a line through it."

I nodded glumly. "I'm sure she does."

"But." Stella leaned forward, her elbows on the table, her eyes lighting up. "Emme loves a big romantic gesture. I think you could get her to give you another chance."

"A big romantic gesture?" I blinked. "I've got no idea what that could be."

"Me neither. And it has to come from you. Something to show her that you love and accept her for who she is and you want her in your life. I don't think she's looking for promises beyond that, Nate. And I don't think you have to offer her anything but your willingness to be open to the journey with her."

"I am." I swallowed hard. "I'll try."

"Good." She picked up her coffee and sipped.

"You know, I looked at some houses this week," I went on, surprising myself. "And I was in this one, and it was like I could see it all so clearly—me and Emme and a family. I got chills."

"You're giving me chills." She smiled. "So it's all right there in front of you."

"You're right. It is." I picked up my coffee and took a

drink, although it was only lukewarm now. My mind was spinning—how was I going to make it all happen? There were so many pieces that needed to fall in place. How was I going to get her to listen to me?

"She's visiting Mia this weekend," said Stella. "She left about an hour ago and will be gone until Sunday." Then she must have seen how crushed I was that more days had to pass before I could set eyes on Emme again because she laughed gently. "That is a very sad face."

"I feel sad," I admitted. "I don't want to wait. I want to fix this."

She tilted her head and shrugged. "You could go up there and surprise her."

I sat up taller in my seat. "You think?"

"Sure. Why not?"

The gears in my head went into overdrive. "Stella, do you happen to know where she's staying?"

"At the winery. Our cousin Mia's place."

"Could I ask you for contact information for Mia?"

She thought for a second, then pulled her phone from her purse. "Sure, why not? Mia loves a good romantic gesture, too."

"Thanks." I put Mia's cell number into my phone, still not exactly sure how I was going to win Emme back, but positive I was going to try.

Tonight.

FIRST, I called my boss and asked for the day off tomorrow, offering to work overtime next week to make up for lost billable hours. She said it wouldn't be a problem.

Next, I called Rachel and told her I'd be coming from a

different direction tomorrow and might need a slight adjustment on the pickup time, depending on traffic.

Finally, I called Mia Fournier.

"Hello?"

"Hi, is this Mia?"

"Yes. Can I help you?"

"I hope so. This is Nate Pearson. I'm a friend of your cousin Emme?"

"What can I do for you, Mr. Pearson?"

I detected a note of cool formality in her voice, and I didn't blame her. She'd probably heard what a first class asshole I'd been to her cousin.

"For now, just hear me out." I signaled, veered onto the on ramp to I-75, and hit the gas.

"I'm about to sit down to dinner with my family. Will this take long?"

"I hope not. Has Emme arrived yet?"

"No. I'm expecting her around nine."

I checked the clock on my dash. It was six-thirty, which meant the timeline would be tight if I wanted to pull this off. But it could be done.

I decided not to waste any time beating around the bush. Mia was a businesswoman with a family and would appreciate my getting straight to the point.

"I'm in love with Emme, but I blew it. I need your help to win her back."

"All right, Nate Pearson, you've got my attention. Speak."

TWENTY-ONE

EMME

Traffic was awful on I-75, and the drive to Abelard Vine-yards was taking longer than usual.

I was cranky and tired. I'd been that way pretty much since Nate and I had split up. I couldn't relax enough at night to fall asleep, and even though I tried to grab the occasional nap before nighttime events, I wasn't always successful. Coco had suggested I take a few days off, maybe head up north and visit with Mia, get some rest. She was confident Amy could handle the events we had scheduled, and even volunteered to be on call if Amy needed help. I'd visited her earlier this week and she said she was desperate to get out of her house.

But she was happy, too. Who wouldn't be in her shoes? Her new baby girl was healthy and beautiful, her husband was over the moon to dote on her, and her mother-in-law was on hand to help with her boys. When I left their house, I recited my affirmation all the way home in an effort not to let envy eat away at my happiness for her. It wasn't Coco's fault I was still hopelessly in love with Nate.

He was never far from my mind. Over and over again, I

went over our final encounter, wondering if I'd handled it wrong. Should I have kicked him out? Demanded more answers? Treated him civilly? Told him the truth—that I wasn't over him and had only taken the job up north to put some distance between us?

But I had no answers. I didn't even tell my sisters about the post-breakup fuck—I was too embarrassed. Somehow I knew neither one of them would have given in. They'd have been stronger, able to resist his kiss and his touch and his cheap shots at my conscience. It was obvious he was miserable, and I was glad. He deserved it.

"I am deserving of a supportive, loving, awesome relationship," I said. I believed my affirmation. I really did.

But I was weak for him, and I feared I always would be. Distance would help.

JUST AFTER NINE, I pulled around the circular gravel drive in front of a beautiful French-style farmhouse. Mia and Lucas came out the front door and greeted me warmly. Lucas kissed both of my cheeks and grabbed the little suitcase from my trunk, and Mia hugged me extra hard.

"I'm so happy you're here," she said, taking my hand. "I have you staying in one of the best little guest cottages on the property. Lucas turned up the heat earlier, so it should be nice and cozy for you."

"Sounds good." It was definitely chillier up here than it had been in Detroit. A cozy little cottage sounded perfect. *It would be even better with someone to share it with.*

I shoved that thought from my mind.

"I'll take your bag over now," Lucas offered.

I smiled at the handsome man, who spoke with a slight

French accent. His scruffy jaw and lean good looks reminded me of Nate. "Thanks."

"Are you hungry?" Mia asked, leading me inside the house.

"Actually, yes."

"Perfect. I'll get you some supper and we'll have some wine. Come sit down in the kitchen. The kids are already in bed, so we'll have plenty of time to catch up."

I followed her to the big airy kitchen off the back of the house, which was modeled after the kitchen at Lucas's family's chateau in the south of France, where they'd gotten married. It was beautiful, of course, lots of natural stone in neutral shades, dark timber beams across the ceiling, walls soft slate gray, white-painted cupboards with open shelves, and Mia's signature pop of color in vibrant pink flowers in a glass vase on the counter. I chose a stool at the marble counter and watched as Mia bustled around the kitchen, warming up something in a big pot on the stove that smelled absolutely delicious. She looked adorable—jeans cuffed a little higher than her ankle, maroon velvet flats, black long-sleeved shirt with a gray infinity scarf around her neck, hair twisted up into a messy bun. And she looked *happy*.

"So we haven't had much of a chance to talk since you texted me," Mia said, handing me a folded linen napkin. "Tell me what's going on with you."

"You mean why I accepted the job?"

"Sure, you can start there."

"I'm looking to make a change." I unfolded the napkin and placed it on my lap.

She nodded, pulling down three wine glasses. "Okay."

"And I really like what I do, but a new scene will be a good creative challenge, I think."

"Sure."

"And things with Nate sort of fell apart," I admitted, smoothing the napkin over my jeans.

"I wondered." Mia pulled a bottle of wine from a fridge beneath the counter as Lucas came in through the back hall.

"Yeah." I took a shaky breath, hoping I could talk about this without crying. "It happened kind of suddenly."

"I'll do that, babe." Lucas took the corkscrew from Mia and opened the bottle.

She gave him a quick pat on the butt before going over to the stove to stir whatever was in the pot. "What exactly happened?" she asked me.

"It's hard to say, *exactly*. We had what I thought was this awesome thing going for a couple weeks, and then boom—it just exploded."

"It exploded?" she asked, rising on tiptoe to pull a big shallow bowl from an upper shelf. "Or he blew it up?"

Lucas set a glass of wine down in front of me. "You know, Mia, this could be kind of a private thing," he said to his wife.

She turned around and gave him a disapproving look. "Girls like to talk about this stuff. Go away if you don't want to hear about it."

He held up two hands. "I'm fine if Emme is."

"I'm fine." I sighed. "I mean, I'm fine *talking* about it. I'm still sort of reeling over the split. To answer your question, yes—he blew it up. I think we got too close for his comfort."

Lucas leaned back against the counter, wine glass in hand, and nodded. "Sounds like a guy move."

Mia ladled whatever she'd warmed up into the bowl, and grabbed a spoon from a drawer, shutting the drawer with her hip. "Honey, will you slice that baguette on the counter, please?" she asked Lucas.

"Of course."

"So you think he sabotaged the whole thing on purpose?" She set the bowl and spoon down in front of me. "Here. Beef bourguignon cures everything."

I inhaled the fragrant, steaming stew and my mouth watered. "You might be right. This smells incredible."

Mia smiled and lifted her glass. "Bon appétit."

I picked up my spoon and dug in, confiding in them in more detail—how careful I thought I'd been, how wonderful it was to see Nate growing to love his baby daughter, how seeing the changes in him had affected me, how learning about his family history and the visit to his childhood home had revealed so much about his emotional makeup. They listened thoughtfully, commented sympathetically, poured more wine.

"But in the end, either he hadn't changed at all and I saw only what I wanted to see, or he got freaked out and decided to end things before they went any further." I mopped the bottom of my bowl with a piece of bread.

"Hmm." Mia lifted her wine glass to her lips. By now, she was sitting on the stool next to me.

"My guess is he freaked out," said Lucas. "Just like Mia did."

I looked at my cousin in surprise.

"What?" Mia shrieked, sitting up taller. "I did not freak out. It was you who was all, *Marriage is futile and I never want kids.*" She imitated his deep voice and exaggerated his French accent.

He laughed. "But right after we met, when we were still in France at the end of your vacation, you wanted to call the whole thing off. *I* wanted to see where it might go."

"Oh, yeah." Mia's spine curled a little. "I always forget that part." She recovered a little spunk. "But I only did that because I thought ultimately there was no hope for us—I wanted a husband and family by age thirty and I was already twenty-eight—"

"Twenty-seven," Lucas interrupted, a rakish grin on his face.

Mia glared at him. "Fine, I was twenty-seven," she corrected, "but I knew what I wanted and it was exactly what you *didn't* want. I didn't see how we were going to make it work, and I didn't want to get hurt. I was half in love with you."

"Oh, you were *totally* in love with me." He drank, his eyes dancing over the rim of his glass.

"How did you?" I asked, looking back and forth between the two of them. "Make it work, I mean."

"I taught her to live in the moment," said Lucas. "To stop obsessing over her silly life deadlines."

"And I taught *him* to be open to the idea of lifetime commitment," said Mia, shooting him a venomous look. "I showed him how amazing it would be to be married to me."

"And she was right. It is." He came over and kissed his wife's lips, leaving a smile there. "Bottom line—it was trust, patience, and compromise." Lucas pulled another bottle from the wine fridge. "Should I open it?"

"What time is it?" asked Mia.

Lucas checked his watch. "A few minutes after ten."

"Yes, open it." They exchanged a look I didn't quite understand.

I was totally into another glass of wine, but I didn't want to keep them up. "If you guys need to go to bed, I'm fine doing that, too," I said, wiping my mouth with my napkin. "I know it's late, and the kids will be up early."

"No!" Mia turned to face me with a smile so bright I

almost thought it was fake. "No, I want another glass too. And we're not tired."

"Not at all," Lucas said, pulling the cork from the second bottle.

I wasn't sure I believed them, but it's hard for me to say no to wine and good conversation, and I loved being around Mia and Lucas. Like Coco and Nick, they were so at ease with each other. They'd found a groove. It wasn't all sunshine and rainbows, there was still a fair amount of teasing and eye-rolling and poking fun, but underneath was this incredible chemistry, unspoken love and support. It was palpable in the air between them. They admired each other and desired each other. In the wake of my disappointment, it was comforting to know that it existed.

We moved to the opposite end of the room and settled on the large, comfortable furniture in front of the fireplace. Mia and Lucas sat next to each other on the couch and I curled up in a chair. I asked about the wine we were drinking, and Lucas chatted enthusiastically about the success he'd had with certain grapes up here that few other winemakers were trying. In the middle of that conversation, Lucas got a text and excused himself to make a quick phone call. When he came back ten minutes later, Mia was talking about the events she had planned for the winery this summer, and how the new guest cottages were almost completely booked from May to September. But I noticed the way she kept her eye on the clock above the fireplace.

Eventually, she yawned and stretched theatrically. "Well, I have to admit, I'm beat."

"Me too," I said. We'd finished the second bottle of wine some time ago, and I was pleasantly drowsy. I looked at my phone. "Wow, it's after eleven already."

"I'll walk you to the cottage," Mia said as she rose to her feet. "Let me grab a sweater."

I stood up and brought my wine glass to the kitchen, setting it on the counter. Lucas began turning off the lights. "Thanks so much for dinner and the wine," I said to him. "Everything was delicious."

"You're always welcome," he said.

Mia appeared wearing a gray cardigan. "Ready?" She tugged on my hand.

"Yes. Night, Lucas," I called.

He looked over at us and smiled. "Night."

Mia practically pulled me down the hall and out the back door. Outside, she took off down a winding gravel path at a pretty good clip.

I laughed, trying to keep up. "Is there a fire? My heels are sinking into the gravel."

"Oh, sorry. No, it's just chilly. I want to get you all tucked into your cottage." But she slowed down a little, pulling her phone from her pocket and checking the screen.

I breathed in the cool night air, scented with wet earth and the coming of spring. Tilting my head back, I looked up at the sky. "Too cloudy for stars," I said with a sigh. "No wish for me."

Mia glanced at me. "What would you wish for?"

I smiled ruefully, dropping my gaze to my boots crunching on the gravel. "Tonight, I think I'd have wished for some sign that I'm not crazy—something to show me that the kind of love I'm looking for is actually possible. Not just a dream."

Mia put her arm around my shoulders and gave me a squeeze.

We passed a couple guest cottages before she guided me off the main path down a narrower one that led right to the door of an adorable little one-story stone structure that mimicked the look of the winery and their house, right down to the steeply pitched roofline and slate blue shutters. At the front door, she pulled out her phone again. "Well, I don't have any stars to offer you, but it is eleven-eleven." She showed me the screen. "You could still make a wish."

I sighed, feeling a little embarrassed I still believed in that stuff. "Nah, it's silly. My wishes never come true."

"You never know," she said. "Better do it, just in case."

Sighing, I closed my eyes and made the wish, altering it a little. *If you're out there, love of my life, come find me.*

When I opened them, Mia was frantically patting the pockets of her sweater. "Oh my God, you're not going to believe this. I forgot the key."

"No worries," I said. "I do it all the time, and Nate always has to rescue me. I'll walk back with you."

"No sense in both of us going. Your boots have heels, I'm in flats. Be right back." Without another word, she took off up the gravel path, leaving me alone in the dark.

It wasn't even twenty seconds later, I heard footsteps again—but they weren't hers. These were heavier, slower. I squinted at the figure coming toward me, someone taller and bigger and broader than Mia. Before I even had time to get nervous, I heard his voice.

"Heard you were locked out."

"Nate?" I blinked as he got closer, but he didn't disappear. He wore a suit and tie like he'd just come from work, and my heart was pounding at the sight of him. "What are you doing here?"

"Well, it was the craziest thing. I looked at the clock and noticed it was eleven-eleven, so I made a wish."

I could hardly breathe. "What did you wish for?"

He was right in front of me now. "I wished for another

chance to tell the most beautiful girl in the world that I love her, that I'm sorry, and that even though I don't deserve her, I hope she'll believe me when I tell her she's the only one for me, and I never should have let her go."

Chills shimmied up my spine. "So here's your chance. Tell me."

He rested his forehead on mine and lowered his voice. "Only you, Emme. And always you."

I wanted to believe him, but I was scared. Placing my hands on his chest, I pressed back. "What's changed, Nate? How can I trust that you won't break my heart again?"

He slipped his hands around my waist and drew me flush against him, solid and secure. "What's changed is that I realized how wrong I was to think I could control my feelings for you. I thought it made me a stronger man, a better man, if I never loved anyone, because I saw love as a weakness. Something to be feared. I always thought I'd be happier alone, but I wasn't. Part of the reason I told myself never to touch you was because deep inside, I wanted it *too* much. It scared me."

"I wanted you, too," I confessed, "but more than that, I wanted to be special to you. I didn't want to be like those girls leaving your apartment Sunday mornings."

He grimaced, his eyes closing briefly. "You were never going to be that. I was struggling with what I felt for you when Paisley came along. You were there for me the whole time, every step of the way. I'd have been so lost without you."

"You had it in you to be a good dad, I knew you did. You just needed confidence."

"I needed *you*. I'm so much better because of you. I get it now, Emme, what you said about alpha males acting the way they do because they have someone they want to protect. For too long, all I cared about protecting was myself. Now, all I care about is you and Paisley, and there is nothing I wouldn't do for you. Nothing. And I'm not afraid to show it."

"Or accept it?" I challenged him. "I love big, Nate. I can't help it. And I don't want to hold back."

"I want it all, everything you have to give." He squeezed me. "Tell me it's not too late."

"It's not too—"

He crushed his mouth to mine, lifting me right off the ground. His body bowed back, and mine curved along his. "I'm going to make you happy, Emme. I promise. For as long as you'll let me."

Maybe I shouldn't have believed it, but I did.

He set me on my feet and pulled a key from his pocket. "Here's the key to your cottage. If you want to spend the night with me, I'll stay. If you ask me to go, I'll go."

"The only thing I'm going to ask you is how you got this key in the first place." I took it from him, and opened the cottage door. "But that conversation can wait."

He grinned. "I'm so glad to hear you say that."

With the door barely closed behind us, we came together, clinging and clutching, desperate to make up for lost time and prove to one another we'd meant what we said. I could feel in Nate's kiss, in his touch, in his body that he loved me without reservation, that he'd broken free of whatever chains had been holding him back. He'd always been a powerful, aggressive lover, but there was something different this time. He was more passionate, more uninhibited, more unguarded than he'd ever been before—especially with words.

Over and over again, he told me he loved me.

Whispered it against my lips as we tore the clothes from

each other's bodies. Murmured it between kisses across my breasts, down my stomach, along every limb. Spoke the words as he carried me to the far end of the cottage where the king-size bed awaited. I realized he must have gone in ahead of time, because dozens of lit candles were scattered around the room, flickering softly in the dark.

He laid me on the bed and covered my body with his, and I opened everything to him—my arms, my lips, my legs, my heart. I, too, held nothing back. I rolled with all my might, forcing him onto his back so I could rain kisses over his face and chest, run my hands along the hard lines of his body, look him in the eye as I lowered myself upon him, his cock gliding slowly inside me.

"I wished for you," I told him when he was buried to the hilt. "For this, for us."

"I did too." He sat up so we were chest to chest, mouth to mouth, arms wrapped around each other. "The very first night when you told me to make a wish, I wished that the next man you fell in love with would love you back the way you deserved. And he does." We began to move together, our bodies a perfect fit, our rhythm in perfect synch. "I swear to God, he does."

Eventually, he took over, tipping me onto my back and driving into me harder and faster and deeper—so deep I gasped for air and cried out in shock and arched up desperately beneath him, my body craving both the pleasure and pain he wrought.

But mostly, I craved that elongated moment of shared bliss, the final seconds of the dizzying ascent, the agonizing hover on the edge of the peak, the feverish breath as we took each other over, the exquisite spiral of the pulsing free fall, our bodies entwined, inseparable, one.

"Tell me again," I whispered breathlessly as our hearts

refused to calm down, even after his body and mine were sapped and his chest was heavy on mine.

He picked his head up and looked down at me. Brushed the hair from my face. "I love you. Only you. Always you."

I smiled. "Told you wishes come true."

"I CAN'T BELIEVE IT," I said, shaking my head. "So it was Stella who convinced you?" We were lying in bed late Friday morning, Nate on his back, me propped on an elbow on his chest. We'd gotten very little sleep, but I felt energized and refreshed. Alive.

"Kind of. I mean, I knew I was miserable without you and that I'd fucked things up, but if I hadn't seen her at the grocery store near that house I told you about, I don't know that we'd be where we are right now." He tucked my hair behind my ear. "You were right about her. She gets underneath the surface fast."

"She does," I agreed. I made a mental note to call her and say thanks, and also to stop being so annoyed by her therapist ways. "And she gave you Mia's number?"

He nodded. "Yeah. She told me you'd left for the winery, and basically said, 'If you want her, prove it.'"

I beamed. "I love Stella. Stella is amazing."

"She is."

"And what did Mia say?"

"Well, at first I could tell she wasn't too keen on me. But after I explained myself, she was up for helping me try to win you back."

I laughed. "I keep thinking about her checking the clock all night as we sat there drinking."

"Oh yeah." His eyes widened. "We were totally nervous

about it. The timing was tight. I didn't even get here until almost ten-thirty."

Something clicked. "So it was Lucas who gave you the key when he *went out to make a phone call*." I made little air quotes and rolled my eyes. "What a sneak!"

Nate grinned. "Yep. I texted him when I pulled up at the winery. Then I walked over to the house."

"I still can't believe it. Those two knew the whole time!" But I was so happy. I felt like this was a completely fresh start.

Nate glanced at the bedside clock. "I hate to say this, but I have to go soon. I need to pick up Paisley at three."

"I'll go too," I told him, sitting up.

He looked distressed. "What? No, Em, you just got here. You should stay the weekend and relax. Visit with your cousin. Talk about the job. Which you can still take if you want. I mean that. We will make this work, no matter what."

"I'll think about it," I said honestly. "I really was looking forward to it, but I love where I am now, too. Your firm doesn't have a Traverse City office, does it?"

He shrugged. "No, but that doesn't mean I couldn't find another job up here. People get divorced everywhere. Every day."

I groaned as I hopped off the bed. "Naaaaaate."

He reached out and grabbed my arm, pulling me back into bed and hauling me across his lap. "Hey."

"What?"

"We're different."

I raised one brow. "Oh yeah?"

"Yeah." He kissed me and touched his forehead to mine. "Only you. Always you."

Somehow, I knew it was the truth.

THREE MONTHS LATER

NATE

NORMALLY, I have a superior poker face. I don't often have to use it outside of work, especially since Emme and I have been together, but every now and again, it comes in handy. Like when I want to surprise her.

Like tonight.

"I'm going to go pick up the food, okay babe?" I grabbed my keys off my new kitchen counter and went over to the couch where she was sitting with a freshly bathed Paisley on her lap. It was my first weekend in the new house—the Dutch Colonial I'd loved on sight—and Emme and I were going to celebrate our favorite way. Some takeout, some cocktails, some Bond.

"Okay." She stood up, moving my daughter to one hip. Seeing them together always made me want to fall to me knees and thank God things had turned out the way they did. "Should I feed her?"

"Sure. Sorry everything is still such a mess in the

kitchen. I swear I'm going to get it all put away this weekend."

"I'll help you. Maybe we can even get some boxes unpacked tonight."

"Maybe." There would be no fucking unpacking of boxes tonight, but she didn't know that. "Be right back." I went out the side door and got into my car, glad she couldn't see the giant smile on my face.

I was also glad she was so trusting. Ever since I'd bought the house, I'd been saying things to her like, *I've got everything I want now* or *My life feels so complete now that I have the house* or *I hope nothing ever changes with us.* She believed me every time, and she always smiled and said she was glad, but I could see the question in her eyes... *Does this mean you still don't want to get married? Like, ever?*

She never asked it, though. And I never brought up the subject, either, even though I'd been thinking about it every day since I brought her to the house and we walked around in it together. The gut feeling I got seeing her move through the empty rooms with a smile on her face was almost eerie— I knew in my heart we would live there together. We would make it our home. We would be a family.

And not only did I want it all, I wanted it all sooner rather than later.

So all that crap about feeling complete was all just part of the setup—I wanted her to be totally shocked tonight.

Stopped at a red light on my way to the restaurant, I glanced beside me at the passenger seat, where a little white bag rested. Inside were two fortune cookies.

And one ring box.

EMME

"SERIOUSLY, Paisley. What's he thinking? Why can't I tell?" I looked down at her face as she drank her bottle. "Do you think he's still totally against marriage, or do I have a chance?"

I had taken to talking to Paisley about it, since my sisters were tired of hearing me worry that Nate might never change his mind if I wasn't going to ask him about it, and I had promised myself I would *not* bring it up to Nate for at least six months. I didn't want to pressure him. We were doing so well, and he was so open about his feelings now. By being patient, I was trying to prove to everyone and to myself that I could be patient and trust in the universe.

"See, I've thought a lot about this, Pais," I went on, sitting her up to burp her. "We had geography on our side all the time—the apartments right across from each other. And timing, too. He happened to be getting home from work at the exact moment I locked myself out. That's how we met, you know."

She burped.

"Good girl." I laid her back again so she could finish the bottle and kept babbling. "And how about his running into my sister at the grocery store the night we got back together? What if he'd gone to a different store? What if Stella hadn't decided to pick up pork chops for dinner? What if her last patient hadn't canceled and she'd gotten out of work an hour later? All that is luck, isn't it? So maybe the universe really is on our side. Maybe Maren is right and everything happens the way it's supposed to and I just need to wait and trust." I sighed. "I really love him. So that's what I'll do."

Nate came in about thirty minutes later. "Let me put

the food in the oven to keep it warm, then I'll get her to bed and make us some celebratory cocktails."

"Okay." I stood up with Paisley in my arms. "Want me to unpack something? A kitchen box?"

"Nope. Just relax." He came from the kitchen into the family room and took his daughter from me, giving her a kiss on the cheek. "I'll be right down."

My stomach flipped over the way it always did when I saw him display affection for his daughter. Earlier, I'd watched him give her a bath in a real bathtub all on his own —I hadn't even lifted a finger. All I could think of was the night she first arrived and he fainted.

Someday, I was going to get him to admit that.

"Night, peanut," I called to the chubby little dumpling he held against his chest.

While he was upstairs with her, I opened my laptop and returned some emails. I also called Coco and left her a message—I'd decided to turn down the job offer up north, but she was actually considering it. Apparently, Nick was interested in some restaurant properties in that area, so the move made sense for them. She and I were going to have lunch tomorrow and discuss my buying her out. It made me nervous, thinking about running a business all on my own, but excited, too.

When Nate came downstairs, I put my laptop and phone away. He switched on the monitor on his way to the kitchen. "Up for a martini?"

"Absolutely," I said. "Want help in there?"

"Since when do I need help making cocktails?" he called. Next, I heard ice clinking into the metal shaker.

The family room and kitchen were open to each other, part of a new addition off the back of the old house. I loved Nate's house. From the moment I saw it, I knew it was the right one for him. Beautiful old street, great neighborhood, kids riding bikes up and down the block, plenty of room in the house for him and Paisley, and even room to grow if he decided he wanted a bigger family.

I really hoped he did.

"Are you hungry?" he asked, shaking up the vodka and the ice.

"Yes." I took off my heels and wiggled my toes. "I skipped lunch today."

"Good, because I have a little treat for you before dinner." A moment later, he brought me a drink and a little plate with two fortune cookies on it. He set both on the table.

I rolled my eyes. "Are you going to tease me about taking these things seriously again?"

"Not at all. I think you should take it very seriously."

"No, you don't. You just want to laugh at me." I looked at them—one was half dipped in dark chocolate, the other was half-dipped in white. "Are these from The Peterboro?"

"Nope. I got them made especially for you. Did you know it's our anniversary today?"

A funny little shiver moved through me. I looked at him, but his expression gave nothing away. "It is?"

He nodded and sat down beside me. "Exactly three months since the night at the winery."

"Awww." I gave him a quick kiss. He still wore his dress pants and shirt, although he'd cuffed up his sleeves before Paisley's bath. He'd also ditched his tie and loosened his collar. Sexy as hell, even half undone. "And I'm supposed to eat them before dinner?"

"Yes. Or at least open them." He handed me the dark chocolate dipped. "Here. This one first. I'll go get your drink."

With my belly fluttering, I cracked it open. Setting the pieces back on the plate, I pulled out the little paper. It said, *Only you.*

"Awwww." I smiled at him as he set my drink on the table and sat next to me. "So sweet." I set the little piece of paper down and picked up the next cookie, although I knew what it was going to say, because it was the second half of something I asked him to tell me all the time. I cracked it open over the plate, and pulled out the paper.

Then I gasped. Because it didn't say what I thought it was going to say. It said, *Will you marry me?*

And Nate was getting on one knee at my feet.

My jaw hung open. My heart clamored in my chest.

He pulled a ring box from his pocket and opened it up. "Always you," he said. His voice cracked. His eyes were shining. But he smiled at me and everything, *everything* fell into place.

I shrieked and threw my arms around his neck before bursting into tears, clinging to him like he'd just rescued me from drowning.

He laughed. "Is that a yes?"

But all I could do was sob.

"Want to at least try the ring on?"

The ring! I hadn't even looked at it.

Sniffling, I let go of him and he held it out for me again. "I asked your sisters' opinions, but if it's not what you want—"

But I was already blubbering again. I see a lot of rings in my business, but this one took my breath away—a two-carat elongated cushion-cut solitaire with a narrow pave band in white gold. "It's p-perfect," I managed. "Ab-abso-lutely p-perfect."

"I'd like to take more credit, but your sisters said you've

described your dream ring to them so many times they had it memorized." He took it from the box and slid it onto my finger.

I laughed through my tears. "It's true." It took me a few more minutes, but eventually I calmed down enough to speak. "Oh my God, Nate. It's real. It was a dream, but you made it real."

"It's real."

I looked at my hands in disbelief—one held a tiny slip of paper with Nate's proposal on it, the other wore a ring he'd just slipped on my finger. I dropped to my knees and threw my arms around him again, pressing my body against his from knee to chest, burying my face in his neck. I closed my eyes, breathed him in, and saw it all unfold. This man would be my husband. This house would be our home. This life would be ours to share.

"You really want me to be your wife?" I asked, tipping my head back to look up at him.

"Of course I do." He kissed my lips. "But that's not all I want. I want you to help me raise Paisley. And I want to have children with you. And I want to spend every day dedicated to our family and our home and our dreams."

"I want that, too."

He grinned. "Then can I please get a yes? Because I don't think you've actually said it yet. What do you say, Calamity, will you marry me?"

I smiled up at him, my wish come true. "Yes."

THE END

ACKNOWLEDGMENTS

I am so grateful to the following people:

Kayti, Laurelin, and Sierra—you never let the snakes get me.

To Jenn Watson, Sarah Ferguson, and the incredible team at Social Butterfly PR, for all your hard work.

To Melissa Gaston and Candi Kane, an unbeatable team.

To Nancy, once again, for tolerating my last minute begging.

To the Shop Talkers, for being funny and smart and generous.

To my earliest readers, Cheryl Guernsey and Michele Ficht.

To my eagle eyes, Janice Owen and Karen Lawson.

To Rebecca Friedman, for building me up.

To Flavia and Meire at Bookcase Literary, for tireless efforts on my behalf.

To my PQs, who always make me smile.

To the Harlots, for being an awesomely positive and supportive group, always.

To my ARC team—a force of nature. You're the best.

To the bloggers and event organizers who do it all for the love of books and this community. You amaze me.

To my readers, near and far. It's all for you.

To my family, whom I love so. Always you, only you.

COMING SOON...ONLY HIM

Don't miss the next book in this series, ONLY HIM! Dallas and Maren's story will release in June 2018.

He was my first crush, my first kiss, my first everything.

But I'm not a lovesick teenager anymore, and I refuse to let him break my heart again.

So when he shows up out of the blue asking me to take a road trip with him "for old time's sake," I say I will. After all, it's been ten years. I'm stronger and smarter, full of inner peace and harmony.

Except he's still got eyes that make me weak. Kisses that steal my rational thoughts. Tattoos that declare war on my senses and a body that renders me completely defenseless. We're just as good together as we were back then—better, even—and I'm willing to give the only man I've ever loved another chance.

But he's got to tell me the truth.

———————

She didn't need to be rescued. I did.

From guilt. From regret. From the nagging fear that I'd wronged the one person in my life who'd loved me unconditionally.

All I'd wanted was her forgiveness. To know in my heart that she'd made peace with the past and had moved on without any permanent scars.

But that's not what happened.

Because when I saw her, everything came back.

I can make her laugh, I can make her cry, I can make her body surrender to mine in ways that neither of us could have imagined back then. I can—and I do—love her more than she'll ever know.

But I can't tell her the real reason why I needed to spend these days with her.

And I can't stay.

Preorder here!

ARE YOU A HARLOT YET?

To stay up to date on all things Harlow, get exclusive access to ARCs and giveaways, and be part of a fun, positive, sexy and drama-free zone, become a Harlot!

https://www.facebook.com/groups/351191341756563/

NEVER MISS A MELANIE HARLOW THING!

Sign up here to be included on Melanie Harlow's mailing list! You'll receive new release alerts, get access to bonus materials and exclusive giveaways, and hear about sales and freebies first!

http://subscribe.melanieharlow.com/g5d6y6

ABOUT THE AUTHOR

Melanie Harlow likes her heels high, her martini dry, and her history with the naughty bits left in. In addition to ONLY YOU, she's the author of the After We Fall Series, the Happy Crazy Love Series, the Frenched Series, STRONG ENOUGH (a M/M romance co-authored with David Romanov), and The Speak Easy Duet (historical romance). She writes from her home outside of Detroit, where she lives with her husband and two daughters. When she's not writing, she's probably got a cocktail in hand. And sometimes when she is.

Made in the USA
Monee, IL
29 November 2022